Lisette scowled at him. "You don't have to play the tough-guy hero."

"If you ever see me being the hero, keep in mind: I *will* be playing. I like things peaceful and easy. I'll meet David somewhere he wouldn't dare cause a scene. I'll convince him I didn't steal *Shepherdess*, he'll apologize, he'll send you a gift—diamonds, probably—and that will be the end of it."

Jack didn't believe what he was saying, and it was clear she didn't, either, but she didn't argue. Instead, she resettled in her seat, forehead knitted in a frown, and gestured grudgingly at the upcoming highway sign. "Get off here."

He exited and turned toward her neighborhood. A distinctly uncomfortable air settled in the truck rather quickly, but he didn't let it get to him. Irritation, he could take. Threats against her person or her life, he couldn't.

But damned if he didn't like, at least a bit, the idea of being her hero.

* * *

Dear Reader,

I finished writing this book almost exactly on the thirtieth anniversary of the sale of my first book. It's been a fun, exciting, eye-popping, frustrating, happy, sad, wonderful time, but one thing has never changed: my deep, deep gratitude for being a part of this business. I've met incredible friends; I've learned incredible things. One of the best aspects of it all has been the readers. You guys have stroked my ego, made me laugh and brought me to tears. You've encouraged me and made me feel ten feet tall; you've shared your experiences; you've offered friendship; and one of the best things of all: you *get* me. Do you know how cool it is for a sort of, ah, unique person like me to find people who really, truly get her?

Whether you're a frequent flier with me or this is your first time, I hope you enjoy the trip. Thanks for taking the journey with me and for helping me do what I love best. Thanks for the best life ever!

Marilyn

NIGHTS WITH A THIEF

Marilyn Pappano

HARLEQUIN®ROMANTIC SUSPENSE

Recycling programs
for this product may
not exist in your area.

ISBN-13: 978-0-373-28208-1

Nights with a Thief

Copyright © 2016 by Marilyn Pappano

Printed in U.S.A.

HARLEQUIN®
™ www.Harlequin.com

Oklahoma, dogs, beaches, books, family and friends: these are a few of **Marilyn Pappano**'s favorite things. She lives in imaginary worlds where she reigns supreme (at least, she does when the characters cooperate) and no matter how wrong things go, she can always set them right. It's her husband's job to keep her grounded in the real world, which makes him her very favorite thing.

Books by Marilyn Pappano

Harlequin Romantic Suspense

Copper Lake Secrets
In the Enemy's Arms
Christmas Confidential
"Holiday Protector"
Copper Lake Confidential
Copper Lake Encounter
Undercover in Copper Lake
Bayou Hero
Nights with a Thief

Silhouette Romantic Suspense

Scandal in Copper Lake
Passion to Die For
Criminal Deception
Protector's Temptation
Covert Christmas
"Open Season"

Visit the Author Profile page at Harlequin.com for more titles.

Chapter 1

Jack Sinclair put on his first tuxedo at the age of eight, looked in the mirror and told the servant who'd helped him dress, *I look* good. The servant laughed before shunting him off to a corner of the main hallway to await his parents' summons. That was twenty-two years ago, but two things hadn't changed: he still looked good in a tux, and he still spent time hanging out in corners at these formal events.

This particular event was taking place at the Castle, a mansion carved out of Rocky Mountain stone in the 1800s. David Candalaria was celebrating the opening of the *King's Treasures* exhibit at the Denver museum that bore his name, a collection of paintings, statues and carvings from a tiny kingdom that no longer existed. Only serious art lovers or historians remembered it today.

Jack liked art, but the party tonight wasn't about that. The best way to view a treasure was in private, intimately. No, this evening was about seeing and being seen. Photo ops. Who was with whom? Who was wearing what? Who had acquired what?

He sipped champagne as he strolled the perimeter of the ballroom. He'd been there nearly two hours, had talked to everyone he had any interest in and now was avoiding the few he didn't want to talk to. That was why he kept moving; it was harder to hit a moving target.

In keeping with the rest of the Castle, the ballroom was grand. Polished marble tile reflected prisms of light from the chandeliers forty feet above. Eight fireplaces were spaced around the room, each large enough to hold six of Candalaria's bodyguards shoulder to shoulder. Palladian windows lined the three outside walls, opening onto stone terraces that led to formal gardens, then to a vast expanse of lush green lawn that ended in dark walls of impenetrable forest.

Sidestepping a Tokyo collector said to covet all the world's masterpieces, Jack turned his attention back to the guests. Some of them were as beautiful as the room, some as expensive, some as dark as the forest encroaching outside. He estimated the net worth of the attendees easily north of $500 billion: royalty, sheikhs, businessmen, politicians, celebrities. The rich who sought out the spotlight and the even richer who paid a great deal to avoid it.

He was approaching the starting point of his ramble when movement in the nearest corner caught his eye. He didn't see much: a flash of dark red dress, an even briefer flash of honey-toned shoulders, black curls drawn up. The woman had slipped through a barely opened door before his brain registered that much. Along with a sense of familiarity.

Of course she seemed familiar. He'd been to dozens of these parties all over the world. There were always local faces added to the crowd, but overall the guest lists included the usual suspects. But something about this woman… He couldn't quite recognize her—and he never forgot a face. Especially when it was attached to such gorgeous shoulders.

Depositing his champagne on a table, he walked to the corner. He didn't look over his shoulder, glance around or do anything to draw attention his way. He simply turned the doorknob, slipped through the opening and closed it behind him.

The hallway stretching before him made a few turns before reaching the kitchen at the back of the house. It was well lit in comparison to the narrow stairs on the left that twisted out of sight within a few steps. They were lighted by a single bulb on a landing above, then another from the second floor. There they connected to a similar servants' corridor, running the length of the east wing suites.

Along with quarters for the most favored of his guests, David's suite was in that wing.

Jack listened, catching faint bits of conversation and clanging from the kitchen, but no sound from the stairs. A glance up showed no fleeing woman, no shadows or signs of movement, but…yes, there distantly, the thud of a heel on wood. Intrigued by the fact that the woman was slipping into very private quarters in the middle of a grand gala, he followed, listening intently, his gaze constantly searching both above and below.

He was rewarded with another sound, a hushed expletive in a husky voice. As he reached the top of the steps, he moved closer to the wall and recalled the layout of the second floor. To the left, the hall extended across the wing, with doors opening into discreet niches in the main corridor, allowing the maids and kitchen help access to the rooms without being visible for more than a few seconds. Candalaria was a big believer that the help should be neither seen nor heard.

To the right, the corridor covered only fifty feet before it ended at a dark, heavy door opening into Candalaria's own suite. All Jack knew about it was what a chatty housekeeper had shared after a few glasses of wine last visit. Unlike the rest of the mansion, the space was modern, austere, one large room bigger than most people's houses. There was a sitting area, an office area, a well-stocked bar, a sleeping area and, behind an undulating wall of water, a bath.

From beyond the door came another muffled sound.

Only a servant would enter by this route. Any woman with an invitation would be escorted along the main corridor, steps muffled by the red-and-blue Serapi carpet, given a chance to admire the Elizabeth Turk marble sculptures, the Lalique tables and the Devine metal pieces on the walls.

Only a servant…or someone in the same line of business as Jack.

Interesting. Who had targeted David, and which of his treasures was she after?

Jack's curiosity was purely that. He wasn't there to study the security setup or to check out the priceless baubles worn by the guests. He wasn't meeting a prospective client or eavesdropping on gossip. He was on vacation, had come for the company, the food and the infrequent chance to admire David's personal collection up close.

But he couldn't help but be interested in someone who was on the job tonight, especially a woman. There weren't many females in his field, and he was pretty sure he'd met all of them except...

Bella.

His stomach tightened.

It wasn't her real name. Twelve years ago, when she'd waltzed into the Italian villa of a designer who'd given Armani and Prada a run for their money, she'd left with the crown jewel of his fancy red diamond collection: a flawless four-carat brilliant cut worth a million or so for each carat. With that one act, she'd become a legend, and like any good legend, there was a shortage of hard, cold facts.

She was fair, with green eyes, so blue they couldn't have been natural, and brown the rich shade of cacao. Her blond hair cascaded over her shoulders...when it wasn't short and sleek and fiery red or pale brown with silvery highlights. She was tall, thin, rounded, danced like a prima ballerina and walked with a limp, spoke with a Southern drawl, sounded French or had an accent too exotic to identify.

The only thing anyone agreed on was that she was a beautiful woman. *Bella donna.*

The designer's fancy red had disappeared, along with, over the years, various other items from London, Berlin, Dresden, Hong Kong. None was ransomed back to its owner, offered on the black market or ever seen again, and after each theft, Bella remained as mysterious as ever.

Up to this point, the highlight of Jack's career had

involved the penthouse suite of Dubai's tallest hotel, rappelling gear and a two-hundred-foot slide onto the balcony of a room occupied by honeymooners so involved with each other that they hadn't even noticed him slipping past and into the hall.

Meeting Bella Donna, being the first to do so…

He climbed the last step onto the landing and turned to the right.

That would be a *very* significant highlight.

It never got old.

Every time Lisette Malone laid eyes on a work of art for the first time, her reaction was the same: goose bumps raising all over, muscles tightening, a quick intake of breath. Tonight was no different.

She stood in the dim room, aware of light, noise, time, but her core was focused on the canvas unrolled on the desk. Its colors were vibrant, the brushstrokes delicate, the pastoral scene so real that it was surreal. It was titled *Shepherdess and Her Sheep*, and for an instant she could actually smell the grass and feel the slight breeze lifting the woman's apron. Two hundred years old, and it stole the breath from her lungs.

Oh, Lizzie, isn't it fabulous?

Lisette didn't look for the source of the comment. She would give everything she had if her mother was hiding in a shadowy corner, or if the voice was coming through the tiny bud concealed in her ear, but neither was possible. Marley Malone had died seven months ago, and Lisette's heart had broken from the aching.

Until the last few weeks, when Marley had taken up residence in Lisette's head with no intention of leaving until her dearest dream had been fulfilled: the return of *Le Mystère* to its rightful owner.

Lisette.

Though she could sense her mother clapping her hands in delight, the emotions inside Lisette weren't so light. *Le Mystère* was a priceless statue, and her father had been killed for it. So had his great-great-grand-father. Some might consider it cursed: by the Toussaint who'd given the statue to the Blue family as a token of appreciation? The next-generation Toussaint who'd tried to take it back and killed its rightful owner in the process? Her father, who'd died to protect it? Or the Toussaint who'd left Lisette fatherless?

It's justice, Lizzie. That statue belongs to you. It's your heritage. It's your father's legacy. He did die for it, and I promised his spirit that we'll get it back. His death won't have been in vain.

"Not now, Mama, please. Stay out of my head."

Lisette had to stay ready just in case company showed up.

This company had better be Jack Sinclair. She'd put herself near his path in the ballroom twice, had paused at the door long enough for his gaze to lock on her. She'd even made sure to scrape a shoe and swear, difficult tasks to carry out when she'd been taught stealth her whole life.

Her gloved hands steady, she rolled the canvas once again and slid it into a mailing tube she'd found in a supply closet. It was a sorry home for such a wonder, but only for another twenty-four hours.

Before capping the tube, she bent close to the desk to examine what looked like colored stones thrown into a glass dish. Given time, she could examine each one and total up their approximate values, but it didn't really matter. The small fancy red was delicate, its colors fiery, and would bring enough to cover her and Padma's expenses for a while.

She sealed the red inside an envelope from Candalaria's desk, dropped it into the tube, then taped the cap securely before glancing around the room once more. There were so many other masterpieces to study if only she had time, but time was never on her side. If she was caught with *Shepherdess*, if she was even caught on this floor of the house…

Shrugging to loosen the tension in her shoulders, she started toward the balcony. If she was caught, she would have to move on to plan B. She always had a plan B—and a C and D. And now, to Marley's delight, a plan IDS, for Île des Deux Saints, the island where *Le Mystère* resided.

Lisette turned to the east wall. There were no curtains on the windows or the French doors—just stunning views of the mountains during the day, near-darkness at night. Little of the outdoor lighting reached this high up, leaving the murky shadows she liked best.

Now for the hardest part of the job. She opened the door just wide enough to slide through to the balcony. Barely ten by twenty feet, it had been built more for looks than function, though it did hold two elaborately carved chairs. She didn't move toward the chairs, didn't go one inch nearer the knee-high balustrade than she had to. She dragged a few oxygen particles into her lungs, pressed her back against the stone wall and tried to ignore the fact that she was standing on a monstrously heavy stone ledge fifty feet above the ground.

She didn't like heights. Didn't like the idea of falling to her death.

It's not the fall that kills you, Lizzie. It's the landing. But you'll be okay.

There'd been a time when Lisette had believed those last three words, no matter the situation. But that was before she'd crashed a party with more security than any presidential visit, sneaked into the owner's quarters and stolen a canvas valued around a million dollars, and now had to climb her way down from the high-in-the-sky balcony and leave the grounds without anyone noticing.

Besides Jack Sinclair. Even with him on her trail, *okay* was still a long ways out of her reach. And if it wasn't him moving quietly in the suite behind her...

"Hey, sweetie, look up." As usual, Padma, Lisette's best friend and partner in crime, was right on time. Though her voice came softly from the bud resting in Lisette's ear, her tone was warm and cheery, meaning everything from her end was going according to plan.

Lisette tilted her head. The bright lights below deepened the contrast with the inky sky. Generally, this far outside Denver, the night put on a pretty spectacular show, but tonight the sky was dark, hiding its gems with a thick cloud layer.

No, it wasn't totally dark. A tiny red light hung a hundred feet overhead, slowly descending. After a moment, its soft whirring buzz reached her, and half a moment after that, the machine stopped in midair in front of her.

"Smile for the camera, sweetie."

Lisette bared her teeth. Technology was Padma's passion. She never missed an opportunity to buy a new toy, and the drone was her latest and favest. Since it was

proving to be of use on the job tonight, she was happy
to call it her favest, too.

Cautiously she reached out to disconnect the bag
hanging beneath the camera. She took out a grappling
hook and line, the metal clanking softly on the stone,
then grabbed a pair of climbing gloves. The *Shepherdess*, with the fancy red in her tube, went into the bag,
the zipper rasping as it closed. Once it was secure, she
backed to the wall again and gave a thumbs-up, envisioning Padma's beaming face.

"Okay, sweetie, I'll get this baby safely out of here,
and you do the same with yourself. See you at home."

I hope. If her dress didn't get in the way. Her heels.
Her fears. A security guard. A nosy guest. But she had
a talent for managing risks.

"FYI," Padma added, "countdown to fireworks, four
minutes. People should be gathering outside the ballroom. Be careful."

Lisette watched the drone disappear into the sky,
making no more noise than an annoying cicada. Once
she lost sight of it, she turned her attention to the grappling hook and the 9.5-millimeter line attached to it.
What goes up must come down. Of course, going up a
flight of stairs was so much safer than sliding down a
piece of rope.

Heart pounding, she knelt even though her entire
body agreed that edging closer to the balustrade was
a really bad idea. She pushed those voices to the back
of her head and concentrated on securing the hook and
the rope with clammy hands. She wasn't as expert with
her climbing gear as she should be, since she tried to
avoid self-induced terror as often as possible. Everything else about her job—the ingress and egress, the

intel, the plans, the backup plans, the disguises—all that was dangerous but fun. Climbing, whether up or down, was just plain scary.

"What're you doing?"

Lisette jerked, spinning around like a turtle hunkered on the ground to face the man who'd spoken, her feet sliding between two squat columns, dangling in air. One shoe slipped, then slid off her foot in slow motion, landing somewhere below without a sound.

For an instant, she wanted to strangle Jack Sinclair, but that would mean prying her hands loose from the stone, and that wasn't happening until it was do-or-die time.

She'd had two choices for this role in her drama: Jack or his friend Simon Toussaint. It had been no choice, even without her mother's lifelong insistence that the Toussaint family was evil. If Simon had appeared on the balcony, she would have lost her grip and fallen backward to her death. He scared her that much.

Jack, on the other hand, was Prince Charming. She'd never met him, but she'd seen him, mostly on the internet, a few times in person. He was tall, blond, tanned and, even in this light, outrageously handsome.

Her gaze was traveling the fine leather of his shoes up to the incredible weave of his trousers when abruptly he crouched in front of her. His brows were quirked, and so was his mouth as their gazes connected. His expression was tinged with curiosity, but underneath that was tautly controlled intensity. Interest. Even amusement.

She didn't take comfort in that assessment.

"Well?" he prompted.

She swallowed hard. "I'm taking a shortcut downstairs for the fireworks."

He looked at the grappling hook and the line, then freed her right hand from its grip on the rope. "Not with these gloves. They're great for not leaving prints, but you'd better have a heavier pair somewhere, or your bloody hands will give you away."

Those same reactions from seeing the painting—goose bumps, muscles tightening, breath catching—returned, provoking a curious emotion, not as awestruck as the painting but not as, say, nauseating as the height of the balcony.

She was in the process of reclaiming her hand when he stiffened, turning his head slightly toward the room. She would like to think it was just a gesture, listening out of habit, but she'd heard the sounds, too, the opening and closing of heavy doors. The rumble of male voices, barely audible outside.

"You got gloves?" he asked again as he withdrew a pair of his own from inside his jacket. The man carried climbing gloves in his tuxedo? Before she could finish being surprised by that, she accepted it. Tools of the trade. Getting caught without them could cost his life.

She ripped off the thin gloves and replaced them with her climbing ones as more voices sounded in the room. Was it staff sneaking in to watch the fireworks from the best seats in the house? Guards making rounds? Or maybe Candalaria himself had come in to show off a wonder, talk business or get busy with the latest woman on his arm. It didn't matter, though. Getting caught on the balcony didn't bode well for Lisette.

She wasn't sure how it boded for Sinclair.

"Come on, Cinderella, get moving, or I'm hijacking your coach for myself."

Giving herself a mental shake, Lisette tucked the

thin gloves into the bodice of her dress, hiked up her dress and slid her bare foot over the knee wall, curling her toes into the stone as if they might find a lifesaving grip there. Her palms were sweaty, her heart was pounding, and she wasn't sure she could do it. Swing the other leg over. Step into thin air. Have a good fall while avoiding one hell of a bad landing. But she had no choice. She very much wanted to avoid prison, even more to avoid death.

Jack's hand brushed her arm. "Let me go first. If anything goes wrong, I'll break your fall."

Gentlemanly? Or seeing to his own safety first? Either way, she couldn't protest over the knot in her throat. All she could do was watch as he slipped over the wall, then gracefully disappeared from sight without making a sound…and listen as the lock on the French doors clicked. The reflections on the glass panes shifted as the door slowly pushed outward. A gold-and-silver ball exploded in the sky high above the grounds, and a raspy voice said, "We're right on time."

Grasping the rope, driven purely by adrenaline, she swung her entire body over the wall to dangle in the air, nothing more than a thin line and her own ten fingers stopping her from splatting to the ground. Instantly she closed her eyes, unable to look at the sky, the tops of trees, the people made so small by distance they didn't look real.

As she clung to the rope, the swaying caused by the inelegant start of her descent stopped. Time to start moving, to press her knees to the line, to balance her weight on her arms, to slide hand over hand down to the ground… Nothing happened.

Time, she told herself more forcefully. She couldn't

freeze now. She was strong, lifting weights just for this purpose, but she couldn't hold herself forever. Even the thought sent fine tremors through her hands, up her arms and across her shoulders to meet in the middle.

Another starburst appeared in the sky with a muffled *boom*, so bright it would take only one guest glancing about to spot her dangling there. Sadly, there was no contingency for that in plans A, B, C or D.

Panic danced up her back, but before it got close enough to make the short leap into her brain, warm fingers closed around her ankle. Jack tugged on it, not enough to startle her into letting go, too much to ignore. Had he already reached the ground and come back up for her, or had he been waiting all this time?

Either way, the touch of his hand made her feel safer, braver. Focusing on that bravery, she pried up her left fingers one at a time, let her body slide, then grasped the rope again and repeated the action with her right hand. Let go, slide, grab tight, over and over, and the entire time Jack Sinclair's fingers remained around her ankle.

At last, even with her eyes closed, she knew she was only feet above the ground. She could tell it from the overwhelming mix of perfumes that assaulted the air, from the voices, the clinking of glasses, the aura created by too many people jammed into too small a space.

"You can open your eyes."

She didn't want to, not until her feet were on the ground—hell, not until her butt was on the ground. But she forced them open and saw that they'd wound up exactly where she'd planned: in the corner where the east wing jutted out from the main building, in the shadows created by a feathery tree growing in a giant pot. Before she could undo her grip on the rope, Jack laid his hands at her waist and lifted her away.

He set her on her feet in the corner, stone at her back, earth under her feet, and stood close, his gaze crinkled as he studied her. His eyes were the rich, startling blue that she kept in her stock of tinted contact lenses, except his were natural. She studied them, looking for something—suspicion, awareness, too many questions or too many answers. She wondered why he had helped her, if he would now turn her over to Candalaria or figure she owed him a favor for not jamming her up. She wondered if she could escape him.

A very small part of her wondered if she had to escape him right this very moment.

Considering that last thought, she paid little attention to his movements—stripping off his gloves, stuffing them into his pockets, straightening his jacket, smoothing a wrinkle from her dress.

"Stay here." He ducked behind the tree before disappearing around the corner of the building.

This would be the perfect time for her to run, and she even took a few stumbling steps before leaning against the wall again. She'd known better than to wear four-inch heels on a job, especially ones that could fall off so easily, but she'd been swayed by the fact that they made her legs look damn good. But slipping out of the party like this would raise the question of how she'd managed to lose a shoe, and the last thing she wanted was questions.

Especially given that, before long, both the grappling hook's presence and the *Shepherdess*'s disappearance would be discovered.

With the faintest of rustles, Jack returned, her shoe

seeming delicate and small in his hand. Prince Charming, she thought again, at exactly the instant he whispered, "Your slipper, Cinderella."

"Thank you." She took the shoe, wiggled her foot into it, straightened, and…

…leaned to the side and puked.

Jack took a hasty step back even as his hand went automatically to the handkerchief in his pocket. Bella Donna, the most famous thief in his rather elite circle, was throwing up after a relatively simple job. It didn't fit the cool, mysterious persona.

She really was beautiful, even as she dabbed her mouth with the handkerchief. The skin exposed by her dress was a lovely bronze; her body was long, lean and muscular; her breasts were nicely rounded; and her hair was thick with curls. Her eyes were brown—at least for tonight—and her facial structure was classical: smooth forehead, high cheekbones, the kind of nose plastic surgeons offered their less fortunate patients, the kind of mouth made for kissing.

That face momentarily wore a chagrined look.

"You have a place to put those gloves? Because it's time for us to say our goodbyes."

She pulled off the climbing gloves, tugged her dress high enough that a slit exposed a length of long thigh and some kind of black rig vaguely reminiscent of a thigh holster, where she stuffed the gloves. He regretted watching the fabric slide back into place. He wouldn't have thought that second skin of a dress could conceal anything, but when she stepped away from the wall, his scrutiny gave no hint that she was hiding anything more than a breath beneath the gown.

So what had she stolen? he wondered as he followed her, easing out of the darkness between starbursts, murmuring *excuse me* as they wove their way to the doors. Something small enough to conceal, maybe even brazenly wear. Maybe he could persuade her to go to his hotel with him, to let him take down her hair and run his fingers through the curls. To undo the zipper of her dress and slide the fabric down her body, to discover what, besides gloves, was underneath it. Maybe...

Once inside the ballroom, where guests bored by fireworks chatted in small groups, she faced him, all calm and composed. "I appreciate your help, Mr. Sinclair."

He wasn't surprised she knew his name. He'd stopped being modest about his reputation—both of them—years ago. He was sure she realized that his assistance had been unnecessary. She might have balked at taking that first step off the balcony, but she would have found the courage.

"I appreciate your not throwing up on my favorite tux."

The corners of her mouth twitched to avoid a smile. His gaze skimmed from that lovely sight to her ears— bare—then her throat, wrists, fingers, also bare. If she'd stolen one of David's countless jewels, she wasn't bold enough to walk out with it on.

"What were you doing up there?"

"Following you. They chose well when they named you Bella Donna. Most of us shorten it to just Bella."

Nothing passed through her eyes—no recognition, surprise, admission. "I'm afraid you've mistaken me for someone else."

He leaned closer, realizing she wore no perfume, either. Scents lingered, created memories, caused downfalls. "There aren't so many of us that we aren't familiar with one another. The stories about you, Bella..."

An older woman, notoriously passionate for gossip, gave them a curious look as she approached. The diamond studs twinkling in her ears were worth easily twenty grand, and he'd received three requests to relieve her of the gaudy ruby bracelet around her wrist so the stones could be put into a setting that did them justice.

"Are those—"

"Real? Yes. Burmese. Ten stones of ten carats each. Worth somewhere around eight million dollars."

"Where are her bodyguards?"

"Around." When the woman stopped in front of them, he leaned forward to kiss her cheek. "Aunt Gloria, I didn't realize you were here."

He caught the widening of Bella's eyes, along with the gleam in Gloria's expression.

"I imagine you were otherwise preoccupied. I saw you two disappearing from the ballroom. Our host didn't, though. David was regaling a small group of us with stories of his adventures. Do you know how it feels to have every bit of air slowly sucked out of your body to the point you can't think, can't move, can't even try to escape?"

She directed the question to Bella, who mutely nodded her head. Gloria smiled. "That's our David. He has millions of millions, and in spite of that, he is undoubtedly the dullest and most boring man on earth." Then she turned her smile to include Jack. "Of course, we only love him for his money, don't we?"

Jack murmured a noncommittal response, then silence fell. His aunt was waiting for an introduction.

Apparently, Bella figured it out and began to take tiny steps like a drunken crab, sideways and backward at the same time. When she put enough distance between them, her intent, no doubt, was to ditch him. His intent was to not let that happen.

He took hold of her arm, her skin warm and silken, her muscles tightening at his touch. "Aunt Gloria, this is my friend—"

"Lisette Malone. Of course," Gloria said. "Someone pointed you out earlier. The gentleman you work with at the museum, I believe. The one with the damp palms."

Lisette Malone. Most likely not her real name, but one these people would be much more comfortable with than Bella Donna.

Once more the corners of Bella's—Lisette's mouth twitched. "Mr. Chen."

"Yes, that's the one. I'm Gloria Mantegna. Even though I'm his great-aunt, Jack calls me aunt to my face and old bat behind my back."

"Aunt Gloria," he protested, but she patted his hand.

"It's a pleasure meeting you, Ms. Mantegna," Lisette said dutifully.

"My friends call me Gloria. My men friends call me Glory. Most of 'em are standin' at attention when they say it." Bawdy humor brought out traces of the Alabama accent she'd tried very hard to lose, and her bright, lascivious smile took ten years off her face. Considering that she was well-aged and astonishingly rich, Jack had no problem imagining long lines of men friends wherever she found herself.

He just didn't want that image in his head.

Abruptly she made a shooing motion. "David's heading this way. You two go. I'll brave the boredom for you."

Jack flashed a smile at his aunt, turned Lisette in a 180 and began strolling toward the main entrance.

"He won't think it rude, your leaving without saying good-night?"

"It won't be the first time."

"That you've been rude?"

"That I've left without saying good-night." He smiled as a few instances flashed through his mind: Viviana, Siobhan, Celene. Good memories.

Their steps echoed as they entered the cavernous hallway running through the middle of the castle. Servants crossed at various intersections, scurrying to salons, private meetings, up the grand staircase. None of them glanced at Jack and Lisette. The guards stationed every thirty feet did, though. There wasn't a man in the ranks shorter than six foot five, or tipping the scales at less than 250 pounds.

As they passed under the scrutiny of the last guard, Lisette moved a step closer to Jack. "They're a bit scary, aren't they?"

"Just a bit? They terrify me."

When they reached the entrance, staff opened doors tall enough to accommodate a double-decker bus. They walked through, met with cool air and a light breeze and, for Jack, a sense of relief. Not that they were free yet. That wouldn't happen until they drove the four miles to the gate, where more guards awaited.

While valets went to retrieve their vehicles, Lisette tugged her arm from his grasp. "As I said before, thank you for the assistance."

He pushed his hands into his pockets and studied her. "What did you take?"

No shifts in expression gave her away. She simply smiled and extended her arms out from her sides. "Do I look like I'm hiding something?"

His gaze slid over her with fine appreciation. "No. But appearances can be deceiving. And I'm pretty sure you weren't crawling around that balcony just for the feel of the stone against your skin."

The valet with her car returned first, saving her from a reply. There was no sign of the other valet with Jack's rental, meaning she would have at least a couple minutes' head start. "It's been an experience," she said, stepping away as the car stopped at the curb.

"I'll see you again, Bella."

She murmured something, then pulled a bill from nowhere to tip the valet. She gave Jack one last smile, the loveliest, sexiest, most beguiling of all, before getting into the car and driving away.

He hadn't planned to let her go so easily, but plans changed. He knew the name she was using, and he knew where she was working for the moment. He would find her again.

Chapter 2

Certain she hadn't been followed, Lisette drove to the only home she'd ever known. She'd taken her first steps on its floors, eaten baby food at the kitchen table, screamed through too many baths to count in the claw-foot tub. Marley had loved the small house, and because of that, Lisette did, too.

Padma's car was parked in the driveway; Lisette pulled in beside it. Shivering in the chill air, she hustled up the side steps to the porch. As she reached out with her key, the door swung open and Padma ushered her inside. "No one followed you."

That used to be Marley's line, never a question because she'd taught them better. "Nobody."

"Not even Prince Charming?" Padma screwed up her face in disappointment. If Prince—Jack didn't track down Lisette tomorrow, they had a plan B and C for dealing with that, too.

"You got the painting back safe?"

"Of course. Was the party fabulous?"

"Obscenely expensive champagne, priceless antiques, fortunes in jewels, the rich and the filthy rich." Lisette shrugged, and the shimmer of her gown made her long for her usual evening outfit of shorts and T-shirt.

"You look so gorgeous. I can't believe the men left you alone long enough to steal *Shepherdess.* That dress is incredible, and the shoes—! Damn you for being a size bigger than me."

Two glasses of yogurt-milk-mango *lassi* sat on the coffee table, along with a plate of *gulab jamun*, a deep-fried sweet that smelled delicately of rose water. "When was your mom here?"

"She got here right after me. You know, I could learn to cook my family's traditional dishes, but then who would Mommy cook for on chilly winter nights?"

Lisette snorted. Mommy, better known as Dr. Laksha Khatri, was a bioengineer at the University of Colorado Denver, and she was happy enough cooking for Daddy, Sandesh, a gastroenterologist, who was usually trying to diet. "I'm sure Dr. Mom would find something else to occupy her time, like, I don't know, cloning a human or something."

"Could come in handy in our line of work." Padma helped herself to dessert, then drew her feet onto the couch. She wore comfy clothes, all in black, and a sturdy pair of black boots were kicked off nearby. Her hair was pulled into a ponytail, and her jewelry—necklace, earrings, bracelet, watchband—was all black in deference to the job. *You don't know how hard it is for this Indian girl to give up her gold,* she lamented on a regular basis.

Lisette tasted the *gulab jamun* and sighed. "It's settled. Your mom can never leave Denver for more than a couple weeks at a time. I couldn't survive longer than that without her cooking."

"She'll be pleased you said so."

Lisette had been saying so most of their lives. The Khatris had been her and Marley's only family. Even though Padma's mom had worked, she'd always made time for two curious little girls. She was a dark-eyed woman with a ready laugh and enough love for a dozen daughters, and she'd generously showered Lisette with it.

Had the good doctor known she was pampering the daughter of a criminal? When she'd given the girls her regular empowerment talks, telling them to find a career they loved and dedicate themselves to it with passion, to soar into the heavens with it, had she ever suspected that career would be stealing back previously stolen treasures?

"I did some checking," Padma said, wiping her fingers on a napkin. "Jack is staying at Air. You know, that gorgeous old mansion turned trendy boutique hotel for the super-rich?"

"Air? Seriously? What did they name the restaurant? Water?"

"Don't be ridiculous." Padma paused for effect. "Water's the spa. The restaurant is Fire, the bar is Spirit, and the grounds are Earth." If she was kidding, her eyes would dance and the corners of her lips would twitch for the seconds it took her laugh to escape. None of that happened, though, which made Lisette shudder.

If she had that kind of money to invest in a getaway, the inn would be named Inn, with a crudely carved arrow pointing the way to Eat. The beach would require no sign because it would lie fifty paces from her hammock.

"It's insane," Padma went on. "Remember when we used to go there? It was so crazy perfect for its time period, but now everything's all very minimalist. Do you think that's the kind of place he prefers? Do you think he's done that to his home on the island?"

"I hope I get a chance to find out." Lisette spoke without so much as a twinge in her stomach. She'd long ago dealt with the fact that this plan—

A fool's plan, Marley reminded her.

—meant Lisette would almost certainly find herself getting intimate with Jack Sinclair. Her mother had made such a big deal of it—

It is *a big deal!*

—but women had sex with men for a thousand reasons, and gaining access to Île des Deux Saints and *Le Mystère* was the best reason Lisette could imagine.

Besides, he was damn good-looking, too.

"Maybe he just likes staying at $3,000-a-night hotels," Padma said with a sigh. "I'd like to live like that for a while, to know what it's like to have the best of everything."

"Aw, if you had that kind of money, you'd spend it saving the world."

"Schools, water-treatment centers, clinics, sustainable growth." Padma sighed again. Those were her passions. When she wasn't handling electronics on their job, she used her environmental engineering degree to supply clean water around the world. It completed her in the way that returning a person's lost property completed Lisette.

Padma abruptly swung her feet to the floor. "Come see it. Take your time appreciating it because we have an appointment to return it tomorrow afternoon."

Lisette followed her into the dining room, where candlesticks and a vase holding a bouquet of flowers had been moved to the sideboard next to a tea set. Padma motioned that way. "The red is in the sugar bowl. And *Shepherdess...*"

The painting was unrolled in the center of the table, lit by the dozen small bulbs in the chandelier. It was still amazing—still gave Lisette a shiver. She studied it, her fingers itching to mimic the strokes, the colors. Mimic was all she could do. Her talent lay in stealing art, not creating it.

Tomorrow they would return it to a house like this on the other side of town. It would be lovely if Mrs. Maier could hang it in the bedroom once again, but losing a piece once made people cautious. Their recovered treasures usually went into a safe or a safe-deposit box or on loan to a museum. After all, if someone had stolen it once, then precautions must be taken to stop it from happening again.

Lisette and Padma could recover their property, but they couldn't restore their peace of mind.

And that was a shame.

Jack didn't like museums—they were set up specifically to avoid the intimacy needed to truly appreciate the works—but that didn't mean he hadn't spent thousands of hours in them. He'd seen the top collections in the world, roaming galleries the way other people hung out in malls, movie theaters and clubs.

The Candalaria wasn't in the top of its class yet, but

David intended to get there. He'd bought the Castle with the intention of housing his collections there but decided a more easily accessible spot in the city would bring in more visitors. Today it certainly had visitors.

Jack's invitation from last night could have gotten him the VIP treatment at the private entrance half a mile down the road, but he preferred to mingle with normal folk, to wait his turn, entertain himself and count security guards—eight so far.

And, this particular morning at least, to think about Lisette Malone. Was she Bella Donna?

Her plan last night hadn't been complicated, and it hadn't gone off flawlessly. She'd taken too long, risking discovery, and she'd had that frozen moment on the balcony before she'd forced herself over the edge. To be fair, though, his showing up had thrown her off schedule, and she would have dealt fine with her fear. There were things he didn't like to do, but they were easy when the only other options were capture or death.

The Candalaria had only one floor aboveground, with two floors of vaults, offices and work spaces beneath, but the roofline undulating from a mere twenty feet at one end to a hundred or more at the other made it seem huge. There were gardens of every type outside, but few people showed interest in them. Instead, they queued along the sidewalks, awaiting entrance to the museum.

Pushing his hands into his pockets, he studied the people around him. Most looked as if they could be waiting at the local cinema, but the artists stood out: accomplished or novices, young, old and every age in between, carrying backpacks, sketch pads, pencils. An aura of anticipation weaved around them, excitement

and appreciation and the fervent desire to someday create pieces of art that would inspire this same feeling
in others.

"You can pick the serious artists out of every bunch.
They all give off pheromones of canvas, paper, oil and
pastels."

Jack turned to find Lisette—Bella?—Malone standing a few feet away. Her gorgeous black hair curled
around her face and down to her shoulders, and her gorgeous legs were covered by tailored black trousers. Last
night's sexy shoes had been traded for flats, no doubt
more comfortable for work but not the star of many fantasies. A white shirt topped the trousers, long-sleeved,
buttoned down the front, unexpected bits of lace edging
the placket on both sides. With a little silver-and-onyx
jewelry, she pulled off a look of minimalist elegance.

She tilted her head to one side, studying him. Realizing long moments had passed while he'd done the same
to her, he gave himself a mental shake. "Pheromones,
right. Sorry. I was more interested in your pheromones
at the moment."

The intensity of her gaze dialed back to what could
be described as merely curiosity. "Why are you standing in line? Your invitation gives you access to the VIP
entrance."

He gave her a pleasant smile. "I was in the VIP zoo
last night. I'd rather hang out with real people this morning."

"Really." She didn't sound quite convinced.

It was one of the consequences of being born into
a family with more money than most nations. Everyone expected him to be spoiled and demanding, to not

do mundane things, to be incapable of living daily life without an army of assistants to do the heavy lifting.

He leaned closer to her and caught a whiff of perfume. It was sweet and made him hungry. "When I'm at home, I do all the cleaning, cooking, laundry and toilet-scrubbing myself." It was true, too, though he spent only two or three months a year in the house he considered home. The rest of the time he traveled, staying in hotels or Sinclair family homes, always fully staffed with people ready to meet his every need. "Was it as impressive as you expected it to be?"

Her forehead wrinkled, tiny lines fanning away from the delicate arch of her brows. "The party?"

A lesser man might have bought her confusion, but Jack knew how to convey perfect confusion, too, as well as perfect innocence. "*Shepherdess.*"

Nothing flinched, nothing twitched, her gaze didn't shift away, her eyes didn't grow smokier or rounder or flare with alarm. Damn, she was good.

"You must have heard about it at the museum this morning. One of David's recent acquisitions disappeared from the Castle during the party. Seems whoever took it left a grappling hook behind."

"So... I wasn't the only one there with a grappling hook."

The line moved forward a few inches, the art students behind them overshooting and standing too close for comfort. On impulse, Jack took Lisette's arm and turned her toward the sculpture garden. "Walk with me."

"I have work—"

"Tell David I asked you for a personal tour. How did you even know I was out here?"

"Mr. Chen saw you on the surveillance cameras. He sent me to retrieve you."

The gentleman with the damp palms, according to Aunt Gloria. "Is surveilling visitors part of your job?"

"No. But he'd noticed a few female security officers drooling over the monitors. Is it fun, turning heads everywhere you go?"

"You tell me."

With a laugh, she shrugged off the answer. The path they were following wound from sculpture to sculpture, the material ranging from marble to concrete, granite and weathering steel. The mountain scene in front of them—cabin, tumbling river and boulders—created from weathering steel looked as if it had been rusting in its spot for at least a hundred years, even though it had been installed only five years ago.

"So...*Shepherdess.*"

A breeze stirred Lisette's hair, and she brushed it back before he'd finished the thought that he'd like to do it himself. "Considering the level of security at the Castle, I'm surprised anyone would think about stealing even a napkin."

He'd thought about it—not with serious intent. But on his visits, he always looked for weak spots, vulnerabilities. Hell, he did that everywhere he went.

And Bella/Lisette had done more than think about it. She'd stolen a twenty-four-by-thirty-inch painting and somehow gotten it out of the house and, presumably, off the property.

"How did you do it?"

Again she tilted her head to look at him. "Mr. Chen kept me busy most of the evening. The only moment I had to myself was on the balcony, and you interrupted that. And you saw what I was wearing. I certainly didn't smuggle a painting out with me."

Yes, he'd admired what she was *barely* wearing. But she'd concealed at least a pair of gloves beneath that dress. But no painting. "You had a partner."

"Was that why you were there? To steal *Shepherdess*? Is that why you're pointing fingers at me, to divert suspicion from yourself?"

Slowly she started walking again, leaving the cabin behind, and Jack stayed with her. He held up one hand. "My fingers aren't pointing. I would never cast suspicion on an associate. Consider my curiosity professional interest, but if it makes you uncomfortable… I want you to be comfortable with me."

He laid his hand on her arm to stop her, making her face him. "Are you, Lisette?"

Her gaze on his hand, Lisette considered his question. Comfortable? Under different circumstances, definitely. Their worlds were galaxies apart, but common interests and opinions could render that inconsequential. At his core, he was a handsome, charming man whose mere look could stir a sizzle deep inside her. At her core, she was an unattached woman with a fine appreciation of sizzles.

"Is comfort what you look for in a woman?"

"Aw, you know what I mean."

"Then you should say what you mean."

"I do…at least I mean what I say."

She began walking, and his fingers slid away from her arm. Even though her sleeves covered her to her wrists, she missed the contact. It was a sad state of affairs when a simple touch from a man could be so significant.

A dangerous man. A man who was convinced she was a thief. A man she had to use to complete her job. She needed to be coldhearted enough to pull this off.

Lisette retrained her focus on the conversation. "Did your nanny read *Alice in Wonderland* to you when you were a child?"

"Mom did. I never had a nanny. When she had to go somewhere, one of the servants got stuck keeping an eye on me. I've been told not even a bonus in their paychecks was enough incentive to make anyone volunteer, but because they liked working for my parents, they gritted their teeth and bore it."

With the sun highlighting his blond hair and tanned skin, his eyes twinkling and his smile perfect and improbably innocent, it should have been difficult to picture him as a rambunctious little hellion. It wasn't. Add in well-fitted gray trousers, a paler gray shirt, a pair of sigh-inducingly expensive loafers and all the spendy trendy sophistication about him, she found it impossible to believe he'd been anything *but* the pirate that flowed through generations of his blood.

"I can see that," she said, and his smile grew into a grin that was anything but innocent. She was acutely aware when his gaze settled on her. It warmed her skin and sent tiny electric shivers through her.

"I bet you were a perfect child."

"I was."

"An only?"

"Yes. But my best friend lived down the block. Now she's my roommate. We're better than sisters."

"Thick as thieves, eh?"

More heat washed through her, as intense as before, but this time all that current gathered in her stomach to send an unpleasant jolt through her. With sheer will, she kept her gaze steady, her manner easy, her voice serene. "You'd know more about thieves than I would."

"Okay, let's suppose you had a perfectly innocent reason for being on David's balcony with a grappling hook and gloves. What was it?"

Damn, where were innocent reasons when she needed them?

She did the only thing she could: she lied. "Someone asked me to meet him there."

"With a grappling hook?"

"He had some…quirks."

Jack laughed out loud. "So you and this guy were going to indulge in monkey sex from David's chandelier?"

"For some people, the stranger the place they do it, the more they like it."

His fingers brushed her arm, then slid down to wrap around her hand. "So I've heard, but I'd bet my next trust-fund payment you're not one of them."

Trust fund. Briefly she reconsidered the notion that common interests could make vast differences meaningless. In theory, she supposed. But then, he was paid regularly from a large trust fund, while she got paychecks, finder's fees and occasional influxes of operating capital. It sounded better that way than admitting that sometimes she stole modest pieces from other thieves to help fund her retrieval business.

Had Candalaria noticed the fancy red was missing? All the gossip she'd heard so far limited the loss to

Shepherdess, but he could be keeping the red's disappearance quiet for a reason.

"Jack, you old pirate!"

Lisette was so lost in thought that the voice startled her into a stumble. Jack's hand tightened, giving her balance, but in contrast his tone was easy and friendly. "A poor pirate I'd have been, David. You know I get seasick."

David Candalaria was a few inches shorter than Jack, his face less finely formed. He could have been considered handsome, with his muddy brown eyes, his hawkish nose, his strong square jaw, especially when everything about him whispered incredible wealth. But there was a softness to his features, an arrogance, a disdain for all people who were *less*. He shook Jack's hand, but his gaze didn't even stray toward Lisette, and she hoped it didn't. She really preferred being totally off his radar.

"You come from a long line of pirates and blackguards, Jack. I come from a long line of number-crunchers. You've got to admit, yours sounds more fun." Without waiting for a response, he went on. "I heard you were standing in line out front with the provincials. Why would you think you could get away with that here? Chen was supposed to send his assistant to bring you inside, but who knows where she went. You know how hard it is to get good help." Heaving a sigh, he rolled his eyes, then seemed to notice Lisette for the first time. His smile turned smarmy, one she had seen many times but never directed at her. "And who is this?"

"Mr. Chen's assistant," Jack said drily, "who came to take me inside. I persuaded her to show me the gardens instead."

"Hmm. Well, she can get back to work. Come on in,

Jack. I'll show you the *King's Treasures*, then my chef
will work his culinary magic for us."

For a second time, Lisette rethought her common
interests/disparate background theory. Jack Sinclair
clearly didn't mind associating with the provincials.
David Candalaria clearly did. Being young, smart and
passionate about art and earning every penny of her
salary twice over meant nothing to him. Not having
money or a pedigree did.

When she tried to pull her hand from Jack's, he tightened his grip. "Actually, David, I was just persuading
Lisette to have lunch with me at Fire. She's insisting
that work comes first, but maybe you could do me a
favor and give her the day off. Then she can give me
the grand tour after lunch."

Lisette's heart rate doubled. Lunch? The grand tour?
Spending the entire day with Jack? Part of her hoped
her boss refused. She needed time to strengthen her defenses before facing Jack privately again.

And part of her hoped Candalaria valued his friendship with a Sinclair more than he did a full day's work
from a nobody employee he couldn't even remember.
Besides, Padma would be so disappointed if Lisette
missed a chance to experience Fire.

Candalaria looked her over again and, just as easily as before, dismissed her. "Sure, Jack, whatever you
want. Hey, I'm having dinner with Gloria this evening.
Why don't you join us?"

"Sorry, I already have plans."

Thankfully, Candalaria's cell buzzed. Murmuring
"Later, man," he pulled it from his pocket and focused
on the screen as he walked away.

Lisette took a few steps to the side, then folded her

arms over her middle, each fist tucked behind a protective elbow. "Ms. Mantegna seems very attentive to him given that she thinks he's the dullest and most boring man in the world."

Jack nodded toward the museum and the lot where he was parked. Slowly they began moving that way. "Think of Aunt Gloria as a cat and David as her mouse. He seriously covets those rubies, and it amuses her to dangle them in front of him. He's convinced that if he keeps trying, he'll wear her down like water dripping on stone. Everyone else knows there's not a chance in hell, but he considers his refusal to accept no for an answer one of his best qualities."

"Do you accept no for an answer?"

He grinned. "You're having lunch with me, aren't you?"

"You could have asked me instead of my boss."

If he heard the faint chastisement in her voice, he didn't care. "Under normal circumstances, I would think his not recognizing you was just typical David behavior, but these aren't normal circumstances, are they? How much effort do you put into staying invisible around him?"

"No effort. Most of the staff are invisible to him."

"And when you're stealing from him, that's a big plus, isn't it?"

"Again with the thief thing. You need a new song and dance." She veered onto a narrow sidewalk that led to a door marked Employees Only and swiped her ID card through the reader. "I need to get my purse."

He glanced at the long line of patrons waiting outside and at the crowded throngs inside. "I'll wait here."

"Lucky you. I'll be back in a few minutes."

"If I'd gone into the family business, my nickname would have been Lucky Jack." His gaze met hers and held for a long moment. "Nice to know my luck's holding today."

Lisette's breath caught in her chest; her feet refused to step across the threshold. It took raucous laughter inside to startle her into movement. "I'll be back."

His only response was a knowing smile.

It's a fool's plan, baby girl, Marley's voice echoed in her head as she let the door close, then hurried along the corridor.

And Lisette was playing the part of the fool.

"You ever visit this place before it underwent its improvements?" Giving the last word a twist, Jack closed the menu and laid it on the table, watching as Lisette's slender fingers shook out the napkin in her lap, her deep crimson nails a contrast to the creamy linen.

"My mother brought us here every year at Christmas."

"Us?"

"Padma and me. It was our tradition for the Sunday after Thanksgiving. The house was decorated for Christmas, they served the typical holiday dishes and they held workshops on things like making candles, tying bows and making ornaments. A local choir sang carols in period dress, and if it snowed, they got out the family's sleds and let us use them on the hill out back." She glanced around the restaurant. "Is this the kind of place you usually seek out?"

He looked around, too. He'd been through the old house only once, when his family had stopped on their way elsewhere. He remembered exquisite woods and marble and incredibly detailed Persian rugs, heavily paneled rooms with huge fireplaces, elaborate architectural details in every room.

Now there was bamboo, hemp and sisal. Fabric panels draped from the ceiling, covered the walls, acted as doors and curtains, and the bed linens were made from soy fabrics, cashmere and alpaca. And everything was in shades of off-white, cream and tan.

"I usually stay at the Brown Palace, but someone suggested I try this hotel. The name should have served as a warning."

"You visit Denver often?"

"Enough to have favorite places." What was that faint emotion? Simple curiosity. Maybe a bit of pleasure. Definitely a little dismay. It was fitting that someone who'd gone to as much effort to remain anonymous as Bella Donna wouldn't be happy with the idea that someone who'd uncovered her identity might hang out in her city.

"I ski, hike, do some climbing." He paused while the waiter served the most colorless salads he'd ever seen: lettuce, hearts of palm and mushrooms, all anemic. Even the avocados were paler than they should be.

He looked up, saw the mild distaste on Lisette's face, then at the same time they burst into laughter. Other guests in the dining room spared brief disapproving glances before returning to their own business.

She was the first to take a bite, and she made a soft *mmm* sound that rippled through him, leaving awareness and pleasure and anticipation in its wake. "It's delicious."

"It's very good given that the best you can say about its presentation is that it's totally inoffensive," he said after a bite, then returned to the interrupted conversation. "Do you ski?"

"If I had my way, I wouldn't leave the house when the temperature dropped below forty."

"What about hiking?"

"Sometimes. I even run and lift weights. It's one of the requirements of letting Padma's mom feed us."

"And I already know you're not big on climbing."

Her brows arched. "Climbing doesn't bother me at all. It's the falling that scares me."

"You need to work on that. In a field like ours, it can be the difference between success and fifteen to life in prison." He waited for her denial, but it didn't come.

Instead she ate a few more bites of salad, washed it down with water, then asked, "Does Mr. Candalaria know you're a thief?"

Jack shrugged.

"Why does he continue inviting you to his parties?"

"He likes socializing with Sinclairs more than he worries about getting robbed. Most of David's art is an investment. He buys it, holds on to it until he meets someone who wants it more, then he sells it for a profit. The pieces he truly values, if they were stolen, he would hire someone to steal them back."

"Does he truly value *Shepherdess*?"

"He didn't have it on display, which suggests he acquired it under less than legal circumstances, so my guess would be yes. He'll probably want it back."

Again, the waiter interrupted, bringing their entrées, taking away their salad plates. When he was gone, Lisette smiled happily at her plate: grass-fed, wood-grilled steak, baked potato and onions, and sautéed bell peppers of every color. She cut into the steak, took a small bite, savored it and swallowed. "Well, he can't have it back."

"You stole it for the original owner, didn't you?"

She didn't admit it. She didn't deny it, either.

"He had it stolen once. What makes you think he won't do it again?"

"He's free to do anything he wants. But I suspect it won't be so easy to obtain the next time."

Jack studied her. Was that why none of Bella's prizes were ever heard of again? Because she wasn't selling them to black-market collectors but returning them to their owners and instructing them on safer ways to protect them in the future?

It was a better reason to steal than his own. He liked the challenge: researching, plotting, getting in and out, the occasional thrill. He liked the connection it gave him to his family history. And no one ever got hurt. The people he stole from had insurance if the piece had been legally acquired or had too much money to miss a few million if it hadn't. As for the people who hired him, odds were good they would be his target someday, if they hadn't been already. Karma was a bitch in that way.

"What about the fancy red?"

If he hadn't been watching her closely, he would have missed the widening of her eyes. It happened so quickly he could have imagined it…but he didn't.

"What fancy red?"

"The one you took from the Italian clothing designer. The crown jewel of his collection, excuse the pun."

Her expression eased, her voice sounding a shade more normal. She was a good liar, but not as good as he was. "You mean the one Bella Donna took." When he opened his mouth to argue, she pointed her fork at him. "How long ago was that? Had you already made your career choice?"

"Twelve years. I was on the fringes of the business." He'd made his first big score a week later to celebrate his eighteenth birthday. Of course, he hadn't been able to share the news with anyone besides Simon. Even now, though there were rumors, no one in the family admitted knowledge—or suspicion—of his hobby. But then, his family wasn't the sort to do anything underhanded themselves. People had always told him he was a throwback to the pirate Sinclairs, and he'd proved them right.

"Twelve years ago, I was fifteen and in tenth grade, dealing with mean girls, stupid boys and burned-out teachers. Do you really think I could have pulled off a job like that?"

Jack hated when someone made a valid argument when he was already convinced of the truth. The stories about Bella Donna painted a beautiful, sophisticated woman. Could a fifteen-year-old possibly have fooled them all on the fancy red theft?

Maybe. With help from an older, more experienced partner.

But Bella's other best-known hits... A dozen netsukes carved by master Tomotada in Hong Kong, the rare Wari kingdom artifacts from South America or the collection of antiquarian books that had disappeared on their way to the Library of Congress and reappeared in the home of a Dresden businessman? Could a fifteen-year-old have the poise and polish to jet around the globe, mingling with the world's richest and greediest and carrying off their riches right under their noses? Could she have masqueraded as an elegant, cultured, sensual woman when she was really just a girl?

If she wasn't Bella, who was? And if she wasn't Bella, who the hell was she? Where had she come from? How had she stayed so completely unknown for so long?

He gave her a narrow look while chewing a piece of tender, sweet lobster. Her gaze didn't waver from his. "If you're not Bella, how do you know who I am?"

Something very much like relief seeped over her, though she tried to disguise it by smiling. "There's this wonderful invention called the internet. You're probably so used to cameras going off nearby that you stopped noticing them, but it seems you get your picture taken a thousand times a day."

"Aw, now you're exaggerating. It can't possibly be more than five hundred." He paused. "So it says on the internet I'm a thief?"

"Of course not. I bet your family has lawyers on retainer on every continent."

"With extras in the US."

She took a few more bites, a few sips of water. "I work in the art community. There are hints of whispers of rumors. No one says anything outright because…"

"Good thieves don't leave evidence behind." Finished with his meal, he sprawled comfortably in his chair. "Though there are exceptions. You don't worry that grappling hook and line will lead back to you?"

She was silent a long time, debating whether to answer or brush him off again. He figured she would come to the conclusion that she might as well answer. After all, he'd *seen* her with the hook in hand. Admitting to it wasn't admitting to the theft.

"The hook was bought from a climber years ago. The line was picked up at a climbing facility in California. I wasn't involved in either purchase. I never touched them without gloves, never had them in my home or my car."

Though he still believed she was Bella—just considering the odds against it—the more he talked to Lisette, the more he liked her. She was smart and careful. Throw in gorgeous and his weakness for long legs and thick, silken curls, and he was damn near down for the count. Granted, being enchanted by a beautiful woman was nothing new for him…but it was always fun.

"What about the surveillance cameras?"

Lisette set down her fork, blotted her lips with her napkin and crossed her legs. Damn, he wished she was wearing another dress. Some things just weren't meant to be covered up. "You know better than me that surveillance cameras are never fail-proof."

He did know that. He could hack into a few systems, but he had a buddy who helped with the more complex ones. Was Lisette seriously underemployed at the museum, or did she have a buddy, too? Her friend automatically came to mind. Was Padma a tech whiz? Would Lisette look close to home for her own safety, or would she stray far away for her best friend's safety?

"Enough talk about business. Tell me more about you and Padma."

Her fingers exerted the slightest pressure on her glass. "Not much to tell. We grew up together, went to school together. When my mother died last spring, I inherited her house, and Padma and I moved in there together. At our age with our jobs, free rent trumps everything else."

"I'm sorry about your mother."

"Thank you." She pointedly checked her watch, then folded her napkin and laid it on the table. "We'd better

Chapter 3

In all her years at the museum, that Friday afternoon counted as Lisette's favorite. For hours she and Jack had roamed through the exhibits, and the conversation had stayed relatively safe. She made sure not to mention Padma again and deflected any question of a personal nature. When he'd asked her one, she'd steadied her gaze on him and asked, *Why do you want to know?*

He'd looked back just as steadily and replied, *Because I want to know you.*

Her emotional side had gone mushy before her practical side smacked it back in line. She was with Jack Sinclair for one purpose: to reclaim *Le Mystère*. Not to like him, not to get to know him, not to be flattered by his intimate looks or his flirting. All that was just part of the job, the means to the end. Her emotional side had to remember that.

You're all emotion, Marley had once scoffed. *You're not the sort who uses someone else for your own gain.*

"In this case, I am," Lisette murmured as she crossed the parking lot to a silver midsize that looked like every other car on the road. It wasn't dented or spotlessly clean; the windows had only the usual factory tint: there were no stickers proclaiming her university affiliation, her political beliefs or her sense of humor. It was totally unremarkable.

Just the way she needed to be when she was working. Last night she'd ignored that rule, and today she'd thought it had been a mistake. She had to be cool and in control to keep it from becoming one.

As soon as she left the parking lot, she called Padma. Her friend's voice was tinged with excitement. "I've got the package, sweetie. Where do you want to meet?"

"How about behind Pecos Pete's?"

"Oh, yum. Can we eat there after we visit Mrs. M?"

Her favorite Mexican food on a Friday night, then curling up with her tablet and a movie—sounded like a perfect evening. "Sure." Then, because she couldn't hold it in any longer, she said, "Guess who came to the museum and took me to lunch at Fire?"

Padma shrieked. "Are you kidding? Were you excited? Did you swoon?"

Lisette wasn't sure whether Padma was talking about her reaction to Jack or to the restaurant. "I survived without swooning once. I'll tell you all about it when we meet."

"I can't wait."

Traffic was heavy, so Padma was waiting by the time Lisette pulled into the employee lot behind Pecos Pete's. She parked beside the red car, slid out and into the passenger seat. Padma's handbag was on the floor behind the console, and a large plastic bag filled with rolls of wrapping paper occupied the backseat. "What's with the paper?"

Padma accelerated out of the parking lot about twenty miles an hour faster than safe before grinning at her. "Camouflage. Just to be safe."

Lisette shook her head sadly. "Mom corrupted me. She corrupted you *totally*."

Padma's fine hair slapped around as she took a quick look before screeching from the parking lot across four lanes to reach the turn lane. "She didn't corrupt me. She added to my arsenal of tools to use if ever I need them." Grinning, she parroted Marley. "You can never have too many tools."

And Marley had believed it. That was why Lisette could pick any lock she came across, had learned to hack most computer systems enough to help in an emergency, could cry on command and was conversant in seven languages. She kept abreast of all the latest developments in alarm systems and electronic devices, had developed a pretty good range of accents, could make herself look anywhere from twenty to seventy and worked out regularly. *Be a chameleon,* Marley had taught, and she'd become just that.

Recalling Padma's camouflage remark, Lisette took another look at the plastic bag and saw that one roll of paper had a plastic cap covering its core. The design on the paper was happy and innocent—snowmen frolicking in a wintry landscape—and, if not for the cap, wouldn't draw a second look from anyone. Even with the cap, no one would look at it and think *mailing tube with stolen masterpiece.*

Except Jack.

"So start talking, sweetie. You've got a lot to spill in the next seven miles."

Lisette glanced out the side mirror, noting the cars behind them. She wasn't usually antsy, but she'd never pulled a job in her own hometown, either. And she'd never had Jack on her trail. Which was really kind of a nice place to be, though it would be nicer if he didn't think she was a thief. He was comfortable with people whispering that about him, but she'd never experienced the slightest suspicion from anyone, and she lacked the power and fortune behind his family name. No one but Padma and her parents would care if Lisette Malone was accused of art theft.

That fact made her uneasy, so she pushed it away and asked, "What do you want to hear about first—Jack or the restaurant?"

Padma chewed her bottom lip. It was a hard choice for her: handsome, sexy, single rich guy versus trendiest place in Denver. "Restaurant first," she finally decided.

The car ahead of them came to a sudden stop at a yellow light, and Padma slammed on the brakes, then threw both hands into the air as if to ask *What the hell?* Bless her heart, she was so pretty, delicate and sweet, no one ever seemed to take offense at her actions.

After a glance around, Lisette launched into a detailed description of Fire. Padma responded with gasp after gasp. When Lisette couldn't think of a single other thing to add, Padma's mouth formed a thin line, accompanied by a sigh. "All that beautiful paneling and trim and flooring…gone. That's depressing enough to make me do something crazy like ordering *lehenga cholis* on-line or, heaven forbid, answering emails from Raza's incredibly annoying girlfriend."

Grateful for a fresh topic, and having the same opinion of brother Raza's girlfriend, Lisette considered the *lehenga choli*: a long skirt worn with a midriff-baring bodice. When it came to fashion, Padma was more assimilated than her mother would like, so it would thrill Dr. Mom to see her buying traditional Indian clothing. "Ooh, that pink one you showed me? Could you get it a size larger so I could wear it, too?"

"Or here's an idea, I could buy one for you and one for me so they would both fit. Then we could wear them when we go clubbing and tell everyone we're twins."

"You'd get to be the Indian twin with the fabulous hair, and I'd be the island twin with the insane curls." *Island* was the ethnicity Marley had given whenever Lisette asked. *That doesn't tell me anything,* she protested, and Marley had responded, *Get your DNA done if it bothers you.*

"Here we are." Padma turned into a narrow drive that ended in front of a tidy white house. The garage had been converted to a room, and fall flowers bloomed in planters on the porch. The blinds at the window beside the front door swayed, then the door was flung open.

"Lisette! Padma! It's so good to see my pretty girls." Mrs. Maier was old enough to be their grandmother, pure white hair framing a face that was always creased by a smile. Though she wore no makeup, her cheeks were rosy, and her blue eyes popped against her pale skin. She was average height, slender as a reed, and she smelled of exotic fragrances when she hugged them.

Standing on the porch, arms wrapped around the shopping bag, Padma said loudly, "We brought you some wrapping paper. You know, because the holidays are almost here."

Lisette kept her eyes from rolling by squeezing them shut for a moment. Mrs. Maier, though, didn't miss a beat, replying in an equally loud voice, "Oh, that's so sweet. Yes, with my grandbabies, I'll have a ton of gifts to wrap. Come in, and we'll have tea."

Padma flashed a grin at Lisette before following the old lady inside. Her own smile rueful, Lisette trailed after them and into the kitchen. They sat at the round table that overfilled the room, where a tea service and a plate of cookies waited.

Lisette and Padma chose tea bags from the bowl next to the pot, and Mrs. Maier poured steaming water over them in delicate porcelain cups. Next she passed around the cookies, then tended to her own tea before smiling at both of them. "You said you had news, Padma. Have you located my painting?"

Padma pulled the tube out of the plastic bag and offered it to Mrs. Maier. The older woman's brow furrowed, then understanding appeared, and her hands began to shake. "This is…oh, my heavens…are you…?"

She began to unwrap the paper, but after a round or two, she ripped it like an excited child. The top popped off when she pulled, the canvas making a faint rubbing sound as she withdrew it. When she unrolled it, the feeling Lisette had experienced upon first seeing it swept over Mrs. Maier, too: goose bumps, taut muscles, a gasp of pure joy. Tears filled her eyes as she stared at it, her breathing rapid, her entire body trembling.

"Oh, my Lord… I thought I would never see…" Her gaze lifted to them. "You sweet, sweet girls! When I asked for your help, I'm ashamed to admit I didn't think there was anything you could do. I thought you would try your best, and then I could accept that she was gone. I'm so sorry I doubted you and so, so grateful you proved me wrong."

Padma patted her arm. "It's okay, Mrs. M. We have enough faith in ourselves for ten people."

Mrs. Maier beamed through her tears. "Marley was right to be so proud of you two."

"She trained us well," Lisette said before taking a sip of her tea.

Padma's smile faltered. "Mrs. M, what are you going to do with it now? The man who had it stolen…if he finds out it was returned, he may hire someone to take it again."

Carefully rerolling the canvas, Mrs. Maier returned it to its tube. "My sons and I have discussed that. They wanted me to get it out of the house years ago, but… Their father gave it to me when we got married. It hung in our bedroom for sixty years. I just couldn't bear to not see it every day." Sadness slipped into her expression, regret for the loss of her husband, the painting, the innocence.

Then she cheered up. "The Fenwick Center isn't far from here. They're small, but they have a lovely collection. My friends and I, we go there every week to see what's new and admire what's old. They would provide a nice home to her." She patted the mailing tube as if comforting *Shepherdess* before turning to Lisette. "Unless you'd like me to contact the Candalaria."

If she hadn't just swallowed the mouthful of tea, Lisette would have choked on it. "No, no, not at all. The Fenwick is a wonderful place, and she'll be the star of their collection. Until you transfer it, though, keep it someplace safe."

"Not a problem. My sons come over every Friday evening. They'll store it in their bank vault until I can talk to the museum on Monday."

They spoke a few minutes more, finished their tea, got hugged again and finally left as the first son arrived. As she drove away, Padma muttered, "If she'd donated or loaned it to the Candalaria, we'd've had to steal it again."

Absolutely. Or, simpler, tell Mrs. Maier that David Candalaria had commissioned the theft. It was their rule to keep the identity of their marks to themselves. After all, their job was to retrieve the goods, not gather evidence for prosecution. But sometimes they had to break their own rules. And though it was a totally wrong idea, she couldn't help but think of Jack and wonder.

Would a successful heist against the Candalaria impress him even more than the theft from the Castle?

Once Lisette and Padma were out of sight, Jack circled the block and drove past the house they'd visited, making note of the address painted on the curb. At the next stop sign, he checked his files. Yep, the address belonged to Rachel Maier, legitimate owner of *Shepherdess*. Concealed in that big bag Padma carried inside, *Shepherdess* was home again, at least temporarily.

Grinning, he drove to the parking lot where Lisette had left her car. With another woman in another place, he might have felt guilty for slipping a tracking device into her purse earlier, but that was because business was business and women were personal.

Except Lisette, who was an intriguing mix of both.

The tracking app showed that she was inside Pecos Pete's, and a drive around the parking lot located her car out back. After finding a space, he went inside and took a seat at the bar, ordered a beer and took a long drink before gazing around. The women were sitting in a booth near the windows, perfectly situated where he could see their reflections in the mirror behind the bar. Padma's expression was lively, her mood clearly a good one. She was doing most of the talking, accompanied by dramatic gestures. She was a pretty woman who somehow managed to project serenity and tranquillity in spite of her liveliness.

Lisette, in contrast, was quiet, thoughtful, serene in fact and not just appearance. She dipped tortilla chips in salsa and sipped her drink while giving Padma encouragement to go on.

"Excuse me. Could I get a pad and a pen?"

The bartender pulled the items from beneath the counter and dropped them in front of him on her way to other customers. He wrote a note and flagged her down again, pointed out Lisette's table, ordered a bottle of their best wine and gave her the note and a fifty-dollar bill to deliver it. His message was brief: *Congratulations, ladies.*

Five minutes later, a waitress tapped him on the shoulder. "The woman at table fifteen sent this." She laid a crumple of paper in his hand before scurrying away for another customer.

Inside the wadded paper was his tracking device. Lisette must have begun searching her purse the instant she'd read the note.

"I thought you might need that back."

When he raised his gaze to the mirror, she was standing behind him. Sliding the tracker into his pocket, he faced her. "I always travel with a good supply."

"Yeah, I figured you did, but you can never have too many, can you?" She combed back a strand of hair. "How long have you been stalking me?"

"Just long enough to piss you off. And it's not stalking, actually. It's…professional curiosity."

"Curiosity killed the cat."

"My pirate name would have been Lucky Jack, remember? This cat has nine lives." Considering that her annoyed expression wasn't easing, he opted for placation. "I wasn't going to follow you home or anything creepy like that." He didn't need to. David's assistant had already given him all her personal information. He wasn't admitting that, either. He figured Lisette was totally nonviolent, but even nonviolent people could be pushed too far.

"But following me to a friend's house, then to a restaurant isn't creepy."

"Consider it a test of your abilities."

It was obvious his comment raised questions, but before she could get to one, he quickly went on. "I know you returned *Shepherdess* to its rightful owner. Will it be safe there?"

"Yes. Are you going to tell Candalaria?"

Jack snorted.

She studied him a long moment before pursing her lips, looking at Padma, who was watching with great interest from their booth, then gesturing. "Come on. You might as well join us."

The invitation was a surprise. He hadn't intended any real contact this evening. He'd just wanted her to know that he could keep tabs on her, to celebrate their success and to ask for a few hours of her time on Saturday. But he was no fool. She'd offered the invitation, and he was accepting.

He followed her to the booth, where Padma was sitting cross-legged on the bench and literally bouncing in place. "Ooh, I was hoping she would bring you over so I could meet you." She stuck out one hand. "I'm Padma Khatri, Lisette's best friend in the whole world. I've known her forever, and I could tell stories about her that would curl your hair. Not for free, though. I accept any and all bribes. Chocolates and milk shakes top my list."

Other than a quick glance, she ignored the fact that Lisette was trying to get her to slide across the bench to make room for her. It was hard for Jack to not smile at her brazen refusal or Lisette's sullen annoyance as she slid onto the opposite bench. He slid in, too, closer than he needed to be, closer than he should be.

Since Lisette didn't seem inclined to complete the introductions, he offered his hand. "Jack Sinclair. It's nice to meet you. And we'll have to talk about those bribes."

Lisette dipped a tortilla chip into tomatillo salsa, then held it in midair while locking gazes with Padma. "Jack saw the gift we delivered to Mrs. M."

Padma's reaction was pretty much a non-reaction. "Yeah, when you said, 'That jerk, he followed us!' I kinda figured the rest of it. There had to be some sort of transmitter, right, because you were watching traffic, and let's face it, it would be really hard to stealth us when I'm driving."

"She's right," Jack agreed. "In three blocks, she made a turn across four lanes of traffic, almost rear-ended a car, ran a yellow light, and I'm pretty sure I saw a dog-walker scramble halfway up a light post with his pooch.

Trying to keep up with her would draw too much attention to any bad guys following. Which I'm not, by the way."

"Following?" Lisette asked drily.

"A bad guy. And by the way, the gift wrap was a good idea."

As he expected, Padma beamed. "Thank you."

The waitress brought their dinner, then asked, "You want to order, hon?"

"No, thanks."

Lisette paused in separating a tortilla from the warmer. "You can stay."

"Thank you. But there are chili dogs calling my name at a little hole-in-the-wall about thirty minutes from here. Besides, I just came to ask a question." He thought of his so-far unanswered question and corrected himself. "Two questions. But only one right now." He would badger the other from Lisette sooner or later. "I'm going climbing tomorrow. It's always more fun with partners."

"Yeah, so someone can call 911 and direct them to your broken body after you crash to the ground."

"You need to work on that attitude. Someone who uses climbing in their job shouldn't automatically think of broken bodies. It's a necessary skill, and you need to improve yours. Don't be scared of it."

Padma snorted. "Calling her a coward doesn't have any effect on her at all. Believe me, I said it a lot when she refused to go skydiving with me."

Lisette serenely stuck out her tongue at her roommate.

"C'mon." He nudged her with his elbow. "Just think. If you'd had more experience, you wouldn't have frozen on the balcony last night, and you could have gotten to the ground and been gone by the time I came out. See? I'm offering to help you avoid me in the future."

Something crossed her face, serious and dark, just for an instant, then she smiled thinly. "When you put it that way, how could I possibly refuse?"

Victory was sweet, Jack thought before he included Padma. "What about you?"

"Thanks, but sorry. I've got some engineers' asses to kick in our quadcopter games tomorrow."

"Good luck with that. Lisette, you want to give me your address or should we meet back here at nine?"

She gave him a measuring look. Figuring he already had her address? "Here at nine."

"I'll bring the gear."

"I'll bring the coffee and the insecurities."

He picked up the tab and got a half dozen feet away when Padma's words finally registered. Turning back, he found Lisette watching him. "A quadcopter? Really? You *flew* it out?"

Her response was the unleashing of that gorgeous smile. "See you tomorrow."

A quadcopter. Damn. Why hadn't he thought of that sooner?

He's cute.

As Lisette followed Padma onto their block, she tried to count how many times her bestie had pointed that out after Jack left. Padma wasn't shy about stating her opinion often and emphatically. Jack was cute, no denying that. But hiding a tracker in her purse? He could have followed her anywhere, everywhere, to a client, to a target. How had she been so careless?

Because she'd never let her guard down while working a job. She'd never gotten close to a target before. Because she'd expected him to be unaware that he even was a target, when in reality, she was the one unaware.

No more. She would pay attention now because, clearly, Jack Sinclair was better at this game than she was.

Padma was waiting in the driveway when Lisette parked. Jack's scoring a big one hadn't put a damper on her good mood. She was happy and still damn near dancing. "It's a gorgeous night, isn't it?"

"We left 'gorgeous' behind twenty degrees ago."

"How is it that I'm the one from India, and you're the one who gets cold if a breeze blows?"

"I've got tropical blood in my veins, too."

"Yes, but you never lived on the island."

"And you never lived in India, either." Lisette slung her purse over her shoulder, and they climbed the steps to the porch. They hadn't gone more than a few feet when a figure stepped out of the shadows at the far end, tall and muscular.

Jack? No, the stranger's shoulders were broader, and his hair was too dark to gleam in the ambient light. Besides, surely Jack knew after showing up at Pecos Pete's that revealing he had her address wouldn't be wise.

She clenched her keys tighter and stepped between the stranger and Padma, or tried to. Padma, protective friend that she was, refused to be shielded, staying at Lisette's side, their shoulders bumping.

The pounding of her heart slowed enough to let her breathe. Padma's cell phone screen glowed, and a glance showed that she'd keyed in 911, her finger hovering over the send button. There were lights on in all the houses around them, and she and Padma could scream as well as any gaggle of ten-year-olds. The man hadn't made any moves toward them beyond those few steps, his hands hung at his sides, and he was wearing— She squinted in the stingy light. A suit. What kind of mugger wore a suit?

Detectives did. So did Candalaria's security.

She wasn't sure which she was more afraid of.

Channeling her mother, Lisette straightened her spine, lifted her chin and in Marley's voice that brooked no argument, asked, "Who are you, and what do you want?"

The man raised both hands in front of him, indicating he was no threat. Yeah, she wasn't buying that. "Sorry to frighten you, Ms. Malone." He slid one hand to the inside pocket of his jacket and took a few more steps. "My name is McSwain." He held out an ID that she couldn't actually see until Padma used the flashlight app on her phone to show it. The picture was stern and definitely the man in front of her, and the badge was from Candalaria Inc. The museum employee IDs were different, but they shared recognizable similarities. "I'm deputy head of security for Mr. Candalaria. He sent me."

Okay, so she wasn't going to jail. Yet. But rather than reassure her, the words stoked her tension. *Why* had Candalaria sent him? Did he suspect Lisette was the one who'd taken *Shepherdess* and the fancy red? Was this man supposed to get a confession from her?

But if she was a suspect, Candalaria would have sent more than one of his people to interrogate and intimidate, wouldn't he? He wouldn't have trusted a task to only one man. After all, she might just be a lowly employee, but she'd bypassed a *lot* of his security last night.

Then the steps behind her creaked. Her head swiveled around, as did Padma's, to find another tall, muscular man standing there. Like McSwain, he wore a dark suit, his hair was short, and he looked as if he could heave both Lisette and Padma over one shoulder without exerting himself.

She caught her breath literally, hoping the chill air would get her brain functioning, gave a choked laugh and turned back to McSwain. "Oh my God, you guys scared us! Don't you know better than to sneak up on a woman in the dark? I could have shot you."

She sensed rather than saw his perusal and envisioned a dry smile on his mouth. "No. You couldn't have."

He was right in his presumption—she'd never touched a gun in her life—but he didn't have to be amused by the possibility. "What can I do for Mr. Candalaria?"

"You were in charge of the guest list for last night's party, correct?"

"Yes."

"And you've heard about the theft during the party?"

"Yes, of course." Could they hear her heart thudding a thousand beats a minute or guess that a little voice in her mind was doing its best to force a scream out her mouth? "It was all anyone talked about at the museum today."

"Mr. Candalaria would like a copy of the guest list. He was told you could provide it."

The guest list. A sigh of relief shivered through her, loosening muscles and calming the little voice. Of course Candalaria would wonder whether the thief had been a guest at the party, or if the party had merely been a distraction that gave him access to the house. Of course he would want to know everyone who'd been invited.

And of course her name was on that list.

"He wants the list tonight. We were instructed to take you to the museum to get it. Our vehicle is just down the street."

Lisette shifted her gaze to the quiet street. Immediately she noticed the dark SUV three doors down, its engine a low hum, its parking lights on. Go off at night with men she'd never seen before? Candalaria actually thought she would do that for the salary he paid?

You had to choose the most dangerous path to regain the statue, Marley might have scolded her.

The most dangerous path would have been trying to seduce her way to *Le Mystère* through Simon Toussaint. She was hoping for much better results by using Jack. Somehow, though, she hadn't counted on Candalaria launching an investigation. Presumably, previous targets had done so, but she'd been so far off the grid that there'd been nobody to investigate.

At her side, still clutching her cell phone, Padma finally spoke up. "Don't you have that list on your laptop, Lisette? You can email them a copy or print it and give it to them now."

Grateful for the suggestion, Lisette smiled her friendliest smile. "I do have it here. I can save us a trip." Without giving McSwain a chance to refuse, she walked to the door, turning her back on him long enough to slide the key into the lock even though it roused every protective instinct she had. The instant she crossed the threshold, she hit the light switch that turned on the overhead lights. There were times when the lack of illumination was comforting, but tonight the lights calmed her nerves, at least until the two men walked through the doorway and the living room shrank by half.

For two people who looked nothing alike, the men were virtually interchangeable: six feet plus a few inches, regulars at the gym, spit and polished and unremarkable. Put them on a sidewalk in the business district in the middle of the day, and they would fade into the background. It was a good quality for men who worked security.

Right now she wished *she* could fade into the background.

"The printer's on," Padma said, gesturing to the corner where the machine sat on a small table. "You guys want something to drink while Lisette gets the file for you?"

"No, thank you."

Uncomfortable silence fell as Lisette booted the computer, opened the file and skimmed it. The list was alphabetical for the guests, complete with contacts for the many who weren't reachable for just anyone. A smaller section at the bottom contained the names and email addresses of the museum employees who'd been included, and at the bottom of that list was her own name.

Lisette highlighted her info, then hesitated. The conversations she'd had at the party had been superficial, head-bobbing responses to other guests' comments. Hardly anyone had asked her name, and no one would remember, except Jack, his aunt Gloria and Mr. Chen, so no one would notice that her name was missing from the list.

But if someone did… Candalaria had seen her, but he hadn't recognized her the very next morning in the museum gardens. He wasn't likely to think back and say, *Oh, wait, my minion from the museum isn't listed here.*

She opted to remove the information, pressing the delete key before looking up at the men. "Do you want the contact info or just the names?"

"Everything. A print copy and an email to this address." McSwain passed over a business card.

Lisette saved the file, hit Print, emailed the list to McSwain, then stood to collect the printed pages. That sigh of relief from earlier washed through her like a tidal wave as she handed them over. His partner checked his cell phone, then nodded curtly. "It's there."

"Thank you, Ms. Malone." McSwain's gaze shifted to Padma. "Sorry to disrupt your evening." And with that, he walked out the door. The other followed, closing it behind him.

Lisette and Padma stood in silence for a moment, then finally Padma set her own phone on the coffee table and sighed dramatically. "Wow, those guys could go unnoticed in a crowd of two."

"I had the same thought."

"Do you think your boss suspects you?"

"I don't think he knows I exist."

"But you talked to him this— Oh. Yeah." Padma set her purse down, grabbed the remote and turned on the TV, then headed for the kitchen. "I'll get the pop and the popcorn. You find us a good movie to watch."

Lisette dropped onto the sofa again, kicking her shoes off and scrolling through the listings. She stopped on a classic movie channel, scowling at the brief de-

Chapter 4

Carrying his third root beer of the evening, Jack sauntered into the hotel lobby, smiling at the desk clerk before heading to the elevator. His goal was in sight when David Candalaria's voice rang out.

"Jack, you old pirate."

Jack stopped abruptly, sighed and rolled his eyes before pivoting to face his… He'd never found a truly good word to describe what David was. Not a friend. An acquaintance but more than that. A pain in the ass, most definitely. A buddy? Never.

The lobby was filled with conversation spots given privacy by drapes and distance and made comfortable with overstuffed chairs and a waiter from Spirit standing a discreet hand's wave away. David made that wave as he spoke. "Come and sit down. Have a drink."

Jack held up his paper cup. "I brought my own. I thought you had a dinner date with Aunt Gloria."

"She had a headache, so we cut it short. I thought I'd stop by and catch up with you." As the waiter approached, David tossed back the liquor in his glass, then traded it for a full one. "I wanted to ask you something, Jack."

The tone of his voice, the way his eyes shifted, the uneasiness—Jack would have to be an idiot to not guess his question. "I didn't steal *Shepherdess*."

Relief mixed with the lingering suspicion in David's eyes. "Or the fancy red," he said as if the answer were, of course, no.

Jack's heart missed a beat. Throughout his entire career, fancy red diamonds had excited him in ways no other gem could because he always associated them with Bella Donna. After her first job with the large fancy red, she'd taken a small one on every heist. It was her quirk, her trademark. There had been an ongoing joke that the best protection against Bella was to own no fancy reds, and yet each mark had owned at least one.

"The thief took a red?" He tried to keep his voice level, his interest professional, but even he could tell he'd spoken too quickly, too passionately.

Which, in turn, piqued David's interest. "Yes, a small one. My grandfather bought it for my grandmother, but she died before he had it set. I'd pretty much forgotten about it. Does that mean something?"

Taking a long drink, Jack made sure his casual attitude was back in place with a shrug. "That he's got good taste. Or maybe his girlfriend does."

David considered that, his expression still both relieved and distrustful. It always took him a while to wholeheartedly accept whatever Jack had told him. He always did accept it, though. "My security team is looking into the theft. My chief suggested it might be helpful to have an experienced thief help with their investigation. Would you consider it?"

A former mark had made that offer to him once. *Your first-ever legitimate job. Wouldn't that make your parents proud?*

Jack was certainly a good choice in this instance. Now that he'd learned how Lisette and Padma had gotten the pieces off the property, he knew it all—including the fact that she'd lied to him about Bella Donna. What were the odds of two beautiful women operating in the same circle, similar in appearance, both skilled thieves, both total strangers to everyone else in the business and both with itchy fingers for fancy red diamonds?

"Sorry, David. I have an obligation to protect any trade secrets I might know."

Given the way his expression darkened, Jack might guess David's pricey dinner had just turned sour in his stomach. More likely, though, his ego had gone sour at the idea that Jack might side with thieves over him.

"What about your obligation to help a friend recover stolen property?"

Jack's smile was surface deep, nowhere near his eyes. "Last I heard, *Shepherdess* belonged to an elderly woman right here in Denver. A wedding gift from her husband. Hung in her bedroom for sixty years. A lot of people had made offers, but she'd turned down every one of them. Sentimental reasons."

Now it was David smiling, and his didn't reach his eyes, either. "Sentimentality is for people who can afford it. I acquired the painting a short time back for a nice bit of change."

Acquired, not *bought.* And that change had been paid to the thief, not the owner.

"The painting is mine. I want it back. More than that, I want whoever had the audacity to waltz into *my* home and take it out from under my security team's noses. As for the red… It wasn't even two-tenths of a carat and had too much purple in it for my taste. If I get it back, fine. If I don't…"

It was easy to shrug about that. The red was certainly insured, so either way, David wasn't out anything. Since no insurance company would cover a million-dollar painting known to have been stolen, he'd lost the money paid to acquire it and the pleasure of owning it, along with the prospective fortune when he eventually sold it.

After a pause, David went on. "I do wonder, though. The red was in a dish with other unset stones worth a half million, but the red is the only one missing. He could have emptied all of them into his pocket in less time than it took to find that one."

Except Lisette's gown didn't have any pockets. And she wasn't greedy. She took only the treasure she went after, along with the reds.

"Maybe he didn't need the others. After all, he already had a million-dollar painting." Though he was grinning inside, Jack managed to say it with a totally straight face.

Silence settled along with the scowl on David's face. It was broken by the clerk offering a cheery greeting to two men striding toward them. Jack knew men like them in every country he'd ever been: security guards, bodyguards, former cops, current thugs. Some operated with rules similar to a police department, others with all the subtlety of a street gang. The Sinclair family's security team was one of the good ones. They protected their clients and left everything else to the proper authorities.

David's followed a different business plan. It was a sliding scale from good to bad, and Candalaria security teetered in between. Sometimes they stayed on the right side of the line. Sometimes they crossed it.

The first man spoke to David in a low voice while handing over a sheaf of papers. Lucky for Jack that he had excellent hearing or he might have missed a few key phrases: *Ms. Malone, at her house* and *guest list*.

David scanned the thick bunch of papers, then offered it to Jack. "Anyone on that list I shouldn't invite to my house next time?"

Jack took it and settled back. The names were familiar, either from personal experience or gossip, except for the girlfriends or boyfriends who changed every week or every city. The ages ranged from twenty to eighty-something, and the fortunes started at *none*—with a notation that the man in question was damn good fun at these things—and quit counting when the long lines of zeroes made a person see double.

Was there anyone there who would buy stolen art? Of course, starting with their host. Was there anyone who would do the actual stealing? He spotted an occasional accomplice of his, also an occasional rival. He saw a number of people who didn't like David, who'd lost to him in auctions or business deals, who thought he was obnoxious, his money wasn't old enough, or he just wasn't worth their time.

As Jack reached the last page, he saw one more name.

Rather, he didn't see it. There, beneath the heading of Museum Employees, the *M*s were empty. No *Malone, Lisette*. No *lmalone@candalariamuseum.org.*

She'd tampered with the list. Aware of the three men watching him, Jack couldn't decide if that was a good or a bad thing. For Lisette, maybe it was good. David hadn't known who she was just this morning. If she stayed in the background, the next time he saw her, he still wouldn't remember.

Hopefully, his security people wouldn't, either.

He offered the pages as he stood. "They're all lovely guests, and your collections are safe with them. If I'm going to climb a mountain tomorrow, I need to get some sleep tonight."

David gestured to one of the men to take the printout, then nodded to Jack. "Enjoy your climbing. Come back to ski next month. Hey, convince your aunt Gloria to sell those rubies to me, and I'll put together the most incredible ski package anyone's ever experienced."

Jack lifted his hand in silent acknowledgment, then stepped into the elevator and punched the button for his floor. As the doors slid shut, he noticed the three men continued to watch, all silent, and a faint whisper of worry slid down his spine.

"You're the only person I know who can eat popcorn, text and watch a movie and never miss a thing."

Padma looked up from her phone, gaze sliding to the television, then to Lisette. "We're strategizing for tomorrow's games. Those idiots beat us last time, but it's not going to happen again."

"And what if it does happen again?"

Determination tightened Padma's jaw. "I'll have to

consider shooting their copter out of the air." She typed rapidly, then turned the screen to show an image to Lisette. "See? Rocket launcher for sale."

"You don't think that's a little overkill for a quadcopter?"

"You're right." Padma swiped across the screen to pull up another image. "Rocket-propelled grenade. That oughta do it without too much fallout." Her phone signaled a new text, and she went to that, typing an answer without losing a beat in the conversation. "Actually, what I would do is hijack the communications and send false positioning data. Then I'd fly it in circles, buzz the morons, land it on a skyscraper, crash it…" Her innocent smile couldn't disguise the stubborn look in her eyes.

"You wouldn't do any of that. First, I bet it's illegal."

Padma tilted her head to give her a long, steady look. "Really? You're going with that argument when twenty-four hours ago you—we—pulled off a seven-figure heist?"

"Okay, bad choice. Better one—you don't cheat. You're good enough to win on your incredible mad skills, and you wouldn't be happy doing it any other way."

Padma considered the compliment, then smiled before going back to her plotting. "Thank you, sweetie."

With a laugh, Lisette curled onto her side, using the sofa arm for a pillow, snagging the quilt from the back and pulling it over her. She'd already changed into pajamas—shorts and a tank top—and the movie was almost over. It would be easy to snuggle in and go to sleep right there, drifting into a quiet, peaceful, soothing nowhere with no worries until morning…

When her alarm would wake her so she could get

dressed, meet Jack—worry number one—and yippee,
go *climbing* with him. Worry number two or, more
accurately, Giant Supreme Terror. Sure, he was right
that she needed to improve her skills, but why couldn't
they have started with something simple like climbing
a flight of stairs or looking down at the ground from a
fifth-floor balcony? Why did she have to gear up and
climb-belay-ascend-descend-slip-fall-and-die and lose
her best chance to reclaim her father's treasure and fulfill her mother's dearest hopes?

She was trying to coax a picture into her mind, any
picture that didn't involve her broken and bloodied,
when Padma poked her foot. "That one's yours," she
said with a nod toward the coffee table.

Short of oxygen because of her dread for tomorrow—
no, damn it, anticipation—Lisette blinked at the phone,
then picked it up, her forehead wrinkling when she saw
the text from Jack. Of course he had her phone number
and probably anything else he could charm from a person. His message, though, surprised her.

Meet me at the back door.

What back door?

Yours.

Her gaze narrowed. Yep, he'd gotten her address,
too. Why wouldn't someone give it to him? He was a
gorgeous man. He was nice. He was Jack Sinclair, for
God's sake.

It couldn't hurt to talk to him. It was the polite thing
to do, wasn't it, when someone drove across town and

sneaked into your backyard to meet privately with you? Besides, she needed to spend time with him—hence her agreeing to risk death on the mountain. And his would be an awfully handsome last face to see before bed.

She set her phone aside and slid her feet into her favorite fuzzy slippers. "I'll be back in a bit."

Padma murmured, her head bent over her phone.

Lisette padded down the hall, stopping at the closet to grab a long black wool coat. She'd given it to Marley a couple of Christmases ago, and faint hints of her mom's perfume still drifted from the fabric. Wearing it made Lisette feel as if she were wrapped in her mother's safe embrace.

At the back door, she undid the lock. A blast of chill made her shiver, but she stepped out onto the porch, where something else made her shiver again. Awareness. A little dread. A little thrill.

She spoke to the shadow on the bench to her right. "Do you want to come inside where it's warm?"

Jack chuckled. "How can you live in Denver if you think *this* is cold?"

"I didn't have a choice. I came here in utero." She considered turning on the porch light before realizing he probably had reasons for not walking right up to the front door. She closed the door, hugged her arms across her middle, and moved a few steps closer to the bench. Leaning against the railing, she pushed her hands into the coat's deep pockets and looked at him. "Is there a reason you wanted to talk back here?"

"Two of them. They were sitting in an SUV outside my hotel, and they both work for David." The distance between them hummed with tension. "I heard he sent his security guys over here tonight."

She considered the news he'd offered so casually. The idea of Candalaria's thugs watching her would drive her into the darkest corner of her closet, but Jack sounded as if it was nothing, really. "Wow. You do get information. My phone number, my address, my uninvited-guest list. What else have you found about me?"

"I know your birthday was last month. Belated happy twenty-seventh." A pause. "I know you're good at what you do. I know you have great taste in diamonds. I know you're a pretty good liar because if you aren't Bella Donna, you must be her younger sister or her—"

The way he abruptly stopped talking and the aura of surprise around him made Lisette's throat go dry, and heat flushing through her body made her suddenly warm. Anxiety rolled over her in waves, legs unsteady, hands clenched, heart thundering, while the intensity of Jack's stare slashed through her.

"Or her—her daughter," he finished, his voice barely audible. It dropped even more as he continued. "You aren't the original Bella. That's why you were only fifteen when she started. But you were training to step into the role. She was your mentor. She was teaching you to become her."

Lisette wanted to lie, to swear that he was as wrong as could be, but her teeth were clenched together. Her brain was tap-dancing for a credible denial, but the denials weren't credible and anything credible wasn't a denial. *A little help, Mom?*

But Marley's voice in her head remained silent.

Jack stood and stepped toward Lisette. Her sight had become accustomed to the dark, enough to see that he wore running shorts, a thin T-shirt and bright-colored shoes. A dark band encircled his left wrist, a larger one around his upper arm—an activity tracker and a heart monitor. Maybe she could borrow the monitor from him to see if her heart was really going to explode. That would solve her problems, wouldn't it?

"Come sit down." He took her arm, pulling until she took the first step, then guided her to the bench. Holding her shoulders, he turned her around and nudged her down onto the wood. He leaned against the rail, studying her.

Finally her brain found enough words to manage a coherent if totally inconsequential question. "How can you live on a tropical island if you think *this* is warm?"

She couldn't see Jack's expression, but she knew relief had washed across his face. She could feel it in the air. "It's not exactly what I'd call warm. After talking with David, I decided I needed to see you, but he'd left a couple of his guys. I'd already found a back way out that was used by the original staff—"

Lisette did the same thing on every job.

"—but I figured dressing for a run would give me an excuse if anyone saw me. I'd never get up at 5:00 a.m. to run, but everyone knows I'm more than happy to do it at midnight."

Her heart was slowing, her breathing easing slightly. Damn it, she wasn't going to explode tonight. Just her luck. "Does he suspect you?" She hadn't intended for that to happen. With most of her jobs, by the time the theft was discovered, she was in another time zone, another country or another continent. She'd planned this job just like all the others: get in, get the art, get out, return the art. This time she'd added an introduction to Jack to her plan but had deemed the subsequent investigation as inconsequential.

Stupid move.

"He suspects me every time someone we know gets robbed," Jack said in an easy tone. "He stumbles around getting the nerve to ask if I was involved. I tell him no and remind him who my family is, and he bites his tongue and drops the matter. This time he also offered me a job, consulting with his security people. You know, who's better equipped to catch a thief than another thief?" A moment passed, weighted, as if he expected a question from her. When it didn't come, he answered it anyway. "I told him I have to protect the secrets of my trade."

"I knew you didn't accept," she said quietly.

"How?"

She hugged her coat tighter around her. "Because he's David Candalaria. Because you're Jack Sinclair. And because…" *You like me. I like you.* Hopefully, he did. Sadly, she did. But that wasn't how she finished. "Because you're not his kind of thief."

"What does that mean?"

"Did you know he offered Mrs. Maier $250,000 for the painting? She said no. He came back with a half million. She said no again. She told him there wasn't enough money in the world to match *Shepherdess*'s sentimental value. So he hired someone to steal it." She scoffed. "It took real courage to steal a painting from an elderly woman whose house has no alarm and whose door locks could be picked by a slightly skilled six-year-old. If the guy had shown up in the afternoon, she would have invited him in for tea and cookies."

"Just be grateful he didn't," Jack said somberly. "Some people who work for David wouldn't think twice about disposing of a witness."

The thought of her friend coming face-to-face with that kind of thug made Lisette shiver. She wasn't sure if Jack took that as an invitation or if he'd even seen it, but he pushed away from the railing and came to sit beside her. Though he left space between them, it wasn't enough to keep her from feeling the warmth radiating from him. It was nowhere near enough to stop the warmth building inside her.

It was a perk of the job, right—getting hot and bothered and tingly and all that stuff. Her path to the Toussaint collection could have been older, smarmier, eviler, scarier. He could have had a potbelly and gray hair, or no hair at all. He could have had frozen eyes and a dead soul. He could have been married and papa to fifteen little ones.

Of all the things her mark could have been, Jack was the best possible choice. He was the one she could attract, intrigue and seduce to gain access to *Le Mystère*, all in a day's work. No problem, no fear, no stomach-churning or distaste or pure revulsion.

The only distaste or revulsion she would feel would be for her own actions.

She forced a thin smile and returned to his last comment. "See? I was right. You're not his kind of thief at all."

"So." Jack half expected Lisette to echo him, but she didn't. She just huddled in the coat that was too big for her, somber wool, an unexpected look with her frizzy slippers. "David showed me the guest list you gave his guys."

She huddled a little tighter.

"I noticed your name wasn't on it."

She turned her gaze to him, though he couldn't make out any of her features. Her voice, though, was quiet, calm. "Did he notice?"

"I doubt it. David knows every detail about the people he needs to impress. An employee at the museum would never matter to him unless, I don't know, she was dating a really gorgeous guy with a lot of money and a lot of rarely exhibited art at his fingertips."

"Then as long as I don't meet this Prince Charming with canvases and cash, I'm okay."

He snickered. "Yet here I sit."

"As I don't date you, I'm okay."

There was a part of Jack that wished for enough light to read her expression. Mostly, though, he liked having nothing to focus on but the tone of her voice, the words she chose, the emotion she expressed so drily. "Sorry, Lisette, but I'm pretty sure a meal at Fire counts as a date in anyone's book. Add in dinner, sort of, tonight and climbing tomorrow…"

He felt her shudder, heard the tiny whisper of a sigh. "You know I agreed to the climbing in a moment of insanity, right?"

He grinned. "I often drive people insane. It doesn't change things. A yes is still a yes."

"Do you know how many hours I spend making sure there are alternatives to climbing on our jobs? I've changed locations for hits when there wasn't any other way. I even slogged through three miles of sewer once to avoid a 150-foot rappel."

"The more you do, the less scary— Wait a minute. Sewer?" He ran a list of the Malone women's jobs through his mind, then asked, "London?" It was enough to make him gag…and to increase his respect for her determination. So what if she would never take delight in dangling from skyscrapers the way he did? Traveling through sewers was way higher on the toughness scale in his opinion.

"A lot of old cities have underground systems. Some of them are very interesting."

"And some of them smell like the furies of hell, are overrun with rats, and can collapse and bury you alive at any moment. What would Padma have done without you?"

"She had a locating beacon—several of them—sewn into my clothes. Luckily, we didn't need it. However, I did undertake the longest, hardest scrubbing in the history of the world. I swear, I stank for the next six months."

Without thinking, Jack leaned closer, his nose almost touching her hair, and took a slow breath. He wasn't one of those people who could take a sip of wine and wax poetic on its characteristics or identify the ingredients in a dish based on nothing more than a bite. He had no clue whether Lisette's perfume was floral, green or herbaceous. It just was: sweet, a little exotic, a little earthy, a lot sexy.

The dog next door barked, its yip making him realize he was about a millimeter away from pressing his face into her hair. He forced himself back, to breathe crisp air not filled with her scent. "Don't worry. The bad smell is gone."

"God, I hope so."

When a breeze blew across the yard, she drew her feet onto the bench, exposing her legs, then tugged the coat over them again. Resting her arms on her knees, she tilted her head toward him and asked, "Should I have left my name on the guest list?"

His thoughts were stuck on her legs, long and lean and bare from the tops of her fuzzy slippers to somewhere high on her thighs. What exactly was she wearing under that coat? Nightclothes? Lingerie? Nothing at all?

She continued to watch him, the weight of her gaze palpable. Reluctantly he shifted his brain into coherent business-talk mode. "I don't think it matters either way. The majority of the guests were from out of town. They've gone back to running their multibillion-dollar corporations or their countries. A lot of them won't be amenable to answering questions. A lot of them won't remember anyone…" It was hard to finish the sentence the way he'd intended. It sounded spoiled and entitled and so damn snobby.

"Like me. The hired help. I know it was obvious even though I wasn't wearing a uniform." Lisette's voice was steady, even light. "There are advantages to being invisible to the rich. It makes my job easier. Will your aunt remember me?"

"Aunt Gloria remembers everyone. On the way over here, I left a message asking her to keep it to herself. She's never cooperative with David. She takes great pleasure in being a permanent roadblock on his road to happiness."

"Why?"

He slid down far enough on the bench to brace his feet on the railing. "Let's just say David isn't anyone's favorite person—not even his parents, when they were alive. He's smug and smarmy and ruthless and thinks we're all dolts compared to his superior intellect. When his family first put together enough money to start getting invited to a few events, Aunt Gloria tried in the beginning to be nice to him. His parents were idiots, and she was very maternal. He was smart, excelled in school and had tremendous ambition, and she knew what it was like to not be born into that world, having to take acceptance wherever one could find it.

"But David was obnoxious and rude and a huge snob even then. She tried to teach him better manners, to help him fit in, but no matter how she tried, she never could get him to throttle back on the attitude. She lost patience and probably would have disconnected from him completely by the time he was sixteen, but by then, he'd seen her rubies."

"So he was obsessed with her rubies that long ago."

"Remember, I said he had ambition. He was already building his own fortune. He worked at one of his father's businesses and invested every paycheck and every gift in the stock market. He bragged to everyone that he was going to buy Aunt Gloria's rubies. They would be the highlight of the incredible life he had planned for himself. He was so fixated that he was never going to be satisfied until he got them. There was just one problem."

"Aunt Gloria has no intention of ever selling them."

"Exactly." He gave her a sidelong look. "Want to know what my obsession was at sixteen?"

"Pretty girls, tiny bikinis and sunny beaches."

"You could've stopped after 'girls.' I didn't care where I found them. I was just glad I did." He paused. "What was yours?"

"Mastering the Moline 1059 alarm system."

The unexpected answer made him laugh and earned a chuckle from her, too. "They'd already moved on to the 1079 by the time I came in contact with one. And I

pretty much cheated. The wife of the guy I was stealing from gave me the code."

"I guess the honeymoon was over."

"Over, dead, buried and forgotten. He wasn't playing
nice in the divorce so she helped herself—or I did—to
a few baubles to make up for it."

"Mom—" She hesitated before starting again.
"We've been approached a few times about helping to
ensure a fair division of property, but that's never been
our interest."

He'd let his discovery that Lisette was Bella's daughter slide by earlier. He'd admired Bella's work and respected the legend for years, so he really wanted to
know more about it, but not tonight. Lisette needed to
get used to the fact that someone besides her and Padma
knew her mother's secret, and he…

He was having a good time talking about his job.
There were so few people he could discuss it with if he
wanted fate to stay on his side. "So you and Padma are
strictly retrieval specialists."

"Except for the red diamonds that cover our expenses. No reason we or our clients should have to pay
to make right someone else's crime."

"I agree. Especially when the someone else is David."
Jack closed his eyes and found it too easy to imagine
Lisette dressed for comfort of movement and camouflage, her long curls stuffed under a hat, pack loaded
with the tools of her trade. It was much harder to imagine her slogging through sewers. She was so pretty and
elegant and girly. How could she have taken that first
step when she'd known the alternative was mere moments of sliding down a line?

At least she'd persevered. She hadn't backed out and

left her clients hanging. She'd done the job no matter how messy it had been. "How are you with safes?"

"I manage them if I have to. I got a diamond core drill and a fiber-optic scope for Christmas a few years ago. Most of our jobs, though, safes don't get in the way. There's a thing about black-market buyers—they're proud of their purchases. They want them nearby or on display so they can enjoy the newness. We've only had to crack a safe maybe four times. Padma hacks way more computers."

Off to the left, the back door creaked open a few inches. "Hey, Lisette, we're done strategizing for tonight. I've got to get to bed so I can knock those guys out of the sky tomorrow. You can bring Jack in now if you want."

"We're comfortable here, but thanks. Good night."

Padma snorted before she closed the door, at the thought, Jack assumed, that Lisette could be comfortable in the cold.

Lisette sighed softly. "I hope their strategy doesn't involve signal-jamming or laser-guided weapons on their copter."

"She takes her games seriously, huh?"

"You have no idea. She's the most competitive person I've ever known." After another sigh, she went on. "I guess I should go to bed, too, if you're still planning to risk my life tomorrow."

Damn, he didn't need that image in his head: the wool coat sliding off her arms and landing in a pile on the floor; the minuscule whatever she wore underneath it; turning down the covers of a warm, cozy, snuggly bed with room enough for two; soft lights, sweet scents and a beautiful woman. Aw, jeez.

He forced himself to focus on the more hopeful part of her statement. "Little risk, lot of fun. I promise. We'll just give it a try. If you really can't do it, I'll concede."

Her gaze narrowed, lines crinkling her forehead, as she stood up. He didn't catch even a glimpse of her long legs, though, before she hugged the coat tight and headed to the door. "I'll be at Pecos Pete's at nine."

Grinning, Jack stepped off the porch and started through the shadows to the far corner of the backyard. A step up and a leap landed him in the neighbor's backyard, shadowy to hide him to the next street. All in all, it had been a productive conversation. He knew now that his initial assumption about Lisette had been both right and wrong. She wasn't Bella, but she was. She was protective of her mother. She trusted him enough to discuss work with him.

And Padma wasn't the only competitive person living in that house.

Chapter 5

Saturday was a beautiful morning, warm enough for shorts, cool enough for a hoodie. The sky was a clear blue, the only clouds thin wisps on the horizon, perfect weather for something benign like watching Padma's quadcopter games. Lisette hoped her friend got through the day without causing physical damage to the opposing team or their fliers.

And that she got through the day herself without any damage.

She shut off the engine and reached for the nearest coffee cup nestled in the console. Pulling off the lid, she closed her eyes and inhaled deeply of the steam rising into the air with promises of rejuvenation, mood alteration and sleepy brain cells jolted back to full function.

The coffee was brutally hot, the brew strong, and once she added sugar and cream, it would be elevated to drink of the gods. Returning the cup to the holder, she began her ritual: cream, sugar, a moment of stirring—

A horn beeped nearby, stopping her midstir. Her gaze went to the rearview mirror first, then she looked to the left, where a monster-sized pickup had parked a few spaces away. Jack came around the truck to her side, key fob in hand, grin on face. He looked far too cheerful for a man who'd taken a late-night run in the cold. After she'd gone to bed, she'd tossed all night, and it showed in shadows under her eyes and in the brain fog that muddled her.

She opened the door, then went back to stirring her coffee. He ambled over, rested one hand on the roof of the car and bent to see inside. "Did I interrupt your morning salutation to the high holy coffee beans?"

"Yes." She handed the other cup to him. "Sugar? Cream?"

"Nope."

"You clearly don't know how to do this salutation properly."

"You do it your way. I'll do it mine." He popped off the lid, sniffed, then took a careful sip. Miraculously the coffee didn't scald his tongue. "I don't drink other people's coffee very often. This is pretty good."

She waved him back, then climbed from the car and leaned against it. "Other people's?"

"The family owns a coffee plantation in Brazil. They ship it everywhere we go. If you want, I'll have them send you some beans." Balancing the coffee, he took out his cell, typed a few lines one-handed, then grinned. "Done."

He shifted to lean beside her, looking like the high holiness of gorgeous men in the morning light. Damn, last night's in-the-dark visit had robbed her of an incredible sight. His hair was the perfect shade of blond, the perfect example of tousled. His skin was perfectly gold, and his smile was perfectly white, his eyes perfectly blue. If he had a physical flaw, she couldn't find it.

Which was fair enough, since she could recite his character flaws without even thinking. Superconfident, arrogant, stubborn, impossible to discourage, sexy and, most unexpected of all, nice.

What has life come to when being nice is a flaw?

"I brought some of Dr. Mom's pastries," she said. Retrieving the plastic container, she lifted the lid, setting spicy, sweet, buttery aromas adrift into the air. "*Nariyal burfi*, *puran poli* and *besan halwa*. They're incredible…but I didn't think to ask if you like Indian food."

Jack leaned close, and his scent distracted her: perfectly clean, fresh, intriguing. Eau de Rich Guy. It could compete with Dr. Mom's baking even on an early Saturday morning. That wasn't a good sign for Lisette. Coffee and Dr. Mom's pastries had long been *the* most important scents of her Saturdays.

"I'll eat anything," he replied, helping himself to a sweet bread. "Except for the time in Korea, where they served me a live baby octopus. The poor guy kept trying to save himself by wrapping his tentacles around my fingers and nose and mouth. They laughed at me when I went outside and released him into the sea."

Shuddering, Lisette took her own sweet bread. "I may never eat *tako* again."

"You like sushi? I know the best place."

"In Denver?" she asked, pretty sure the answer was no. She'd figured out before they even met that she and Jack didn't live in the same universe. She worked for a living and considered it a good month when she added to her savings account instead of depleting it, and he jetted around the world on a whim. Meal and shopping options were limited to her finances and her local area. His weren't limited by anything.

"Tokyo. It's the best sushi in the world. We should go sometime."

She considered how totally decadent it would be to fly via private jet to Tokyo, eat sushi prepared by a master, then fly home again. The idea of such a once-in-a-lifetime splurge appealed to her almost as much as it appalled her.

"The heights are awaiting us. Let's get going." Jack gave her a sly look as he claimed the box of sweets. "I'll carry these."

She got her purse and gear bag, then stepped up into the truck's passenger seat. Turning, she tossed both into the backseat. This time she would look for trackers when she got home.

He kept his attention on the road ahead and the snacks on the console at his side until they were clear of the city and steadily climbing into the mountains. Lisette didn't ask where they were going. Thinking about it would just twist the knots in her stomach a little tighter.

"Is Dr. Mom Padma's mother?"

"Yeah, she is. She was Mom's best friend. They and Dr. Dad pretty much raised us."

"Where was your dad?"

There was a flood of grief, an ache around her heart, made more acute by the loss of her mother. The sad truth was that talking about her father generally wasn't a difficult topic. She'd never known him. Never seen his smile or heard his voice singing horribly off-tune ballads to her mother. Never laughed at his jokes or argued with his opinions or even given any thought to what kind of father he would have been. What was the point of imagining someone who could never be in her life?

Sometimes, that pointlessness made her sad. "He died before I was born."

Jack's somber gaze flickered to her, then away. "I'm sorry. That's tough."

"Hmm." But tougher for Marley than for Lisette. Marley had lost a living, breathing person. Lisette hadn't lost anything but possibilities.

But, oh, what possibilities.

It got quiet in the pickup after Jack's question about Lisette's father. Clearly, she didn't want to talk about him, and Jack should have suspected that by the fact that he didn't appear to have played any role in her life. When she talked about family, it was her mother, Padma and the Doctors Khatri. But he hadn't thought before he'd spoken, resulting in a few degrees of discomfort inside the cab.

Relieved when a sign appeared for his exit, he glanced to the right before switching into that lane. Most cars on the interstate drove at a fast clip as if speed limits were merely suggestions, not laws. The exceptions on this stretch of road were him, a beat-up sedan that didn't appear capable of going any faster and a dark SUV a short distance back.

"Which park are we going to?"

"It's not a park." He steered onto the exit ramp, then merged onto the two-lane highway. "I've got a friend who lives up here. He's a climber, and the property's got a lot of great rock formations, plus a few manmade ones." He grinned at her. "Don't worry. His six-year-old daughter has mastered all of them with a little help from her eight-year-old brother."

"So it's not enough that I might die today, but I'll do it with the knowledge that I've been bested by a six-year-old. Thank you."

Jack laughed. "It's too bad they're in Italy now, or Filomena Jane could be your guide."

"Bested by a six-year-old named Filomena Jane." Lisette shook her head woefully. "Padma's going to love this."

The road began a steep ascent, mountain on the right side and, on the left, twelve inches of shoulder that gave way to a car-crushing plunge. The road, along with the treacherous winter weather, was one of the reasons the Iannuccis had moved on to their home in Southern Italy. They believed mountains were for climbing, not crashing off, and winters were best spent in warm places.

As the view behind them disappeared around a curve, a dark flash caught Jack's attention. It could have been anything—it seemed half the vehicles on the roads around Denver were black—and it probably meant nothing. Still, he kept his gaze alternately on the roadway ahead and in the rearview mirror.

"I have to say, you having friends with children surprises me."

He slowed his speed a few miles per hour, then spared a second to grin her way. "Why is that?"

"We-ell…"

"You're cute when you're trying not to offend me."

Pink tinged her cheeks. "You're not married. You spend a lot of time going a lot of places and doing…

well, nothing. You look good for the cameras, you party a lot. Parents generally are a little more..."

"Settled?"

After a moment, she said, "Yeah, sure. *Settled* will do. Responsible. Not so much into taking risks."

"To be fair, a lot of what I do is for my job. Like you going to David's party for your job—both of them." He checked the rearview mirror again and saw nothing. His hands relaxed on the wheel. "I wouldn't stop being friends with someone I liked just because they lived differently. Besides, marriage and kids are just a part of life I haven't gotten to yet."

"Do you intend to?"

"Sure. Don't yo—" Damn. Coming around the last curve was a dark gray SUV, definitely the one from the highway, similar to the one parked outside his hotel last night. Though he felt Lisette's curious gaze on him, he didn't say anything. Instead, he increased his speed back to the limit and consulted the GPS screen for options. The remaining six miles to the Iannucci house were highlighted, with nothing between here and there but a roadside convenience store.

Lisette was very still, half turned toward him, not looking anywhere but him. "Are we being followed?"

He released one hand from the steering wheel long enough to rub an ache starting in his neck. "I don't know. Maybe."

"The business we're in can cause a little paranoia."

"What's the joke? Just because you're paranoid doesn't mean they're not out to get you."

She made a face. "Thank you. That makes me feel better." She resettled in the seat, made a point of exhaling quietly and looking calm and relaxed. If he didn't know better, he would believe the facade, but this was Lisette channeling Bella. This calm-cool-innocent act was the main reason she succeeded as a thief.

After a moment, she pleasantly said, "I don't think David believed you when you denied being involved with the theft."

"I know. I think I'm offended. David's always been so eager for approval that he's even a bit gullible."

"Maybe he's tired of being gullible."

Jack smiled at her. Her own smile was sunny, but it didn't reach her eyes. She didn't like being under close scrutiny, and she didn't like having dragged him into it with her. Not that she'd done any actual dragging. He'd been the one to notice her at the party, to follow her upstairs, to track her down at work the next day. Simon had always warned him that he would find himself in serious trouble someday, and it wouldn't be the plotting and stealing and working with criminals that caused it, or the thrill-seeking or the recklessness. It would be a woman.

And Simon, blast him, was always right.

The roadside store appeared ahead: small, dusty, plastered with signs. The prices at the gas pumps were outrageous, but a line of cars waited at each one.

"It's good for business to be the only place for miles around that sells gas, milk and beer." Lisette's head was turned to the right now, tipped down so she could watch the SUV in the outside mirror as they passed the store. A moment later, a small breath escaped her. "They turned off."

Again, if he hadn't known better, he would have missed the wealth of relief flooding from her. He felt it, too. He worked awfully hard to avoid dangerous situations when he was on the job. He knew his strengths and his weaknesses, and dealing with physical threats was definitely a weakness. Sure, he could throw a punch, and take one, but he was seriously averse to weapons of any kind. Knives were for cooking and climbing. Guns were for cops. The closest thing to a lethal weapon he'd ever used was a stun gun when a security guard had made an unscheduled patrol, and he'd apologized repeatedly before leaving the guy incapacitated on the vault floor.

He would really prefer Lisette didn't know he was no white knight who could save her from peril.

By the time they reached the Iannucci driveway, Jack's tension had drained away, replaced by anticipation. It was a lovely morning, he was about to get some climbing in, and he was going to do it with Lisette—his definition of a good day.

Before they reached the first of two massive electronic gates, they passed four private road and no trespassing signs. Lisette's brow arched. "Are the people around here a little slow to get the point?"

"You'd think one or two would be enough to get the message across, but people trespass out here all the time. When the family's in residence, they have a full contingent of security guards patrolling day and night."

"Why don't you?" She watched out the side window, where the only thing to see besides trees was more trees. There were the occasional large ones, but most of them grew so close together that the best they could manage was spindly height.

"There are security guards at home."

"Why don't you have them when you travel?"

He'd heard that question enough times in his life

from his parents. He couldn't remember them ever
going anywhere without at least two bodyguards plus
their well-trained driver tagging along, and when he
was little, his tutor, a former Mossad agent, had been
as much protector as teacher. "I don't need them."

She scoffed. "You're worth a kajillion dollars. You
go for runs late at night in strange cities by yourself.
You wander around like a common person."

He sent a charming smile her way and asked, "How
much is a kajillion?"

"A bazillion times more than a billion. Don't change
the subject."

At the first gates, Jack typed in the code, pressed his
index finger to the scanner, then rubbed his neck again.
"I've had bodyguards before, and I don't want them
again. Try kissing a Dutch tourist from the next island
over when Hulk and Hulk Too are hanging around. Or
dancing with the very hot Princess of Perfect from some
tiny kingdom no one's ever heard of at a club in Paris.
Or sneaking away from a party to break into our host's
office to pick up forty carats or so of gems that belonged
to his ex-lover. Besides, I've been traveling by myself
for years, and nothing's ever happened."

Another scoff. "You would be so easy to kidnap."

"I'm observant," he said smugly, driving through the
entryway, watching in the mirror as the gate closed behind them. "I pay attention to my surroundings. I can
take care of myself."

"I'm a thief. I could steal you without any problem."

He put on his best leer. "You wouldn't have to steal
me, Lisette. I'd go willingly. In fact, we can do that
later, when we're done climbing. Where do you want
to stash me, and what do I need to do to be released?"

She looked as if she wasn't sure whether she should appeal once again to his sympathy to get out of the climbing or react to the rest of his words. What would that reaction be? Amusement? Maybe a little interest? Maybe even a real answer?

Hands clasped in her lap, she settled for a chagrined look tinged with a pout. "You realize if I don't survive the climbing, there won't be a 'later.'"

"I was going to keep you safe anyway." He grinned. "Now I just have extra incentive."

Three hours later, Lisette wasn't more confident in her climbing abilities. In fact, she would say she was simply less dismayed whether she died while climbing. Every muscle in her body had tensed so often that she had aches everywhere. She'd taken so many deep, calming breaths that her nose was sore, and her teeth had been clenched tightly the entire time to keep an ever-growing list of bribes inside. She was willing to offer almost anything if they could quit while she was still functional.

Filomena Jane's home was a perfect playland for kids. The back wall of the house did double duty as a climbing wall, and a zip line was strung from the third floor to the roof deck of the pool house. A line dangled from there for a quick descent to the ground.

Lines dangled everywhere—from century-old trees and twenty- and thirty-foot stone cliffs. Climbing walls of varying materials and sizes dotted the backyard—though Filomena Jane considered them cheats, since the hand- and toeholds were designed into the surface. When it took every ounce of determination Lisette possessed to climb the first wall and Jack had shared that

tidbit, she'd crabbily thought to herself that the kids at
school probably shortened the kid's name to Mean Jane.
Then she regretted being jealous of a six-year-old just
because she was braver than Lisette.

A laugh escaped Lisette, drawing Jack's attention to
her. He swiped sweat from his forehead with his sleeve,
then raised his brows. "What's funny?"

"Nothing. Maybe I'm light-headed because it's
lunchtime, or maybe I'm hysterical because I'm still
in one piece."

His smile warmed his entire face, and his gaze moved
lazily over her body as if confirming the one-piece remark warmed her. "You're like a dog with a bone. You
grab on to some little thing like dying and milk it for
all it's worth. You're not dead, are you? You're not even
close to it. No bruises, no scrapes, no horrible falls...
You didn't even freeze, not once."

He was right, she realized. Sure, they'd worn har-
nesses and safety equipment, but that in itself didn't
calm her fears. She'd hated slipping off into space,
climbing over balconies and up or down lines and trust-
ing her body not to fail her...but it hadn't. It hadn't been
pretty or graceful, but she'd completed every task Jack
had set for her.

"Huh. Maybe there's something to this partner
thing."

Jack came closer to her, invading her personal space
but not touching her. Heat radiated from his body, and
his hair looked perfectly adorable sticking up in sweat-
slicked spikes. His Eau du Rich Guy still smelled incredibly enticing, and his eyes still looked perfectly
blue, only serious this time.

Suddenly her breaths were harder to take, her lungs

tougher to expand. Maybe it was the thinner air or a delayed reaction to all the times she should have hyperventilated on taking those first steps.

Or maybe it was just Jack.

"It's not a partner thing. It's an I-make-you-feel-safe thing. You can admit it. It won't puff up my ego. I'm used to it. In fact, feel free to show me how grateful you feel. I won't mind."

You be careful just how much gratitude you show him. Remember Le Mystère. The silent whisper in her head made Lisette feel a flush of guilt. "But we're not done yet. How awful would you feel if I thanked you now and then fell to my death?"

"Gee, like you couldn't thank me now, then thank me again later?" he grumbled good-naturedly. "Come on, let's get down off the rock." Abruptly, a wicked grin appeared. "And then we can talk about you kidnapping me."

They stood atop a rock outcropping that jutted into the air like an arrowhead pointing the way home. Jack had climbed it the hard way, using nothing but his hands and feet, his equipment there just in case. Lisette had come up the easy way, walking a meandering path up a hill that was steep in only a few places. She'd made enough ascents for the day. Besides, in her experience, it was the descents she had to worry about.

The drop to the ground from one side of the arrowhead was far; from the other side, it was even farther. Jack walked to the southeastern edge, and she followed at a safe distance, keeping her gaze on the rock and not on the empty air at its edge. "Remember," she said, keeping her thoughts off the inevitable. "I don't steal for fun and profit. Well, not for profit. I retrieve things.

Someone else would have to take you, then I could retrieve you."

"Couldn't we just skip the first step?"

"Can we skip this last descent?"

He shook his head.

"Then I can't rescue you until someone else kidnaps you." She drew a deep breath. This was for her job—a worthy effort, right? After all, she prayed never to see the inside of a sewer tunnel again. Besides, she'd easily picked up all her mother's skills, and Marley had climbed like a three-year-old on an epic sugar high. She could manage this, and then she'd be safe. For a while. Until she persuaded Jack to take her to the island.

"There are rappel anchors here, and the gear's in good shape," Jack said, "so it's up to you whether you want to rappel or downclimb. Either way, the hard part for you is going to be getting started, so I'll stand by to give you a shove."

She smirked at him, even though he was right. Taking that first step was the hardest. She'd done her share of rappelling, but Marley hadn't given her much experience with downclimbing. Scrambling down a steep slope with shifting surfaces could be a useful tool in her bag of tricks someday.

"It's a fairly easy descent. Face out, keep your back to the wall, and keep your weight on your feet as much as possible. There's a lot of scree, which makes it easy for your feet to slide out from under you. You want to pretty much scoot your way to the bottom. We're only about thirty-five feet up here. Normally, I wouldn't use a safety rope, but you should, given your preoccupation with sudden death."

"And yours with getting stolen." She considered leaning forward to check his estimation of the height but thought better of it. "Only thirty-five feet? Really?"

"Really."

"And I bet Filomena Jane has been downclimbing it since she learned to walk."

Jack gave her a curious look, but with half a laugh, she waved off the comment. "Okay, let's get this show—"

Lisette wasn't sure what stopped her: a flock of birds taking flight from a grove of distant trees; the sharp report that was slow to reach her ears; or the puff of dust and chips rising from the rock where they stood, close enough to bite into her calves. But the words stopped, and her body tensed, and she jerked around to look for the source of the disruption. Then her feet slid, and she was thrust into her worst nightmare, gracelessly, terrifyingly, rushing toward the ground. Her own mulish insistence was the last thought racing through her mind in the seconds before impact.

Damn. I really am going to die today.

"Lisette!" Jack flattened himself on the rock and shimmied to the edge on his belly, praying he would find her dangling from a fingerhold that had miraculously appeared exactly where she needed it. No such luck. He crabbed a dozen feet to the right, where a natural scoop in the rock made for the best start for downclimbing, and he slid over the rim, sliding and staggering his way toward the bottom. She had landed about halfway down, sprawled on her side against a mound of stone, and damn it, she wasn't moving.

He shouldn't have insisted she do this descent. Downclimbing was as dangerous as ascents. He should have belayed her to the bottom. Hell, he should have let her walk down the way she'd come up. But this was an easy descent. He'd never thought she might slip.

Loose dirt and rock shifted beneath his feet, sending him on a precarious slide to where she lay. He crouched next to her, reached out but stopped short of touching her. She was so still, her ponytail spread in curls around her head, her hands splayed as if she'd tried to slow her fall. Careful not to touch her, he leaned forward so he could see a portion of her face. "Lisette? Lizzie? Can you hear me?"

After an instant of silence, no movement, he leaned closer, and his voice got edgy. "Come on, Lisette, talk to me. Open your eyes and say something. You know, like 'I told you so.'"

Seconds dragged out, echoing in his ears, before a tiny, barely-there movement began so slowly he wasn't sure it was real or his imagination. Then, with a distinct flutter of lashes, she opened one eye and fixed her gaze on him. "You are in so much trouble." Gingerly, she swiped a clump of curls from her face. "Oh, and I told you so."

Relief swept through him, slowing his heart rate to a mere gallop. The trembling in his legs dropped him on his butt next to her, and his breath left his lungs with a huge whoosh. He'd taken plenty of short falls himself, and they were kind of fun when he was all hooked up in safety gear, but in all the years he'd been climbing, he'd never seen anyone free-fall. He hoped to God he never did again.

With a groan, Lisette rolled over. Jack helped her into a sitting position, his gaze searching her face, arms, legs. She was covered with dust, and a few small rocks tumbled from her curls when she shook them out. There were abrasions on the front of her calves, a couple of them trickling blood, but she was moving okay, and her breathing wasn't labored. She looked remarkably good for someone who'd fallen ten feet and slid another fifteen.

"Are you okay? Do you hurt anywhere? How's your head?"

She shifted a few times, probably looking for a stone-free place to sit, then leaned heavily against his bent leg before squinting at him as if his questions puzzled her. "I *fell* off a *cliff.*"

"Well, more like a boulder." Her gorgeous eyes narrowed on his face, and he relented. "All right, a cliff. A huge giant cliff. Where do you hurt?"

She twisted her neck, rolled her shoulders and flexed her fingers. After doing the same with her legs and wiggling her ankles side to side, she replied, "I don't think I actually do. I slid mostly on my butt before hitting the rock. I'm a little stiff." She brushed at her shirt, sending puffs of dust into the air. "I'm dirty, and I imagine I'll have some bruises tomorrow, but I'm okay."

Then she turned to look at him, her gaze narrowing again. "What the hell was that noise?"

He moved so she could lean more comfortably, her shoulder resting against his, then dragged his fingers through his hair. "I'm no expert, but it sounded like…"

Abruptly he looked in the direction the sound had come from, where the birds had launched. There was nothing to see now: trees, rocks, thick scrub. It was a hundred feet past the west edge of the manicured lawn, a spot no different from a hundred others around the house, except it had a bird's-eye view of the boulder above them.

A bird's-eye view of *them*?

He didn't know, but damned if he was going to wait to find out. "Can you get up? Can you walk?"

For an instant she looked as if she was going to remind him again that she fell off a *cliff*, but after studying his face, she nodded. Scanning the area around the trees once more, he stood, then helped her to her feet, wincing when a groan escaped her. He slid one arm around her waist and lost no time leading her as close to the rock face as the scree allowed. It was a harder path than continuing the route her fall had taken, but in a few yards, the cliff would hide them from view of anyone in the direction of the house.

"You're no expert on what?" Lisette asked, holding tightly to his hand while stepping from one exposed vein of rock to the next.

"More things than you would guess." He was aiming for humor, but neither of them appeared particularly amused as they neared the point section of the arrowhead. Once they circled to the other side, a person would have to trek through the woods to locate them.

Which these guys, because there had been two of them in the gray SUV, just might have already done. Might be out there waiting for another chance.

The cliff sheltered them from the sun when they reached their goal. Lisette sat on a boulder, propping up first one foot, then the other, checking the abrasions and blood on her calves. The small injuries didn't seem to interest her. After removing the band from her hair, she shook out another cascade of pebbles and dust and put it up again. Then she placed her hands on her hips and faced him. "Did someone shoot at us?"

"You were thinking that, too, huh?"

Her skin paled, leaving even her lips a lighter pink than usual. Letting her feet slide to the ground, she bent over at the waist, leaning against the boulder so she didn't have to support all her weight, and breathed slowly and deeply. Jack watched her, thinking that she'd been in so much more danger before: every time she'd sneaked into a party, trespassed onto an estate, broken into a house, circumvented an alarm, bypassed security guards, and stolen million-dollar masterpieces. She stayed cool through all of that, but the idea of someone taking a shot at them really unsteadied her.

Aw, hell, it unsteadied him, too. The burglary stuff—that was the known risks of their profession. There was always the chance for things to go wrong and contingency plans to deal with it, but most well-planned heists were executed neatly. This…this was personal.

Slowly she straightened. "Well, if someone wanted to scare me, they succeeded. What do we do now?"

Jack grinned at her. He couldn't help it. It was his go-to response for just about every situation, and she looked so damned dusty and disheveled and beautiful and a whole lot more in control than he was. "You have any suggestions?"

She left the boulder and sat down with her back to the cliff base. It was a good choice: she could see anyone approaching from the front, and with the overhang, no one could surprise them from above. "Do you think they're still around here?"

He sat down beside her, close enough that their shoulders bumped. "I don't know. I'm guessing they didn't mean to actually hit either one of us. It was a long shot. Anyone who could put a bullet between your feet could have just as easily put it three feet higher."

She nodded, her hair tickling against his skin. He studied the curl that caught on her hoodie, a soft black spiral dusted with dirt. The scent of her shampoo drifted on the air, vanilla and something sweeter, also dusted with dirt. Who knew he could be so attracted to the smell of dirt?

"Which would make it a warning," she said thoughtfully. "I'm guessing to you, since no one knows I exist."

Jack's shoulders hunched as he gazed at her legs stretched out in front of her. Smooth bronze skin, a mere twelve inches of it exposed between her snug-fitting yoga pants and her shoes, marred as a result of the shot. "So David's thugs shot at you because of me." The words were morose, but inside him anger was rising, fed by guilt. He rarely got angry—rarely felt guilty—and he didn't like the edgy irritation spreading through him.

"No."

When he looked at her, Lisette shrugged. "Yes, they shot at me to give you a message, but only because they don't have a clue what's going on. Apparently, David believes you stole his painting, so yes, they warned you." Her expression turned somber, regret clear in her eyes and the set of her mouth. "I'm sorry. I didn't mean for you to…"

"Become a suspect?" he asked when she didn't finish. He nudged her gently with his elbow. "It's a novel experience. Usually, even when I'm guilty, people are too scared to suspect me—at least, to say so out loud. Besides, I get in trouble by myself all the time."

Her look was skeptical. "How many times have people shot at you?"

"None," he admitted. "Most of them fantasize more gruesome demises."

"I don't suppose this will change your mind about traveling with a bodyguard."

Before he could answer, a voice broke the silence from some distance away. "Jack Sinclair? Jack, can you hear me? It's Dominic." For an instant, every muscle in Jack's body tightened, and so did Lisette's, but on hearing the name, the tension fled. Rising, he extended his hand to Lisette and pulled her to her feet.

"We're over here, Dominic," he called, then grinned at her. "I don't need a bodyguard. I have guardian angels everywhere."

Chapter 6

Dominic Caruso was head of security for Filomena Jane's family. He looked a great deal like Candalaria's guys, except he had a pleasant face that became ridiculously beautiful when he smiled. He'd stayed behind when the family decamped to Italy and kept things under control at the house. Usually.

Lisette sat on a patio bench while the men walked to the trees, looked for signs of intruders and climbed to the top of the arrowhead to inspect where the bullet hit into the rock. They climbed the formation even faster than she'd fallen down it, she noted with a wry smile.

The smile faded. She'd never made even minor mistakes in planning her jobs before; Marley had taught her such care it hadn't even seemed possible she could royally screw up. But that was exactly what she'd done this time.

She had only wanted to meet Jack, to get his attention. She hadn't expected Candalaria to see them together at the museum, and she'd certainly never thought Candalaria would suspect him of taking the painting.

You could have pulled off the job and gotten out of the Castle. Get in, get out, fast and safe.

That still wouldn't have stopped him from following her. Though that wasn't entirely true. She had loitered in the ballroom, letting his gaze land on her a time or two before slipping out. She'd wanted him to follow. She'd thought…

And she knew what her mother would say. That she had an important job to do, and involving that man… he'd break her heart.

A small smile quirked Lisette's lips. Without that man, she couldn't get close to *Le Mystère*. Once she managed that, it would be like taking candy from a baby.

But what about after?

She stretched out her legs, tilted her head back and closed her eyes. After, she would come back home to Denver. She would pick up life as usual: her and Padma, righting injustice one theft at a time. She would hear about Jack from time to time—maybe even see him— but there would be nothing between them. Once she reclaimed the statue, he would want nothing to do with her, and she would want nothing more from him. It would be finished.

She knew Marley would have one last thing to say to her. *Lying to others, baby girl, is part of the job. Lying to yourself… That'll come back to bite you.*

Lisette had learned a lot of things from Marley: career lessons, life lessons, responsibilities, ethics. There

was also one other thing she'd picked up: hardheaded
determination compounded by tunnel vision. When she
focused on a job, she focused narrowly, and she'd never
yet let a situation make her back off. If she ran into
roadblocks, she looked for detours, and if there weren't
any, she went over—or, on the London job, under—the
obstacle. She wasn't going to let a little thing like possibly getting her heart broken sway her from reclaiming her father's property. It was what she'd been taught
her whole life.

When she heard voices behind her, she straightened
on the bench, swearing quietly. It was a good thing
she'd landed on her backside when she'd slipped, but
there would still be pain. Maybe she would spend Sunday wrapped in a quilt on the couch with Padma and
Dr. Mom coddling her all day.

The men were talking about skiing, resorts and
opening dates. Dominic's voice was deep, his language
more formal, his accent Italian enough to make a grown
woman swoon. Jack's voice was more everyday, and his
accent was a blend of Caribbean, French, British and
sometimes pretty darn near American.

And he could make this grown woman swoon.

They stopped in front of her, and Dominic gave her
the angel smile. "May I help you to the vehicle, Ms.
Malone?"

She envisioned him hefting her under one arm and
hauling her quite easily around the house to the truck,
setting her inside as if she weighed no more than Filomena Jane. Smiling, she said, "Thank you, Dominic,
but I'm fine." When she started to stand, he offered
his hand, pulled her to her feet and didn't miss her gri-

mace as her body reminded her that she'd fallen from a huge giant cliff.

Before releasing her hand, he leaned close. "Ice packs. Rest. No hot baths for a few days. No alcohol. Ibuprofen. Lots of fluids."

"Well, darn. I was just envisioning a long, hot soak and a glass of red wine."

"That will be your reward for being a good patient the next few days."

"I will be. Thank you for the advice."

Dominic walked them to the pickup and helped Lisette into the passenger seat. She watched while securing her seat belt and was surprised that, instead of a simple goodbye, Jack hugged him. She hadn't had a lot of men in her life, and while Dr. Dad was very affectionate, neither he nor Raza was demonstrative about it.

Would her father have been a hugger? Would he have expected her to recognize his love in the way he looked at her, talked to her, provided for her, or would he have been, like Marley, lovey-dovey huggy-huggy?

Deep down inside, an ache throbbed, the loss that had been with her her entire life. Usually it lay quiet, dormant, but she suspected the closer she got to the statue, the more it was going to make itself felt.

Jack slid behind the wheel, started the engine and followed the large circle drive back to the lane they'd come in on. "You sure you're okay?"

"I am." She shifted position, and her tailbone immediately contradicted her. "In fact, I learned an important lesson today. There *are* worse things than rappelling from a balcony."

"Like falling off a huge giant cliff?"

"No, actually. Like being unaware that someone's

watching you. Like being totally vulnerable to whatever they do. We were sitting ducks."

"Quack quack." His expression was more serious
than she'd seen. He stopped the truck in the middle of
the lane, heavy woods on all sides, and turned to face
her. "I'm sorry, Lisette. When I suggested coming out
here, I never imagined this happening."

"Because you had nothing to do with it." She didn't
want him feeling guilty, because then she would have
to, and she had a lot more reasons for guilt than he
did. "It's Candalaria's fault. Not yours, not mine." *Well,
partly hers*.

His features took on a wry set. "To be fair, he thinks
I stole his painting."

"Which, to be fair, he stole himself from a defense-
less old woman."

"He wants it back."

"He can't have it."

Laughing, he set the truck in motion again. "What
if he manages to get it?"

"I'll steal it back."

Jack gave her a long, amused look. "You're going to
be a problem for him in the future, aren't you?"

The thought interested her enough to widen her eyes
and raise her voice half an octave. "His guys took a shot
at me and made me fall off a cliff. Hell, yes, I'm going
to be a problem. When we're between jobs, we're going
to start retrieving every piece he's ever stolen. We might
even take a few that he actually bought. Or maybe we'll
recover other stolen art and plant it at his house, then
notify the authorities." She smiled, thinking how easy
it would be. Once they had stashed an adequate supply

of stolen pieces, they could watch from the sidelines while Candalaria's world imploded.

"Remind me not to piss you off," Jack said, grinning at her. "I think for such a beautiful do-gooder, you must have a very bad side, and I don't want to be on it."

Her own good mood slipped. He wouldn't piss her off. He would never get the chance until she was done and out of his life. And then he would know for sure that she did indeed have a bad side, and he wouldn't want to be on *any* side of her. He would wish he'd never heard her name.

But she could live with that. As long as she recovered *Le Mystère*, she could live with anything.

Jack had a lot on his mind on the drive back. Should he insist Lisette get checked out at the hospital? Was he a fool for planning to confront David about the afternoon's incident? Should he make a report to the authorities, though for both Lisette's and his own safety, he was pretty sure the answer to that was no? Should he hire a few thugs of his own to protect Lisette?

This trip had become serious business, and he was so thoroughly not the man for serious things. He didn't like violence or guns or, as far as that went, even being serious.

Maybe it was time to go.

And take Lisette with him.

He glanced at her. She didn't look comfortable, making microadjustments to her position every few minutes. He'd heard her stomach rumble a few miles back and decided to pick up burgers at the first fast-food place they passed, then take her home. Then he would decide about David.

When a sign advertised food at the next exit, he changed lanes, earning a smile from her. "I was wondering if you could hear my stomach. Oddly, my stomach growling is much more pleasant than me growling."

"I doubt you've ever growled once in your life."

She bared her teeth at him. "Are we paying a visit to Candalaria today?"

"I am. You're not." Huh. Apparently, his mind had decided he *was* a fool.

"I want to go, too." Then she backtracked. "I really don't, but you can't go alone. You need thugs at least twice as big as his."

He grinned at her. "Where do I get those? Thugs R Us?"

"Or you could take me and Padma and Dr. Mom with you. We're scary when we want to be. *No one* disrespects Dr. Mom."

He believed that. No one disrespected his mother, either, and lived to tell the tale. "I'm taking you home so you can rest, and then I'll go see David." When she opened her mouth, he raised one hand. "I'll meet him someplace public. His guys won't be able to do anything."

"After what they did today, you think he'll just agree to meet you?"

"He won't have a choice." He slowed at the top of the exit ramp, then turned toward the drive-through on the right.

"So you'll remind him you're one of *those* Sinclairs, and he'll jump to obey."

"No. I'll have Aunt Gloria call and ask him to meet me for drinks." He grinned. No, he wasn't above asking his seventysomething great-aunt for help. "No matter what else is going on, he would never say no to Aunt Gloria."

"You don't think he might threaten her?"

Jack's first urge was to laugh. "I'll put that down to you meeting her only once. She took up martial arts in her fifties and earned black belts in three different disciplines. When she decided a few years ago that she should cut back on the five-day-a-week classes, she bought a Glock. Because she can't take the gun everywhere she goes, she also carries a stun gun and a canister of pepper spray. No one disrespects her, either."

"Ooh. A new role model for me."

"Now, that's scary. I'm not sure the world can handle both you and Aunt Gloria."

Easing the truck forward to the speaker, he ordered, handed the bags to Lisette to sort through and headed back to the interstate, thinking about the meeting. He was expecting the usual dolt he'd always known, but people could change. Maybe David was done being the obsequious one, the suck-up who was never going to be treated the same. Maybe he'd reached a point where he didn't give a damn what anyone thought of him anymore. Maybe he'd decided respect was more important than acceptance, fear more satisfying than friendship.

Maybe Jack's status as a Sinclair wasn't going to protect him this time.

Heavier traffic signaled that they were back in Greater Denver, only a few miles from their destination. Jack polished off the last of his meal, then watched Lisette from the corner of his eye. She'd eaten without complaint, though it certainly wasn't the meal he'd planned once their climbing adventure was over. Now she sat, bedraggled and dusty, eyes closed, so still she might have been asleep.

She could have been badly hurt today. Could have died. The knowledge sent a chill through him. As she'd pointed out, it hadn't been his fault. Of the three major players in this game, he was the only one even close to innocence. His only fault was being attracted to a beautiful woman.

"What are you thinking?" she asked without moving, opening her eyes or giving any other sign that she was aware of him.

"That the weather at home is gorgeous this time of year," he lied. Home was always with him—its serenity, its beauty, its security and Simon—but today it was pushed back so far he'd had to call it out of thin air. He might be the crown prince of taking things easy, but even he understood there were more pressing issues at the moment.

"And home is?"

"Île des Deux Saints. It's in the Caribbean. A hundred and fifty miles from anywhere else."

"Island of Two Saints?" She gave him a look, as if he couldn't possibly be one of the two. She was right, too.

"My however-many-greats-grandfather and his best friend discovered the island and settled it three hundred years ago. Granddad was a Saint Clair, and his friend's name was Toussaint, so two saints." He shrugged. "It's been in the family ever since. Simon, the current Toussaint, lives there full-time, and I visit four or five times a year."

She faced him obliquely. "Do other people live there? Are there any cities or towns?"

"There's a village not far from the Toussaint house where the staff live. It doesn't have a name."

"You have enough staff to fill a village?"

"There's maybe 150 people. The office and house staff, the gardeners, the farmers, the fishermen and the ones who have retired and the families. There's a store to supply things they can't make themselves, a nurse practitioner, a teacher and a priest. No tourists, no one wandering about where they don't belong and plenty of security."

And very private. Anyone visiting without an invitation was met by armed guards and politely escorted away. Anyone there for photos, a tabloid story or an unauthorized look at the families' art collections was not-so-politely escorted away and dealt with.

"It must be the best-kept secret in the Caribbean."

"Not in terms of the existence of the island, but as far as what's on it, yes. Simon can probably tell you exactly how many outsiders have been invited in over the last hundred years."

The interest in Lisette's eyes was similar to the interest he'd seen in countless other eyes when it came to the island. It was the uniqueness; even he didn't know many people who owned their own island. But when she spoke, her comment was unexpected. She didn't coo that she would love a tropical vacation, or ask how spectacular the houses were, or remark on the luxury of life in paradise. "Deux Saints. Your great-great-grandfathers thought pretty highly of themselves when they chose the name, didn't they?"

He laughed. "Considering that they were pirates, yes, they were very impressed with themselves." He feigned a wince. "Yes, it's a trait that's been passed down through the generations. All Sinclair and Toussaint men think they're special. But I really am."

With a smug smile, she reached across and patted his hand. "Of course you are."

His gaze slid from the road to her hand, cleaner now than the rest of her, thanks to a good scrubbing with napkins before she ate. Despite the gloves she wore when working, there were slight calluses on her palms, but the surrounding skin was soft and warm. The polish on her nails, the color of scarlet, was chipped, and one nail had broken in her fall. It was a little thing, easily fixed, but the sight of it flared his temper, reminding him of all the big things that could have broken instead. Her arm, her leg, her spine, her neck.

He might be averse to violence, especially when it involved him, but some vengeful spot deep inside him wanted to break David's neck in exchange.

"I have a suggestion. Let's stop at my house so I can shower, and then we'll meet David together and—"

"No."

She scowled at him. "You don't have to play the tough-guy hero."

"If you ever see me being the hero, keep in mind—I *will* be playing. I like things peaceful and easy. I'll meet David somewhere he wouldn't dare cause a scene. I'll convince him I didn't steal *Shepherdess*, he'll apologize, he'll send you a gift—diamonds, probably—and that will be the end of it."

He didn't believe what he was saying, and it was clear she didn't, either, but she didn't argue. Instead, she resettled in her seat, forehead knit in a frown, and gestured grudgingly at the upcoming highway sign. "Get off here."

He exited and turned toward her neighborhood. A distinctly uncomfortable air settled in the truck rather quickly, but he didn't let it get to him. Irritation, he could take. Threats against her, he couldn't.

But damned if he didn't like, at least a bit, the idea of being her hero.

"Doesn't look like luck was with Padma this morning," Jack commented, directing her attention to the house, where Padma sat on the porch steps, knees drawn up, arms around them, chin down. She looked bereft, *not* her usual reaction to losing a competition.

"Padma doesn't pout when she loses. She immediately starts scheming how to win next time—and there's always a next time. I wonder if her copter crashed or something." As soon as Jack parked, Lisette undid her seat belt and opened the door. She'd hoped to get home before her friend, to clean up and change and totally minimize what had happened, but no hope of that.

When she slid out of the truck, the moment her feet touched the ground, a gasp escaped her, and she grabbed the door for balance. Ah, jeez, every place on her body throbbed, from the cuts and abrasions on her calves to the scalp that she was sure still hosted a load of dirt and pebbles. Moving hurt. Breathing hurt. Even the fresh air on her bloody scrapes hurt.

Jack came around to her as Padma launched off the steps and headed their way. He slid one supporting arm around her waist and murmured, "You still sure you don't need to go to the hospital?"

She pasted on a cheery smile. "I'm sure."

"Oh my God, Lisette, you won't believe—" Rounding her car, Padma came to an abrupt stop, her dark eyes widening. "What happened to you? You look terrible. Are you all right? Do I need to call Daddy?"

Though there was a part of her that wouldn't mind one bit being fussed over by Doctors Mom and Dad, Lisette shook her head. "I'm fine. Just bruised a bit."

"And filthy. You both look like you rolled around in the dirt. What happened?"

"We rolled around in the dirt," Jack replied cheerfully, earning himself a scowl from her normally cheery roomie.

Lisette hesitated. She would tell Padma the truth— they might lie to everyone else but not each other—but not this minute. Not until she found out what had upset her. "Remember how Mom used to say it wasn't the fall that killed you, it was the landing?" When Padma bobbed her head, Lisette smiled wryly. "Well, I got lucky with the landing. What's going on with you?"

Padma gave her a head-to-toe look, reluctant to let go of the subject so easily, but then her eyes clouded and she stepped a few feet closer, her voice lowering. "Someone broke in while we were gone. They ransacked every room. My laptop's in *pieces*."

Her lower lip trembled for a moment, stirring Lisette's sympathy. Her own laptop was a convenience. Padma's was her auxiliary brain. She'd had it built to her specifications, paid a small fortune for it and was rarely more than arm's length away from it.

Lisette gritted back a groan and hugged her. "Oh, Padma, I'm so sorry. But all your stuff was saved elsewhere, right? All your work stuff?" She felt selfish asking but went on. "All our work stuff?"

"Yes, of course. But I *loved* that computer." For half a second, she rested her head on Lisette's shoulder, then abruptly pulled back and grasped her arms. Even though they stood only a foot apart and no one was in sight in any direction but Jack, Padma still lowered her voice to a stage whisper. "They took the fancy red."

Lisette's stomach dropped, and it wasn't entirely the realization that the credit card bill for her party dress and shoes would be arriving soon, a staggering amount for her working woman income, or the fact that she owed Padma a share of the quadcopter costs, since they were using it for pleasure and business.

No, this was fear. Shock. Consternation that for the first time someone could actually connect her to a burglary. The fact that it was David Candalaria, the man with more millions than brain cells, didn't soften the blow to her ego one bit.

"Crap," Lisette muttered at the same time Jack murmured an earthier version. She met his gaze. "Do you think it's laser-inscribed?" An identification number etched onto the girdle of the stone could prove it was David's stone, and from there, the likeliest conclusions to leap to were that the thief had given it to her or she *was* the thief. The first didn't bode well for Jack. Neither boded well for her.

Jack shrugged. "He didn't seem to care much about it when we talked last night. He didn't even connect the red as Bella's trademark. He did say it had been bought by his grandfather. Laser etching wasn't available back then, and I doubt David bothered to have it done when it became available. He said he kept the red in a dish with other stones that were worth about a half million dollars."

Padma's jaw dropped. "A half million dollars? You

could have taken the entire dish, and you took the time to pick out one small stone? What were you thinking?"

"That I was covering our costs. We were never in this to get rich. That would make us no better than—" She broke off abruptly, her gaze darting to Jack's handsome face, then quickly away.

"No better than me?" He didn't sound offended, and when she finally peeked, he didn't look it, either.

"No," she snapped, exhaling sharply. "I didn't mean— We'd be no better than our targets. We're bad guys because it's the only way we can help the good guys."

Padma hastened to reassure her. "I know, I'm just teasing. I admire that you weren't even tempted, because I would have. Been tempted, I mean. I wouldn't have stolen them." Her expression grew more somber. "Sweetie, Candalaria knows. *No one* has ever known. What do we do now?"

Lisette didn't want to admit that she didn't have a clue. No one in the entire art world had any idea who Bella Donna was. A lot of people believed she was just a myth created by another thief for the fun—and protection—of it. The fancy reds had been the only link between the crimes, and they had never led anyone anywhere.

Except Jack.

Lord, all she wanted right now was a shower, ibuprofen and her bed. Closing her eyes for a moment, she tempted herself with the image: the water pounding to beat away her pains, the superthick fluffy towels so big that she could practically swaddle herself…and maybe Jack doing the swaddling. He would be gentle toweling the water from her hair and patient working the comb through her nightmare curls, and when he was done…

The image swept away like a balloon pricked by a pin. When he was done, he would tuck her in, maybe kiss her forehead and leave her there while he went off to confront David because she'd made such a mess of things.

"He doesn't have proof," Jack said. "Not the sort that matters."

Lisette opened her eyes to join Padma in studying him. He looked as if none of them had a care in the world. Given that he'd had more near misses than Bella would ever have, and that he'd never once been arrested for theft, he had to know more about that sort of thing than she and Padma did.

"What do you mean, no proof that matters?" Lisette asked. Her last word hadn't disappeared into the air before Padma came close to screeching.

"No proof? He's got the red! His guys found it hidden *in our house*. You think that doesn't make us look guilty as hell?"

"They found it during a break-in. They can think you're involved. They can tell other people. They can sully your reputation with rumors and gossip, but the one thing they can't do is take that diamond to the authorities." Jack ran his fingers through his hair. "As far as David's concerned, *I* stole the stone and gave it to Lisette. He wouldn't believe she was capable of planning and executing the theft because she's…"

Now it was his turn to catch himself before saying something insulting. Lisette shifted her weight, taking more support from his arm around her, and offered him a choice of words to finish the sentence. "Common? Working-class? Inferior? Female?"

"Yes." His gaze locked with hers.

She nodded in agreement. "It took me just two months at the museum to find out that he has excellent taste in art and is an incredible snob and a huge misogynist. He resents people who have more money than him. He envies people who were born into your world. He considers himself far superior to everyone, and the only acceptable places for women are working at the computer, cooking at the stove, cleaning house or faking it in bed."

Jack gave her a sidelong glance. "You learned that in a few months and stayed eight years?"

"The sacrifices we make for the job." The easy shrug she intended made her bite back a groan. "You'd be amazed how much information and gossip I pick up in my world about yours."

"No, I wouldn't. My world consists of some vapid and self-centered people with limited conversational skills because they've been raised on twenty-four-hour care, to spend money like confetti and to never overtax their brains. All that leaves is gossip.

"So David's got the red back, but there's nothing he can do legally besides fire you, and he's fired so many people for such inconsequential reasons that it's not even a black mark against them." He grinned. "The curator of my family's collections was fired by David years ago. My uncle who hired him considered it a glowing recommendation."

Though Lisette smiled at his remark, inside she was thinking what David could do legally wasn't the problem. His guys had followed them into the mountains.

They'd taken a warning shot at them. Other guys had broken into her house, and they'd found proof, usable or not, that tied Lisette to the theft.

With a deep breath, she pushed one last longing thought of a shower away and straightened her shoulders. "Let's see how much work they've created for us."

Padma led the way inside, Jack bringing up the rear. Lisette steeled herself before walking in the door, but the mess inside still took her breath away. She couldn't find a single item that hadn't been tossed, upended or broken, from the pictures on the wall to the sofa pillows to the television. Every piece of china, crystal and porcelain in the dining room was broken; the kitchen looked like a tornado had torn through; the contents of the coat closet were on the floor. The bedrooms upstairs, the attic and the basement were the same. The back door had been kicked in, and apparently they'd left the same way, with one of the jerks oh so politely putting his foot through the screen door.

She wanted to cover her face and weep. This house had been her safe haven her whole life. Nothing bad ever happened here. Her memories were sweet enough to send a diabetic into a coma, all because of Marley. She had picked this place, this furniture, those dishes, had painted the walls and refinished the wood floors, had cooked in the kitchen, told bedtime tales in the bedroom and passed on two lifetimes of experience and love to Lisette in these rooms—her own and that of her father, Levi.

Suck it up. Keep calm and forge on.

"Should we call the police?" she asked Padma as they returned to the first-floor hallway.

In any other situation, Padma's astonishment would

have been comical. "Two thieves calling the police because other thieves broke in and stole back the gem they'd stolen? Are you crazy?"

"I wasn't thinking of mentioning our own stealing," Lisette answered drily. "But if we want to file an insurance claim to replace all the broken stuff—especially your computer—we'll need a police report."

"Don't worry about the insurance."

Jack's voice came from behind her, where he was picking up coats and jackets and rehanging them in the closet. She watched his strong fingers curl around the collar of Marley's wool coat, give it a shake, then he lifted it and ducked his head, and his nostrils flared at the faint scent. Was it just Marley's fragrance, or had he recognized a little of her there, too?

"Sorry, Jack, but we work for a living—Lisette for your big bad friend, and me for a nonprofit. We have to worry about insurance." Padma filled a basket with gloves, scarves and hats that were scattered across the floor and began organizing them.

"Don't worry. I'll take care of everything. David will repay me when I'm done." Jack's determined tone was unfamiliar and oddly comforting. Lisette had no doubt he did prefer things the peaceful, easy way, but she was also certain he could take care of himself when circumstances demanded it. And it looked as if these circumstances she'd gotten him into most certainly would demand it.

Good thing for him, the blood of pirates ran through his veins.

Chapter 7

They'd restored order to the living room before Padma forced Lisette upstairs to clean up. While she escorted her to the bathroom, Jack started on the dining room. It was a cozy room, the table, chairs and buffet taking most of the space. He used a broom and dustpan to clear a path while avoiding forcing the chunks of broken glass into the pine floor.

When Padma returned, he'd crouched to pick up a few larger pieces of china: fragile, a delicate pattern of pink flowers on a creamy base, not overly valuable but probably filled with sentiment. She held out her hands for the pieces so she could dump them into the wastebasket she'd set on the table, but she clutched the remnants of the sugar bowl a moment.

"Marley bought all these dishes at an estate sale when we were kids. Every meal, even every cookie, we had here was on these dishes at a formal table. She wanted us to use our linen napkins correctly, to treat the dishes with the care they required, to know which fork or spoon to use. She promised that someday we'd be grateful for the lessons. Once we truly understood what she was grooming Lisette for—or in my case, when I had to attend a formal banquet my senior year in college—we were very grateful."

Jack imagined them: dark-haired, dark-eyed little girls trying not to squirm in their chairs, wishing for paper plates and plastic utensils but doing their best to learn the lessons Marley was teaching them. He understood, having gone through the same lessons himself because at the tables he'd frequented, paper plates and plastic utensils didn't exist.

"How did you get involved in the grooming? Surely her mother didn't decide to train you as a thief without consulting your parents first."

Her smile was merely a shadow of the usual million-watt glow. "I wanted to do everything Lisette did. Marley taught her things, and she'd turn around and teach me. About the time we were twelve, Marley finally agreed to teach me, too, just to broaden my education, but I wasn't supposed to *ever* use any of it. I never actually did until I was grown, after spending a tremendous amount of time convincing her that I was an adult and it was totally my choice and I wouldn't do anything dangerous. I'm a complete wiener. I would never take the kind of chances that they did—that Lisette does." She shrugged, her hair falling over her shoulders. "That's how I became Bella Donna's support staff, because I don't have the nerve to be an actual thief."

Falling silent, her expression darkened, then suddenly she smacked him on the arm. Jack yelped. "What was that for?"

"You were supposed to keep her safe today!"

"Hey, falls happen. It wasn't my fault. And she did really well on everything else. Better that she get bruised a little now than get caught in some mark's mansion because she froze."

"I guess," Padma grudgingly agreed before scowling fiercely at him. "But you're lucky she wasn't seriously hurt. Then you'd have to deal with me, and while I'm all sweet and friendly on the outside, there's a little bit of Satan living inside. You don't want me to let him out."

Lisette had been right: they could be scary when they wanted.

Over the next few minutes, the only disturbances in the house were their sweeping and scuffing, glass clinking off glass and the rustling of trash bags.

And the sound of the shower running upstairs. Water cascading down, warm enough to provide comfort, not so hot that it could worsen Lisette's bruises. Washing away all the dust and sweat and grime. Cleansing, soothing, relaxing... And she, of course, was naked beneath all that lovely warm water, lathering her skin, rinsing her hair, wet and gleaming and—

Damn, how did it get so warm in here?

Looking for a distraction, he seized on an earlier remark Padma had made. "You said you work for a non-profit. What do you do?"

"I work primarily on water projects—better filtering systems, purification plants, accessibility, conservation. Did you know these guys in Britain created a water bottle that you can actually eat when it's empty?"

"I did not know that. That's a cool idea."

"Very cool. Did you know that 780 million people don't have access to clean drinking water? That's about one in ten. Very *un*cool. There are tons of agencies working on it, and we've made a splash—sorry for the pun—but it's a very big problem. What's the situation at your home?"

Jack picked up a heavy piece of crystal and dropped it into the trash. "Um…"

"Come on, Jack. The Caribbean got hit by a drought. Don't you watch the news? How's the water supply on Deux Saints?"

"I, uh, don't know. I'll have to ask Simon." Heat warmed his neck at the admission. Granted, he didn't live on the island, but he was half owner. He should know about something as important as water. It was an island, after all, surrounded by millions of gallons of the stuff. Of course, those gallons weren't drinkable without treatment, calling to mind the Coleridge quote: *Water, water, everywhere, nor any drop to drink.*

Upstairs, the shower shut off. His gaze lifted toward the ceiling, his imagination all too ready to fill in sights he hadn't yet had the luck to see, but he forced it back. "I hate to leave you with all this work, but I need to talk to David, and if I don't get out of here while Lisette's otherwise occupied, she's going to insist on coming with me."

Padma's gaze narrowed. "You're meeting him alone?"

"Oh, hell, no. There will be plenty of people around. Even so, I've already told her she can't go, and she's already insisted she should. Tell her I'll let her know what happens." He started toward the door, then turned back. "Maybe you guys should leave this for later, pack a bag and go stay somewhere else, at least for tonight." He didn't add *just to be safe,* but Padma heard the words anyway.

"Yeah, we'll do that. Do you think my parents' house— No, we'll go to a hotel." The bathroom door creaking drew her gaze upward, too, for a moment. "It'll take her a while to get dressed, but go on."

He was about to disappear around the corner when she quietly added, "Be careful."

"I do my best." He all but sneaked past the stairs and out the door, not taking a deep breath until he was backing out of the driveway and listening to Aunt Gloria's phone ring. By the time he got to the hotel, she'd called him back with word that David had agreed to meet him in one hour at a bar near her hotel. Though she'd been curious, she hadn't questioned him. She knew she would get the details eventually.

In his suite, he showered, changed into black trousers and a sapphire-blue shirt, grabbed a well-worn leather jacket, then dialed Simon's number on the way out again.

His best friend and good-as-a-brother answered, his accent far more of the islands than Jack's. "It's eighty-three degrees and sunny here, and you're scheduled for a cold front, rain and the possibility of snow in the next twenty-four hours. It's good to be me."

Weather had become their shared joke. Simon insisted he had too much tropical warmth, sun and sweet breezes bred into his blood to allow him to live anywhere else, while Jack teased him with gorgeous autumns, incredible springs and winter wonderlands when he traveled. Right now, he had to admit the island sounded pretty nice. Having Lisette on the island with him sounded damn nice.

"It's good that you're you because no one else would want to be."

"Ha. Are you still in Denver?"

"For the moment. Did you hear about David Candalaria losing one his paintings to Bella Donna during his big party?"

"Toinette mentioned the theft. She didn't say it was Bella. I admire the woman's taste."

"You don't even know which piece she stole."

"Knowing she stole it from him is good enough."

It was. Payback was always good. He figured Lisette's payback to David would be great fun—provided she survived to pull it off—and Jack wanted to be a part of it.

"He thinks I took it."

"He actually said that?" Simon's tone was part amusement, part surprise. Though he rarely left the island, when he did, he received the same sort of fawning Jack did—even more so, since time to fuss over him was always limited.

"He asked. I told him no. But today…" Jack hesitated. He normally wouldn't share a secret with anyone, but Simon wasn't exactly anyone, and he could keep a confidence better than everyone. "Lisette Malone works at the Candalaria Museum. I met her at the party, and today we went rock climbing. Someone shot at her, and she fell. No real injuries. But when we got back to Denver, someone had broken into her house and found…"

Simon was always quick to catch on. "The fancy red diamond that always goes missing when Bella's around?" He chuckled. "Well, hell, son, of course you'd be the first person in the world to discover who she is—

and to get blamed for her heist. Is she as beautiful as the legend says?"

"And then some."

"So she steals from David, he believes you did it, and he's seriously pissed. Tell me why you're still in town."

"He's afraid to do anything to me, so he's going after Lisette instead."

"Who's the one he really should be going after, anyway. *You* didn't steal his stuff. *She* did."

"But he doesn't know that. He's only after her because he thinks I like her. If I hadn't brought attention to her, he wouldn't know she exists."

"So he's targeting the right person but for the wrong reason." Simon paused to speak to Toinette, his administrative assistant. "Do you like her? No, of course you do. You admired Bella from the moment you heard her name. Most guys idolize athletes, rock stars, celebrities. Your only idol has ever been Bella. It doesn't even matter how she looks. You were predisposed to be enamored of her anyway."

Jack didn't argue with him. Lisette's being gorgeous was merely the icing on the cake.

"You know, that jet sitting idle at the airport carries eight passengers. You and Bella could disappear where Candalaria would never find you."

"The only place he could never—" Jack broke off. Simon didn't love art, though he collected and protected it. He might not warm to the idea of inviting a thief into his home, but he wouldn't say no to Jack, and Jack would truly enjoy showing her the island and the tropical weather she loved.

"I'm having drinks with David in a few minutes. If

that doesn't go well, you might be seeing both of us—um, all three of us—soon."

"Three?"

"Padma, Lisette's friend. If David's stalking Lisette to get to me, then we have to assume if we leave, he'll stalk Padma to get to her. We can't take off and leave her here unguarded."

"No, of course not." This time Simon was amused. "You know, you really should hire that bodyguard your mom nags about. If you stay there more than another day, I can arrange a couple of guys."

"I hope that won't be necessary. I'd better head off to the meeting. Don't worry. Aunt Gloria will be nearby if things get ugly." Jack was about to sign off, but abruptly he asked, "Hey, how's the water situation on the island?"

Simon's silence indicated his surprise at the question. "The ocean's still there, though not as clean as we wish. We haven't gotten as much rain as usual, but our freshwater sources are maintaining. Why? You've never cared about water as long as you had plenty to dive, bathe and drink."

"Yeah. Don't tell anyone that, will you? It makes me look like a jerk. I'll let you know how it goes with David."

"I'll have a few rooms readied," Simon said drily, then added in a serious tone, "You know David doesn't have an honest bone in his body. Be careful."

"Who went and made today 'everybody-tell-Jack-to-be-careful day'? You guys are making me feel incapable of carrying on a simple conversation without getting into trouble."

Simon laughed. "It's been that way every single day

since you were two. It's not our fault you were adventurous."

"Skydiving, skiing, trekking across entire countries—those are adventurous. All the skills I need for the thief gig—those are adventurous, too. Confronting ol' David, the jerk, the dolt… That actually sounds a little fun."

"Sounds stupid to me," Simon helpfully disagreed. "Maybe you should blow him off and get that bird in the air."

"Run away? From David? The only time people run from David is to avoid being bored to death."

"Forget he's David. Just think of him as a psychopath with a boatload of money and the belief that he's entitled to take whatever he wants."

"Thank you for that reassuring description, Simon," Jack said. "I'll try to brighten your day sometime soon."

"I can't believe he sneaked off to meet Candalaria alone." Lisette swept up the last broken glass from the kitchen floor, then lifted a bucket filled with hot soapy water from the sink. The astringent floor cleaner competed with the sticky-sour-sweet condiments dumped from the refrigerator, but that didn't stop her from dipping in a mop and dousing the floor.

"Of course you can believe it. He's Jack Sinclair." Padma had located supplies from previous projects in the basement and was in the middle of a temporary fix on the back door. "You told him you wanted to go. He told you no. He won that round."

Of course he won. Lisette just hoped his luck and influence continued to protect him. "Why did these idiots have to make such a mess? Sure, the diamond could have been hidden anywhere, but *Shepherdess* was too big for most of the places they looked."

"Not idiots, sweetie. Punks. Bad guys. They wanted to cause as much damage as they could." Padma nailed a board across the upper part of the door, getting out some frustration with the hammer, then added another near the bottom. "Maybe their boss thought you had other stuff Jack had given you."

"But nothing of his."

Padma gave her a sympathetic look. "I know you're tired and you hurt and it kills you to see your mom's house like this, but we're talking about Candalaria. You know he has no qualms about stealing. You think he would leave anything of value behind just because it wasn't his?"

"The bastard. This is all his fault." Lisette dunked the mop into the bucket again. "And my fault for stealing from him in the first place. And my fault for dragging Jack into it. I could have put off meeting him until later. I didn't have to do it the same night I took the painting."

After hammering in a third board, Padma faced her. "I'm not laying blame, because at the time we both agreed it was our best plan A at the time. But in hindsight, yes, you could have met Jack later. But we didn't know his part of our plan was going to turn out so well. I mean, he really likes you."

Ignoring the warm little quivers in her gut, Lisette corrected her. "He really likes Bella."

"Bella was just part of the hook. He likes *you*."

"I don't want him to like me." Lisette's words came out grudgingly as she dunked the mop again. She wanted him to experience a short-term infatuation with her: long enough and serious enough to get her onto the island. A little flirting, a little romance, a little sex, all running their course about the time she disappeared with the statue. Then he would be too upset about the statue to give the romance a second thought. And he was an easy-come, easy-go sort of guy. He would forget her with the very next party he attended, the very next pretty woman who smiled at him.

And she would forget him…well, sometime.

"As soon as you're done, let's get out of here. Pack some clothes, whatever you need for a few days, and anything you don't want to leave behind."

Lisette didn't want to leave *anything* behind. This was her home. Her safe haven. The only place in the world where she truly belonged. "Where are we going?"

"To a hotel."

"Why?" Lisette could already hear her friend's answer: *because Jack said we should.* She was surprised when Padma said something totally different.

"Those bastards violated our home, Lisette. I hate knowing they touched our stuff and had fun destroying it. I'm pissed off and scared, and I don't want to stay here tonight. I want to go someplace nice and safe, and I want to put on my pajamas and order room service and distract myself from all this for a few days until everything is back in order and the door's replaced and I don't feel threatened anymore."

Lisette plopped the mop in the bucket, tiptoed across the wet floor and awkwardly hugged Padma. "I'm sorry. You're right. 'Home, sweet home' doesn't feel so sweet or homey right now, does it?"

"No, it doesn't." After a moment, Padma mumbled, "Besides, Jack said we should go."

Lisette rolled her eyes. By the time she'd rinsed the

bucket and mop, Padma had put the supplies back in the basement. They climbed the stairs together, separating in different directions at the landing.

Like the rest of the house, Lisette's bedroom was a disaster. The drawers and the closet had been emptied, the mattress heaved against the wall, her makeup and jewelry scattered. She located a small suitcase that usually resided in the linen closet, now upside-down in the hall, and threw in enough clothes for several days, a swimsuit and as much makeup as she could gather. Her essentials were packed in minutes.

It took longer to pull back a piece of carpet from the bottom of the closet, pry up a section of floorboards and remove a thick stack of file folders. She also took an envelope filled with cash and a small velvet pouch that held two of her mother's three treasures: her wedding ring and a crudely fashioned necklace strung of wooden beads, both gifts from Lisette's father.

What's the third treasure? Lisette had asked every time Marley removed the pouch from its hidey-hole to reminisce, and Marley always brushed her curls back and said, *You are, baby girl.*

Lord, Lisette missed her!

After making certain the storage space was concealed again, she pressed a kiss to the pouch, then tucked everything inside her suitcase. She zipped it and met Padma at the top of the stairs. "Ready?"

Padma's bag bumped from step to step to the living room, where she stopped and took a long look around. Her expression was grim when she quietly replied, "Ready."

Lisette retrieved jackets from the closet and walked outside before stopping to lock the door, resting her hand on the knob. It felt wrong, letting a bunch of punks chase her out of her own house. She should stay, barricade the doors and make a stand, but she was neither stupid nor stubborn nor heroic. Candalaria had cast her as a pawn, and after his meeting with Jack, who knew what actions he might take? Lisette wasn't going to die so Candalaria could get back at Jack. She wasn't going to stay in the house Candalaria's men had broken into, making it easy for them to find her again, lowering her guard, going to sleep.

And she and Padma would be back.

Pain throbbed when she hefted her bag into the trunk of Padma's car. She'd become accustomed to the aches from her fall while cleaning, but now that they were in retreat, her body was yearning for relief. Food, bed, a couple of pills and blessed sleep to put this day behind her.

Plus a phone call from Jack to let her know he'd survived his meeting with her boss. Maybe now that Candalaria had his diamond back, he would back off.

Sure. The diamond he didn't care about versus the painting he desperately wants. Yeah, that'll make him stand down.

Lisette closed her eyes. Couldn't a physically bruised and emotionally battered woman hope? Even when it was hopeless?

"Where are we headed?" Padma backed into the street, drove to the end and cruised through the stop sign onto the main avenue. "Are we just seeking safety or splurging on refuge? And before you answer that, let me remind you—I really want room service."

The fancy red that was to have paid their expenses for the next months was gone, but what the hell? Everyone deserved room service sometimes, didn't they? And it wasn't as if she and Padma lived outrageously. "I haven't been served dinner in my pajamas since high school. Definitely splurging." Lisette gasped as Padma whipped the little car around a monster pickup that had failed to yield.

"Don't give me that look." Padma wagged a finger at her. "I'm a good driver. I only take calculated risks. Besides, it makes it easier to tell if anyone is following us."

Remembering Jack's comment about forcing a dog-walker and his dog up a light pole, Lisette grinned, feeling better for the first time in hours. She settled comfortably in the seat, easing the tension knotted in her neck, and did the best thing she could while her best friend was driving.

She closed her eyes.

Lisette's nap was short and sweet, lasting mere minutes according to the dashboard clock. She lifted her head, looked around to see where they were, then looked at Padma. "You're awfully quiet."

Padma held the wheel with both hands, and her gaze was shifting steadily from the street ahead to the rearview mirror. "You were asleep. I always try to be quiet when you're asleep. Not that you've ever fallen asleep in the car before. By the way, it's much more peaceful than your usual cringing and squeaking."

Something seemed odd about the scene, but it took Lisette a moment and the sound of a *click-click-click* to realize what it was: Padma was driving the speed limit, signaling a lane change, then a right turn. She never signaled lane changes or turns until she was halfway through them. *I like to keep 'em guessing what I'm going to do.*

"What's up? Is there a cop behind us?"

"Nope." Padma flashed a smile that didn't reach her eyes. "I kinda wish there was."

Lisette's head started to swivel to look over her shoulder, but Padma cautioned. "Don't look. There's a dark SUV that I think is tailing us."

"Tailing?" The word didn't belong in their vocabulary. They weren't cops or criminals—well, not the kind who had to worry about someone tailing them. But when she checked the outside mirror, there was indeed an SUV, very much like the one from the mountains. There were a couple of cars between them, but when Padma made two more quick turns, the vehicle followed.

"They got behind us back by the Asian market. They didn't follow us from the house, so they must have expected us to go somewhere. They probably had cars on all the major streets."

The sourness of fear settled over Lisette, dark and edgy, but she tried to keep her voice light. "I can't believe they kept up with your normal driving."

"They caught my attention so I slowed down to see if I was just imagining things." Padma made one more turn, and a moment later, so did the truck. The maneuvers had taken them back to the broad avenue. "Should I lose them?"

Their gazes met for an instant, Padma's reflecting Lisette's uncertainty. *Could* they lose them? The car was reliable transportation, purchased more for its good mileage than its engine. The SUV was big enough and powerful enough to roll right over them if the driver so chose, leaving nothing but mangled bodies in flattened metal.

For all the teasing, though, Padma was a good driver, and going fast and wild came naturally to her. What seemed risky and reckless to others was business as usual for her.

Before Lisette could choose an answer, a roar sounded behind them, then she and Padma were thrown forward with surprising force. The seat belt caught, burning Lisette's shoulder, and her ribs ached as she braced herself with both legs and hands. She thought she made a choked sound but wasn't sure, since her lungs were resisting her effort to force air into them.

"They hit us!" Padma shrieked, fighting to control the car. With cars stopped ahead of them for a red light, she slammed on the brakes and jerked the steering wheel hard to the left, spinning the car a complete 180 degrees and still pulling as hard as she could. "Those idiots *hit* my car!"

"Go," Lisette croaked, still strangled for air. "Go, go, go, *go!*"

The car fishtailed before the tires found traction, squealing as Padma accelerated. Lisette turned to see the SUV driver try the same maneuver, but his vehicle was too big. He drove over the curb, skidded on the grass and plowed over a street sign before bumping back into the street, heedless of traffic. She imagined she heard the big engine even over angry horns and struggling brakes when he straightened and pointed the vehicle at them again.

"Here." Padma thrust her phone at Lisette.

"Who do you want me to call?"

"Gee, I don't know. Maybe the *police?*"

Of course. Hands trembling, Lisette punched in 911. All her life, she'd been taught to be unflappable under pressure—and to stay away from the police—but on this Saturday from hell, all her unflappability was gone. Her entire body shook, and when the dispatcher came on the line, so did her voice. She reported their location, the SUV following them, crashing into them and now chasing them, and gave a great shudder of relief when the operator said officers were on their way. The wail of a siren a few seconds later allowed her to take the first deep breath since the moment of impact.

The patrol car hauled past in the opposite direction, lights flashing, siren piercing the air. A second car joined it, both of them closing in on the SUV, which made a sudden turn onto a narrow side street. The cars followed while more sirens sounded nearby.

Padma slowed for an upcoming intersection, easing into the right-turn lane. More police cars flew through the intersection, some going south to follow the suspects, others turning east to presumably try to block them from exiting the neighborhood they'd entered. "Though we called, I really don't want to actually talk to them. Do you?"

"No." Too many lame or half answers always yielded more questions, along with suspicion and distrust. She didn't want the police in the city where they lived to think they had something to hide.

While Padma drove like a law-abiding citizen, Lisette dug out her own cell phone. "I wonder if Jack's met with Candalaria already. If he hasn't—"

"He shouldn't." Padma's brows knit. "Tell him it's gotten dangerous. Tell him they *hit* my *car*."

The whine reminded Lisette of herself that morning—*I fell off a cliff!* Her smile was tough to pull together, though, and it didn't last long. She located Jack's cell number and dialed it, praying he would answer.

Her heart stuttered when it went to voice mail. "Jack, it's Lisette. Call me, please. It's important."

Padma leaned across the car. "They hit my car!" Once again she wagged an admonishing finger. "A crisis is no time to be calm and cool. You've got to get your point across."

Wishing she'd heard Jack's reassuring voice instead of the canned message, Lisette wondered what the hell to do next.

Jack took his time getting to Rory's, the bar David had chosen for their meeting. David was as punctual as a second hand on a finely made timepiece. Tardiness in others drove him nuts, and of course Jack liked to drive him nuts.

Stopping on the next block down from Rory's, he scanned the vehicles outside, particularly the three SUVs right in front. With the tinted windows, it was impossible to tell whether they were occupied. His best guess was yes: at least two bodyguards inside the bar with their boss, one waiting in each of the trucks.

When a Humvee blasting music pulled up behind him, he made a quick right turn before the driver could blow the horn. A drive around the block showed no more suspicious vehicles—and also no way to enter Rory's without walking right past the guards.

"You're really not made to be a pirate, Jack. Are you sure you want to do this?"

Actually, he was sure he *didn't* want to. Since getting off the phone with Simon, he'd had a bad feeling in his gut. Maybe it had been sneaking off without Lisette, or Padma's uncharacteristically sober warning. Maybe Simon's psychopath comment had sounded like less a joke and more reality. Maybe Jack really was a coward, or he had better sense than people gave him credit for, but the meeting didn't feel like his best decision ever, and he already got enough ribbing about his bad decisions.

"Okay." He parked around the corner on the side street, out of sight of the bodyguards. He'd give himself a pep talk if he thought it would matter, but it wouldn't. He was going to force himself through the next however many minutes: one step, one word, one threat at a time.

He was about to walk away from the pickup when he remembered his cell phone. He took it from the charger and was surprised to see a missed call from Lisette listed on the screen. He'd had music on, not that loud, but the combination of nerves and dread had been a pretty potent distraction.

Instead of retrieving her message, he called her. She sounded breathless but fairly normal. "You guys find a hotel for the next few nights?"

"Um, we had a bit of a problem with that," she answered, followed immediately by Padma's irate voice. "They hit my car!"

The hairs on the back of his neck prickled. "Who hit what?"

"Someone in a gray SUV followed us, rear-ended the car, then tried to chase us down."

Damn. "Are you all right?"

"Yeah, just shaken."

"Shaken, hell," Padma muttered. "I want my mom."

"We, um, aren't used to this sort of thing," Lisette said, her voice cracking. "We don't know what to do."

Jack wasn't used to it, either, but there was always one place problems couldn't follow. All he had to do was get the women to the airport. The problem of David wasn't going to magically disappear, but they would have help in figuring out a plan of action, and they would be untouchable until then.

"Where are you now?"

"At the Presbyterian/St. Luke's parking garage. We thought it was safer to get off the streets, and Padma's father's on staff, so we came here."

"Okay, good." Jack slid back into the driver's seat, made a U-turn and left the area. "Tell me how to find you."

She gave easy directions, waiting until he'd reached point A before trying to send him to point B.

"I'm coming to you, then we'll get a cab. They'll be looking for your vehicle, not a taxi."

"And where will we go?"

"Doesn't it seem like a good time to spend a few days down south? Warm water, sunshine, cool breezes, beautiful art…"

She was silent a moment, broken by an audible swallow. "Where south? The Florida Keys? Cozumel? Jamaica?"

"Why would I take you to any of those islands when my own is just a little farther?"

It was just a few hours ago that he'd told her outsiders were rarely allowed on the island. Was she considering that, wondering if the invitation meant something, if it was more than mere protection from David? After all, he could fly her anywhere in the world and hire enough security to be equally safe. He didn't have to take her—them, he reminded himself; Padma, too—to his private ancestral home.

But he wanted to.

"Don't we need our passports?"

"There are ways to get around that. And I'm at the intersection you said."

She gave him a direction and distance to the next landmark, then her voice became more distant. He imagined her turning in the car seat to face Padma. "You want to check out the water situation on a Caribbean island for yourself?"

"Yes! Oh, crap, no, I can't take off work right now. The deadline for my grant proposal is coming up. But we don't get to travel that often without paying for it ourselves because we run on donations, and that would be so cool to learn firsthand. And I can work while I'm gone. My computer may be smashed, but I've got my tablet in my bag, and I—"

Lisette interrupted her, used to her meandering. "We'd be grateful for the break. You should see the hospital campus by now. We're on the third level of the garage. Drive slowly, and Padma will honk the horn when we see you."

"Okay. I'm turning in now." The garage wasn't made for oversize vehicles, so any speed besides *slow* wasn't an option. Appreciative that there wasn't much traffic this late in the day, he followed the narrow lane up to the second level, then the third.

With the echo of Padma's honk fading, he stopped behind them and got out, blinkers flashing. The women met him at the trunk, lifting out suitcases, tote bags and coats. "Wow, this was all for two nights away?"

"We believe in being prepared." Lisette grimaced when she lifted her bag. He pulled it from her hand, took Padma's, too, and stowed them in the backseat of the truck.

Buckled in again and waiting for them to settle, he studied the damage to the car. There was some crunching and broken plastic around the right taillight. Part of the bumper was missing, and the trunk, though operational, was crumpled. David's people hadn't been trying to hurt them, he suspected. Yet.

"Not so bad. It doesn't look like your airbags even deployed."

"What?" Padma leaned forward from the rear seat, mouth gaping. "I was so terrified, I didn't notice! That rotten dealer sold me a car with *broken* airbags!" She slumped back. "Oh, they are in so much trouble. Sell me a car with no airbags…"

Lisette's smile was sweet and indulgent. Though there was no blood between them, their relationship went beyond best friends to family of the best kind. He understood because he and Simon were the same way. They didn't see each other as often as they should, but they were still best everythings.

"It's good they didn't hit you harder." He directed the quiet comment to Lisette as he shifted into gear and continued up the incline.

"I think their goal was to scare us."

"Or to stop the car so they could take you." He spoke without thinking, felt the sudden stillness in the air and glanced at her. Her expression was stark, making him apologetic. "David's threatening you to get to me. If I was meeting with him, then I couldn't be with you. Having a hostage would certainly give him the upper hand. It was an ideal time for him to make his next move."

When her mouth turned up in a faint smile, surprise raised his brows. "Instead, it became an ideal time, while they're waiting for you, for us to make a run for it."

He smiled, too. "Exactly what I was thinking. Can you call a cab and have them meet us a couple floors up? Offer them an extra thousand if they get here quickly. I'll alert the pilot that we're on our way." While dialing the pilot's cell, he made a mental note to send the truck's location to the rental company and to ask the hotel to send his belongings to the island. He would let Simon know they were coming, too, so his friend could gloat about being right, and...

He couldn't think of anything else. All they had to do was reach the airport unscathed, and within minutes, they would be out of Denver. Out of David's reach. Home. Safe.

At least, for a while.

Chapter 8

The trip to the airport was the most uncomfortable one of Lisette's life. Sharing the cab's backseat with her, Padma gazed out the window, a glum look reflected in the glass. Was it finally hitting home with her, all that had gone wrong today? She'd started out with such excitement about—

"Ooh, how did you do in the quadcopter games?"

Padma's brows drew together, then a smile burst across her face. "We kicked their butts. The guys took the trophy and my copter home with them to do a little tune-up on it. It's good to be team leader." After a moment, she asked, "How was the rock climbing? I mean, besides falling."

"It's better climbing with someone who knew what he was doing, truly enjoyed it and had enough confidence for both of us."

Padma raised her voice to carry. "Jack has enough confidence for twenty people. That's one of the perks of being Prince Charming."

He grinned at them over his shoulder but didn't interrupt his conversation with the cabdriver. He had a few unconfident moments, Lisette had seen for herself, and she liked him more for them. They made him seem more...

She couldn't say accessible. He was friendly, open, traveled by himself without the squads of bodyguards he could easily justify. He was nice. Interested in others. He didn't give the sense that he was slumming, didn't let on that his everyday life was so privileged and luxurious that she could imagine it only because of the glimpses she'd gotten on the job.

His moments made him less a rich man, more a man.

"Can you believe we're going to Île des Deux Saints?" Padma whispered. Plan A hadn't included her in the trip; she was supposed to stay home and provide long-distance support. Between Lisette's faulty choices, Jack's sense of right and David's violence, there wasn't going to be much that was usual about this job.

And there was no need now for sex. The whole point of the seduction was to get Jack to take her to the island. Once she set foot there, the hard part was over. All that remained was not to fall into bed with him, thwart their security and escape with *Le Mystère*.

It was for the best, after all. She'd been willing to sleep with Jack to get what she needed, and she would have felt bad about it. Sex with Jack deserved to be so much more than that.

So why did that relief feel so much like regret? Because she hadn't had a date in months? Because she

hadn't had sex in even longer? Because she'd enter-
tained fantasies about how handsome he was, and nice,
and interesting, and sexy, and the body, damn, to make
those fantasies steam? Because she *liked* him? Because
once this time with him was over, there would never
be another chance?

Her sigh was soft, but Padma understood, squeezing
her hand again. "It'll work out okay. You and I have a
knack for that, you know. We've tempted fate a million
times, and yet here we are."

"Don't be feeling too smug yet. You've still got to
call your parents, tell them someone broke into the
house and rammed into your car, and that now you've
taken off on a spur-of-the-moment trip to the Caribbean
with me and a man you've known twenty-four hours."

Padma's expression morphed into dismay. "Thank
you for reminding me of that. *But* I also get to call my
boss and tell him that I'm doing on-site research on the
islands' drought conditions at no expense to us. He'll be
so amazed at my good karma that he'll make me team
leader next time."

When it came to confidence, Padma could match
Jack one-to-one.

The roar of a jet engine overhead drew Lisette's gaze
out the window. Denver International spread out, with
more traffic, people and planes than she wanted to face
in one location. The cabdriver continued past the signs
for the passenger terminal, curving around the property until at last he made a turn into a less chaotic area.

A lone plane stood on the tarmac, sleek and powerful. The airliners she was used to compared as favorably
to it as a tricycle to a Tesla. The air stairs were down,
and a man in uniform stood next to them. The engines

were already running. By now, Candalaria had realized Jack wasn't coming to the meeting. He'd probably sent his thugs out to look for him, and the airport must be high on their list of places to look.

Getting out of the car, she turned in a slow circle, searching for anything that seemed out of place. Since *she* was the main thing out of place, she gave up and turned to find Jack reaching for her arm. "Do you think... Never mind. I don't want to know." She softened her words with a smile as he and the cabdriver hustled them to the plane, Jack escorting her and Padma, the driver hauling the luggage.

Another man stood just inside the cabin at the top of the stairs, nodding politely. He directed them to the middle of the plane, where Padma spun gleefully. "Aw, man, it's gonna be hard to go back to flying coach after this."

"It won't be so hard when you have no choice." Lisette chose a plush leather seat and sank into its comforting depths with a silent *ahh*. Padma chose an identical chair across the aisle. There was room to stretch out their legs without menacing another passenger, or to curl up and sleep without folding into pretzels. Not that that would be necessary, since a sofa several feet longer than they were tall lined the wall farther back.

The rich were different.

She'd enjoy it while she could, because every job ended eventually.

Had Deux Saints changed since her parents' time? Twenty-seven years ago, it had been so oppressive, and Marley's and Levi's desire for freedom so strong, they'd risked their lives to achieve it. Her father had died for it. Her mother almost had.

And the direction of Lisette's life had been chosen before she'd even taken a breath.

Jack slid into the chair nearest her as the plane began taxiing. "You okay?"

Worried what emotion thoughts of her parents might have brought to her eyes, she stared blankly out the window and nodded.

He leaned closer to gaze out the same window. From the corner of her eye, she caught his mouth quirking. "Man, this is really going to piss off David."

Curiosity focused her gaze on the two dark SUVs stopping about the same place the cab had, and her mouth quirked, too. She wondered for one wild moment if the men would chase after the plane, guns blazing, and try to prevent them from taking off like they did on TV, but neither vehicle moved.

Jack clicked together his seat belt, then swiveled to face her, his normally cheery expression semi-serious. "David's a patient man. He doesn't care how long it takes to achieve his goal. He suspects where we're going. As soon as we land, he'll know. Then he'll start plotting what to do when we return, because eventually we will return."

Padma's gaze turned darker. "My parents—"

"Someone's watching them. Don't worry. They won't even know."

"Mrs. Maier…" Lisette felt bad that she hadn't thought to warn the old lady. She'd just been too caught up in what was going on. Lord, she'd had way too much confidence in herself before this whole job went to hell. A little failure was a good thing, Dr. Mom insisted, especially when it meant you were getting too big for your britches—or, in Padma's case, sari.

Their deconstruction of this case when it was over was going to cover a whole lot of new lessons learned.

"Someone's watching her, too."

Jack looked entirely too pleased with himself, but that was okay. Lisette was pleased with him, too. "When did you take care of that?"

"I texted Dominic while Sa'id, the cabbie, was listing all the ways the Broncos had disappointed him." He gave a shake of his head. "You Americans take your football seriously, don't you?"

"Just like the rest of the world and their soccer."

"Real football," he and Padma chimed.

As soon as the plane was airborne, Jack stood up. "I'm going up front to make a couple calls. I'd suggest you two call everyone you need to talk to, then turn your phones off for the rest of the trip. Once we land, you can use island phones for check-ins."

He went to the front, Padma to the back, and Lisette remained where she was. There was no one for her to call. Padma was here, and Mr. Chen would surely hear on Monday that she'd been fired. The only other people who might miss her would be their regular waiters at their favorite restaurants.

On another day, that realization might bother her—or maybe not. Her mother had taught her, more by actions than words, that a few good friends were double the worth of a hundred so-so friends. In the Khatri family, Lisette had people who loved and trusted her. She didn't need or want more casual acquaintances to round out her world, not when she had secrets to keep.

Padma knew all her secrets. And Jack knew some. Except for the one concerning him. Wouldn't it be lovely if she could find a way to reclaim her family's statue without him finding out? If he never had to know, if they could still be friends after, if there would still be a chance...

With a faint smile, she shut off her phone, tilted her head back and closed her eyes. Jack might be Prince Charming, but she was no fairy-tale princess.

There would be no happily-ever-after ending for them.

When Jack finished his calls—Simon was gloating quite capably—he shut off the phone, slid it into his pocket, gathered the makings of dinner and returned to Lisette. He dumped everything onto an empty seat, then positioned a table between their chairs. "I've been trying to sit down to a spectacular meal with you since Friday morning, but something keeps getting in the way."

Her smile was wan. "Fire was pretty spectacular."

"Though the ambiance was lacking." He opened packs of cheese, crackers and tiny tomatoes; crostini and finely diced olives, peppers and feta; thin slices of prosciutto paired with Parm. There were fresh grapes, too, and the miniature oranges he liked best and, still on the galley counter, trays of desserts. The pilot took care of the plane, and the copilot handled the shopping. He was good at it.

Jack glanced at the couch in the rear. "Is Padma still on the phone?" She sat sideways on the sofa, her back to them. She was quiet, possibly listening to her mother, but she was also still.

Lisette glanced over her shoulder and turned back wearing a grin. "She's probably snoozing. Between her job, our work, her family and the rest of her life, she's spinning like a top all the time. She's learned to grab a break any time she can."

"Hey, sometimes a whole night of sleep just isn't on the schedule."

"I'll bet you've seen a lot of those nights."

"I bet you have, too."

"But for very different reasons. I'm neither a jet-setter nor a partier nor a risk-taker nor a ladies' man. When I'm operating on limited sleep, it's because I'm working."

Jack considered whether to take exception to any of the things she'd called him and decided no. It was tough to be insulted when everything she'd said was true. Except the part about being a ladies' man. Sort of. He liked women. Some of them liked him back. All of them liked his bank account. And it was easier to be nice to people even when he intended to never see them again than it was to keep everyone at a distance.

Instead, he focused on her casual mention of her job. "How do you get clients? It's not like you can hand out business cards. How do people contact you?"

She paid great attention to picking up a crostini, spreading olive salad over it, scooping out a chunk of feta to perch on top, then sliding it into her mouth. He let her delay, enjoying the simple act of watching her chew, catching her eyes rolling upward with unspoken appreciation, delicately patting her mouth with a napkin after swallowing.

Forget conversation. He could just sit and watch her for the rest of the trip.

"On occasion, we approach them. We hear about a particular robbery, and if it seems right, we offer our assistance. Some of our clients are word of mouth.

Mrs. Maier has sent several people our way. The bulk, though... My mother had a friend who manages insurance coverage for some of the top collections in the world. His client suffers a loss, he contacts her—now me—and we get it back."

"Do you get finders' fees from the insurance company?"

She tilted her head to one side. "Oddly enough, the law doesn't make allowances for the reason a thief has taken something. My stealing a million-dollar painting to return to its real owner isn't looked on any more kindly than Candalaria's thief stealing it in the first place. It's still a felony. It still involves prison time."

"But surely insurance companies can find ways to pay out a ten or fifteen percent fee without anyone in law enforcement knowing."

"I'm sure they could, but as a whole, the insurance industry is incredibly tightfisted. When they do pay a finder's fee, it's more likely to be to an investigations firm that locates the stolen piece. Then the company works with the authorities to retrieve it legally, which can take years. I prefer a quicker schedule. Candalaria had *Shepherdess* less than three months before we recovered it. Besides..." She reached for another piece of crostini. "If the insurance company paid me, even off the books, my name would eventually come to the attention of the wrong people. The cops would want to arrest me. The criminals would want to stop me." She shook her head, her curls shimmering. "No, thanks. I'd rather take a trinket to cover our expenses. We're not trying to get rich here."

"A fancy red trinket." He finished off a piece of prosciutto and Parm before asking, "Are you ever tempted to keep one?"

"I'm not a fancy red person. I'm not even much of a jewelry person." Just like the night they met, her delicate fingers were bare. No bracelets dangled from her wrists, not even a watch, and no necklace draped around the slender warm-cocoa column of her neck. *All* that warm-cocoa skin would be gorgeous decked out in gold and gems. He'd once stolen a necklace, ninety-two carats of cascading yellow diamonds that gave the illusion of floating against the skin. She would look incredible wearing that.

Especially if it was all she wore.

Which rooms do you want prepared? Simon had asked. *Your house is ready, of course, but what about Bella and her friend?*

It was too easy to imagine Lisette in his house. The pastel colors, the airy spaces, the furniture that faded into the background…she would fit as perfectly as if it had been designed with her in mind. The house would provide the setting, and she would provide the color. The life. The subtle scent she wore would seep into the surfaces. Everything she touched would retain her imprint. She would make it more of a home than it already was.

And then she would leave.

For a while. Maybe.

He'd taken a long moment before finally replying. *Put them both in the main house.* The distance between the two was minimal. If she chose to visit him some evening, or if he chose to lure her away, it would be simple enough. But it would be a choice. She would make the effort, or he would, but there would be no temptation prompted by proximity, no spur-of-the-moment splurge that she might later regret.

And there *would* be lots of privacy.

A snore interrupted his musings, drawing both their gazes to the rear of the plane. Lisette left her seat, took hold of Padma's ankles and tugged her until she slid down onto her back on the sofa. Padma neither twitched nor mumbled, but the positional change did stop the snoring.

"You two are close," he remarked when Lisette sat down again.

"Twins separated at birth, with different parents, from different backgrounds and of different ethnicities." She picked up her drink and sat back, legs crossed, looking so very relaxed. He hadn't been through all that she had, but to achieve that level of relaxation, he would have to break into the liquor cabinet in the galley. "What about you? Who are you close to?"

"Simon. Also twins separated at birth, with different parents. Same backgrounds and ethnicities, though."

"Which are?"

"Both descended from pirates. Still living off their bounty. As far as the ethnic stuff…we're French, British, Spanish, African, Dominican, Portuguese. You name it, someone in our family tree represents it. Deux Saints is truly a melting pot." In the history of the world, there had never been any shortage of people willing to strike out and explore, seeking adventure, riches, a better life or even just a different one. He was grateful his ancestors had been in that group. "And you?"

Shadows darkened her eyes before she took a long drink of soda, a delaying tactic he could recognize with his eyes closed. When a smile curved the corners of

her lips and her gaze returned to him, though, it was
as if the moment—the shadows—had never existed.
"I'm not totally sure. White, black, brown. No specif-
ics, just some mix thereof." After another moment, the
smile formed fully. "My mother came from the Caribbean. She didn't like to talk about it. That was her old
life. Denver was her new life."

Jack could have asked a dozen questions, but he had
the distinct impression that Lisette didn't like to talk
about it, either. Instead, he shifted to a different angle
of the same subject. "What about your father?"

"Ethnically, he was more of the same. He died before
I was born. Boating accident." Again came the shadows
and, again, quickly gone. "I suppose that was why she
didn't like to talk about home."

"I'm sorry."

"Sometimes I think I can't miss what I never had,
but that's not true. I used to watch Padma with Dr.
Dad. He was so fierce about her. Even though I'd never
known my father's fierceness, its absence left a place
in my life." The look on her face was melancholy. She
appeared to savor it for a minute, maybe two, before
pushing it away. "Does the shop on your island sell
clothing?"

"A few essentials. Anything else has to come from
Santo Domingo in the Dominican Republic. That's
where we trade the plane for the helicopter."

"Padma and I will need a shopping trip. We weren't
expecting to leave Denver, so we brought jeans, sweat-
ers, boots and coats. I did toss in a swimsuit, since the
hotel would have an indoor pool, but nothing else suit-
able for a tropical escape."

She said swimsuit, not bikini, but he was imagining

her long, lean body covered with the merest of triangles and strings. More specifically, he was mentally drooling over all the skin *not* covered by the tiny triangles and strings. It took a measure of pure will to concentrate on the jeans and long-sleeved shirt she was actually wearing, and on the conversation. "We'll make a couple stops in Santo Domingo."

"Won't it be late?"

"It's six now. Five hours or so, plus the time change."

"But the shops—"

"Open when there's money to be spent. I know a few people. I'll call when we get closer."

"And you'll make it worth their while."

He wasn't sure if the words were a simple comment or if there was censure hiding inside them. "I don't make a habit of regularly inconveniencing someone with special requests. In this case, the goal is to get us out of David's reach and to keep us safe. But you need clothes, and the stores will be closed. Rather than take you out again tomorrow, when David could conceivably have people down there, I'd prefer to pay my friends to open their shops tonight. They do it for other people, for various reasons. They know they can tell me no, and someone else will say yes, so they'd rather say yes and get the extra cash themselves. It's business."

"Did you make it worth Sa'id's while to pick us up so quickly? Did you give him the thousand-dollar tip?"

"No. I gave him a two-thousand-dollar tip."

"Oh." She stood, got halfway through a stretch, then stopped and opted instead to take a few creaky steps to work out the aches. "Sorry. I'm just cranky."

Jack made his eyes pop. "Really? This is cranky? The last time my mom got cranky, she threw the whole family out of the house, all the relatives visiting from a dozen different countries plus Dad and me, and wouldn't let us come back for three days. The last time Simon was cranky, he took me out to the north side of the island where the jungle's nearly impenetrable and left me there. I hadn't been there in years, the sun was setting, it took *hours* to find my way home, and I was convinced the entire time that the spirits were watching me. As soon as I got to the cleared fields, I ran the rest of the way like a little girl."

He stood up and had the good luck to find himself only a scant foot from her. His fingers itched to touch her, to feel the warmth radiating from her, to see if the skin on her throat was as soft as it looked, to see just how well their bodies fit together, but the aches she still suffered stopped him. "You aren't cranky. Gorgeous, but not cranky."

Then his restraint said *what the hell,* and he leaned forward to kiss her mouth. It was a chaste enough kiss, nothing to stir blood or passion or need, but it was sweet, and it did make her dark eyes lighten and her cheeks turn rosy. It wasn't much, but it was enough.

For now.

Long after he'd moved to the back of the plane, Lisette stood motionless in the aisle. She'd experienced a wide range of kisses: okay, so-so, toe-curling, forgettable. She'd gotten a lot more than kisses with some of those guys, but never had they left her feeling…

She didn't even know what. Touched. Stunned. Overwhelmed by the pure simplicity of one kiss. Who would have believed a kiss worthy of a mother's or a grandmother's cheek could so rattle the cool, controlled, elegant Bella Donna?

But Jack hadn't been kissing Bella. He knew Bella was a persona, a disguise made not of clothing and cosmetics but of calm, confidence, brazenness and determination. If he'd been kissing Bella, she would have known, and it would have disappeared, forgotten, into the air, as quickly and permanently as all of Bella's flirtations. No, that so-sweet kiss had been a kiss for *her*, and that was why it flustered her so.

The large-screen television flickered to life, the sound muted. Jack was stretched out on the second couch, a pillow under his head. She gathered the remains of their dinner, repackaged the leftovers, threw away the trash and found a coffeemaker with a dizzying array of flavor pods, most marked with the Saint Clair logo.

And many of them bore family names, as well. There was Graycie's Choice, Glorious Gloria, Simon's Curse, Lucky Jack and probably two dozen more. Feeling about fourteen, Lisette slipped a Lucky Jack into her pocket for a souvenir before starting the machine. Eyes closed, she waited peacefully until a sputter of water and rich aroma signaled her coffee was done. She sprinkled in sweetener and more cream than was good for her. "Do you want a cup?" she asked Jack.

"No, thanks. Come sit down."

She'd really rather stand or pace or roll Padma to the floor and take her place in snooze land, but she wanted to ask Jack about something he'd said earlier. She sat in the chair nearest him, propped her feet on the table and blew lightly on her coffee to take the burn off.

"What blend did you choose?"

"Graycie's."

"Aw, you should have tried Lucky Jack. Graycie's a girly coffee. Lucky Jack is bold, stimulating, surprisingly complex and, I've been told, somewhat addictive."

She laughed. "Are you sure you're talking about your coffee and not yourself?"

He gave her a sly wink. "You'll see."

Judging the coffee cool enough, she sipped it, then took a larger drink. She wouldn't admit to him, but it was, well, a girly coffee. It was a pleasant drink, but she was pretty sure small children could down a pot or two of it before nap time without suffering any ill effects.

"Told you so. I'll make you another—"

"This is fine." She waved him back and took another sip of the coffee-flavored drink for people who wanted the taste but not the full impact. After her day, she needed the whole big boom. "I want to ask you about something you said."

His brow furrowed, his eyes raising to the ceiling as if he was trying to remember all the many things he'd said. She cut him a break and asked outright, "What spirits?"

"Oh." He kicked off his shoes and stretched his feet out at a right angle to hers. "Maybe I should have asked how you feel about ghosts before I brought you onto the plane."

"Your island is haunted?"

"From the beginning. The saints were bloodthirsty pirates. People died, and some of them, apparently, didn't want to go into the light."

Marley had told her a few stories of restless spirits wandering the island, souls who couldn't or wouldn't settle. It had made sense to Lisette that something remained when a person passed, far more sense than the idea that a person died and everything about him just blinked into nothingness, like the light that simply vanished when a bulb was shut off.

As a kid, she'd loved the ghost stories, huddling in bed at her mother's side and pleading for more. As an adult, she'd never given any real thought to ghosts until the first time Marley appeared in her head. At first, she'd thought she was so grief-stricken that she was imagining her mother's voice, but now she wasn't so sure.

Could her father's spirit remain on the island? He'd died in the ocean but not so far from land that his soul couldn't have found its way back. Could he have been waiting there all these years, hoping for Marley to return, longing for one look at his baby girl, one last look at his wife?

Her mother chose to remain silent on the subject. Her spirit was no different from the woman she'd been: wise, worried and more stubborn than any dozen mules.

Lisette moved from the chair to the end of the sofa opposite Jack. "What kind of things do your ghosts do?"

"Eh, we hear them sometimes at night, singing. People have seen lights moving through the jungle. A few employees have reported late-night encounters with what they believe are spirits." Jack turned so they faced each other, two good-sized cushions between them. "The creepiest part is the watching. It doesn't matter what time of day or night. There are always places where I *know* someone is watching me. It's kind of freaky."

Lisette had a vague fear that anyone who watched her long enough might get a glimpse of her true selves, every one of them. The idea of ghostly spies in the middle of the day on a sunny, bright, paradise-perfect island raised goose bumps along her arms and neck. "I assume your family organized search parties to make sure no one had taken up residence on that end of the island."

"Oh, yeah, more times than anyone counted. They hiked in from the south and anchored small boats off the coast and swam to the rocks. Simon's dad put the helicopter up, flying at treetop level. I don't think anyone ever managed to explore all of it because—well, you'll see. But no one ever found any sign of life besides the creatures that belong there, and the incidents have continued, like I said, for three hundred years."

Jack stretched his arm along the back of the couch. If she did the same with hers, their fingers wouldn't touch, but they'd be close. He could scoot forward...or she could, until they made contact. In fact, if she turned around and kicked off her shoes, she was pretty sure she could slide right over next to him, and he would wrap that arm around her, holding her as close as she wanted to be.

All the little goose bumps created by otherworldly promise combined into a giant bump of anticipation that made her shiver.

"You're not afraid of three-hundred-year-old singing ghosts, are you?"

Not afraid...though wouldn't it be incredible if the ghosts could be held responsible for *Le Mystère*'s disappearance? If she didn't have to betray him? But it was a long way from their harmless actions to stealing a priceless statue.

Carefully she eased one ankle-high boot off, then toed off the other and bent her knees, bringing her feet

Chapter 9

It was 2:00 a.m. Denver time when the helicopter set down a few hundred yards from the Toussaint house. Jack had been holding up pretty well, landing in Santo Domingo and shopping for a tropical wardrobe for the women, but now he was exhausted. The rest of the island had been dark when they'd flown over, making the lights around the house and the landing pad a cluster of brilliance surrounded by velvety black.

"Wow," Lisette murmured, and Padma echoed it half a breath later.

Jack felt that way himself every time he came home. Lush green grass, an abundance of flowers, towering palms and the house itself awed most people. He wondered what it was like seeing them for the very first time and regretted they couldn't have scheduled their arrival for morning when everything was in its best light.

Including them. They would make great targets in morning light.

A small welcome committee waited along the sidewalk: Simon and Toinette, his right hand. Eduardo, who thought he ran the household, and Marisol, who really did, and Ali, the head of security. His sidearm wasn't as noticeable as the automatic weapons carried by the guards around the landing pad. Everyone was sharp-dressed and alert, as if getting pulled from their beds in the middle of the night was a normal occurrence.

"Are you ladies as eager to get some sleep as I am?"

"Actually, I'm pretty much ready to start my day," Padma replied, bouncing on the balls of her feet. Her grin was infectious; sadly, her energy wasn't.

"That's because you slept all the way here." This time Lisette actually sounded cranky. She'd fallen asleep while they'd talked, so he'd shut off the television, and with a bit more finesse than she'd shown Padma, gotten her stretched out on the couch. After dimming the lights in the rear of the cabin, he'd settled up front to make some phone calls.

"She's grouchy when she doesn't get her eight hours," Padma teased. "Let's grab our stuff and get moving."

When both of them turned to the helicopter, Jack turned them back toward their host. "The guys will bring your bags. Come meet Simon and the others."

Tension streaked through them, evidenced by the tightening of their muscles beneath his fingers. They'd been familiar with him before they'd met him. Had they also Googled his friend and been intimidated by his internet presence?

The thought made him smile. Simon was a tough businessman and a fierce negotiator who didn't tolerate incompetence or weakness. As far as business went, yeah, he was a shark and could scare powerful people with nothing more than a scowl. In his personal life, he was far less threatening. Usually.

"Any problems?" Simon asked.

"They missed us by about sixty seconds at the airport, but the flight was uneventful." Except that he'd gotten to kiss Lisette. He didn't think that would impress Simon, though. He made the introductions, his gaze straying a time or two to the lights in the east that marked his house. Marisol would have made sure it was dusted and aired out, the clothing he kept there would have been laundered, and there would be fresh linens on the bed. Incredibly soft sheets. His favorite pillow. The open windows stirring a breeze that would make the gauzy curtains dance.

Suddenly he was so tired, he could barely focus on the conversation.

"Lisette, Padma, we've prepared rooms for you in the main house," Toinette said, her words heavily accented thanks to her upbringing in a French and Spanish home. "Let's get you settled. If you're hungry, we're happy to provide you with food. Otherwise, I think what you probably want most is your bed." Her gaze shifted to Padma, still too energetic by far. "Well, maybe not you. Come along, please, and Marisol and I will show you the way."

Padma and Toinette took a few steps, but Lisette hung back, looking at Jack. They hadn't discussed sleeping arrangements on the plane. He would like to think she was hesitant to let him out of her sight because she felt safe with him. More likely she was reluctant to go off with people she'd known two whole minutes without knowing where the only familiar face would be.

"Where are you staying?" She didn't sound nervous or insecure or saddened at seeing him go—merely asking for information in that business-as-usual way of hers. So much for his ego.

"That's my house over there." He pointed out the two lights on his front porch, then the curving line of dimmer lights that lit the path between the two houses. "If you need anything, I'm number two on the autodial on the phone system."

"Sorry, Jack," Toinette said. "You've been gone a while. You're number three now. I'm number two." With a laugh, she swept them along toward the house, gathering Marisol while Eduardo went to supervise the luggage retrieval. Marisol was beaming when they turned the corner out of sight. Nothing made her happier than to fuss over good guests, and Lisette and Padma would be the best.

"They'll be calling her Maman by morning." In the night, Simon sounded hard, stern, as if he'd never smiled in his life. But there was definite affection for the housekeeper who'd mothered them at least as much as their own mothers had. "Are you hungry?"

"No. Ryne had time to hit the market before we took off."

Simon had begun moving, and Jack followed, not realizing until they reached the pool that they were heading for his cottage. "You got a call from a woman named Rory. She said Candalaria thought it incredibly rude of you to stand him up, and he pitched a right little fit. He told his guards to find the girls no matter what and make you sorry for involving them in this. He also promised no good would come to you."

Jack was pretty sure Simon could have delivered that news in a tone that made it sound much less menacing. Sometimes Simon thought menace was required to make him take something seriously. Well, he was taking this seriously.

Mostly. "Do you think that means I'm off his Christmas list?"

"If you can get in this much trouble when you're innocent, how the hell do you stay alive when you're guilty?"

Jack grinned. "It's a talent. Honestly, who knew this would be the incident that would drive David over the edge? He's had so many other chances to go stark raving. I didn't expect this one to cause it."

Simon shrugged. "You never betrayed his friendship before."

"We never had a friendship to betray."

"No, but you usually treated him well. You didn't exclude him as obviously as most people did. You were friendly, and he read more into it than there really was. Then you accepted an invitation into his home and stole his treasure."

"That he'd stolen in the first place."

Simon, several inches taller than Jack, gazed down at him. "Never thought I'd ever say this, but you're being too logical. Candalaria paid money, and in return he got the painting. It doesn't matter that he paid a thief and not the owner. In his mind, it's now his. And you took it. At least, he thinks you did. So you not only stole his newest treasure, but you spat on his hospitality, betrayed his friendship to do it and ruined the opening of his grandest exhibit ever."

Jack breathed deeply, inhaling the scents of grass, flowers, salt and sea. He'd been gone too long this time, but the usual peace was starting to seep into his bones despite all the distractions. "You're probably right."

Up ahead, a creature rustled in the bushes, heavy panting breaking the quiet. Tension streaked through Jack, but Simon didn't seem disturbed by the sound. An instant later, the varmint burst through the bushes and ran to them, a streak of fuzzy yellow.

"That's Sneezy." Simon picked up the puppy and scratched his chin. "The kids named him."

"You let them name him Sneezy? Poor little guy."

"Hey, I stopped them from calling you Wheezy that time you came running home full-tilt from your last visit to the north side." Simon set the dog on the path again and murmured, "At least, to your face."

"You *left* me there. You took me out, got me turned around and lost, then left me. In the *dark*. With the *ghosts*. Damn right I was wheezing by the time I made it back. I was running for my life!"

"Five years, and you're still whining about it." Simon pulled a set of keys from his pocket, climbed the steps to the veranda and unlocked the front door, leaving the keys in the lock. He shut off the alarm before stepping back outside. "Get some rest. We'll talk tomorrow."

"No one better call me Wheezy."

"Nah, I thought we'd concentrate on our real problems, starting with the fact that a sociopathic billionaire is really pissed off at you and may follow you here."

"And the other?"

"You brought the infamous Bella Donna to stay amid our own treasures."

Just for an instant, the hairs on the back of Jack's neck prickled, but just as quickly he shook it off. "Is anything in our collections stolen?"

"No."

"Then it's safe. Lisette only steals back stolen items to return to their legal owners, plus a few bits and bobs to cover their expenses. Nothing's in danger here."

"Except you, her, her friend and everybody on the island."

Jack hesitated, then carefully asked, "Do you want me to take them someplace else?"

"Of course not. I'll put our people up against Candalaria's any time." Simon pushed his hands into his pants pockets and took the steps two at a time. "Go to sleep. You've got company to entertain and a problem to start working out tomorrow."

Despite her late night, Lisette woke up shortly after eight. Her brain was fuzzy, full of memories and dreams half-formed. She would have given a lot to go back to sleep, but the voices inside her had had enough quiet. They had things to do, they shrieked, and they wanted to do them *right now.*

She winced, squeezing her eyes tight. Why did all the little voices in her head sound like Padma?

A wonderful, fresh, steamy aroma floated on the air, drifting straight to Lisette's nose. Her first breath was curious, the second invigorating. It actually made her mouth water and effortlessly dissipated the fog around her brain. Shoving her hair back, she opened her eyes, saw a large mug of coffee and reached toward it greedily, dimly noticing it was Padma tempting her. Then she let her gaze stray from the mug, noting the size of the room, the three walls of French doors with ocean views and the elegance of the furnishings, and her eyes widened. "Île des Deux Saints!"

Padma laughed. "It sounds like a curse when you say it that way. *Sacré bleu! Île des Deux Saints!*"

Lisette scowled. "I'm still half asleep. Don't be mean to me."

"Yeah, tell me about it. I was about to move on to plan G—throw a bucket of water over you. Nothing else has worked." Padma picked up her own coffee. "Did you know they have their own coffee blends? You're getting Jack's this morning. I'm trying Aunt Gloria's, since she's my hero. Come on, get out of bed. Put some clothes on and let's get downstairs. Maman made a special breakfast for us."

Wishing for more energy and fewer aches, Lisette managed to get her feet from the mattress to the woven rug on the floor, but it took several more sips of Jack's *bold, stimulating and surprisingly complex* coffee to get her to stand and walk to the bathroom. Padma was dressed in one of her new outfits—yellow shorts, a white shirt—and she was already rummaging through Lisette's closet.

"Shorts, please," Lisette requested before she closed the bathroom door. She took care of business, swallowed two headache tablets and was wondering what to do with her hair short of calling for a pair of scissors when Padma came in, hiding behind two hanging garments.

"Those aren't shorts. Why do you get extreme comfort and I get a girly outfit in colors bright enough to wake the dead?"

"When a place is haunted, I doubt it takes much to wake the dead. Besides, every piece of clothing you wear should make Charming want to take it off. This outfit is gorgeous and bright and should pretty much seduce everyone."

"I don't want to seduce everyone."

"You want to seduce Simon into giving you access to their art collections. You want to seduce Toinette into being available for help if we need it. You want to seduce Eduardo into telling you everything he knows about the island. You want to seduce Maman into keeping you well-fed." Padma counted on her fingers while she talked. Now she faked an astonished look. "Oh, look, there's still one left. Who is it, who is... Oh, yeah, you want to seduce Jack right out of his clothes and into your majorly comfortable bed.

"Remember what the shop owners said last night? 'Consider it the price of admission for Jack. He gets to see you in the clothes, and maybe take you out of them, too, eh?'" Laughing, she thrust the clothes at Lisette. "I'll get my hair stuff so we can do something with yours. Get dressed. My stomach's growling."

Lisette fingered the fine fabric of the shirt, a vivid hue of coral, just one of the wild colors in the skirt, and sleeveless with a long row of small buttons. Could Jack's capable hands undo them? Would he have the patience to work at them, or would he be more in favor of pulling the thing off and replacing it later if necessary? She would be happy either way.

The skirt reached down her calves, thin and light and full of movement, while the top did the opposite, hugging her as if it had been stitched into place. With sandals, she felt like what her mother had always told she was: an island girl.

This island's girl. She stared at her image, wondering if any of the residents might see her mother or her father in her face. Would they wonder if they'd met her before, or would they simply write off her familiarity as a Caribbean thing, not a Deux Saints thing?

Padma returned with a case filled with hair clips, clamps, bands and such. As she went to work, she asked, "Do you realize that if your parents hadn't left, you would have been born here? Would have grown up here? You would have played with Charming and Simon when you were kids, and now you'd probably be—"

"The upstairs maid? The lowliest assistant to the lowliest of the gardeners?"

A dozen bobby pins clenched between her teeth made speaking difficult for Padma, but she managed. "Probably Cap'n Jack's mistress."

"You'll be the water goddess, and I'll be a mistress?" Lisette snorted.

Padma poked the last bobby pin harder than necessary, then asked, "What do you think?"

Lisette studied her image. The style was retro, her hair parted, rolled to the back, the loose ends braided and pinned up. It was cool and neat and flattering. "You're good at that."

"My mom hasn't worn her hair down in forty years and I've been the designated braider my whole life." Unexpectedly, Padma hugged her from behind. "I'm glad things weren't different. If you'd been born here, you wouldn't have been my best friend for forever, and my life would have been so much sadder."

Lisette squeezed her hand. "Aw, you believe in karma. We'd've met somehow. It was meant to be."

Padma met her gaze. "I do believe in karma. I believe things happen for a reason, and sometimes it's terribly good, like you and me, and sometimes it's terribly sad, like your mom and dad, and sometimes... Well, we just hope for the best. I'm really hoping for the best for you and Jack."

Lisette considered what could possibly be *the best* for them. Her first vote would go to living happily ever after. Maybe not with each other, but being happy with themselves was important, too. Maybe Jack not hating her was the best she could hope for. Or Jack not being hurt. Or Jack not letting Simon report her to the authorities. Or Jack not regretting the day he'd met her.

Because by the time this was over, she would regret the day they'd met more than any other day in her life.

A phone call from Simon woke Jack at a quarter to eight, dumping the first crisis of the day on him even though he was groggy from too little sleep. Padma, it seemed, was up and being her usual self, and Simon wanted reinforcements. He wasn't the friendliest person first thing in the morning—or, for that matter, middle of the afternoon or late at night—and he seemed to think that being alone with Chatty Padma might be even riskier than having Bella Donna sleeping under the same roof as the family art.

Maman Marisol had set a table on the patio with places for six, meaning Toinette and probably Ali were joining them, but only Simon was in his seat. Thoroughly amused by the wariness Padma had stirred in him, Jack sauntered to the cloth-covered table a few yards away and fixed a cup of coffee before sitting on Simon's left. "Where'd your scary bad companion go?"

Simon scowled. "To wake Lisette."

"I can't believe you don't know how to handle a woman like Padma."

"I know exactly how to handle women like that. I fire them."

"But she's not an employee."

"No, she's a guest—and not even my guest."

Jack wondered at Simon's grouchiness. Padma was energetic and inquisitive and outspoken, but she hadn't yet annoyed him, not even when she'd hit him for failing to keep Lisette safe. "She talks a lot when she's excited. Or worried. Or scared. Enjoy whatever distance you get between you two, because it's not going to last. Remember when I asked you about the water supply here?"

"Eighteen hours ago? Of course I remember."

"That was Padma asking. She works on water projects for a nonprofit, trying to supply clean water everywhere. Once she gets comfortable, she's going to have a lot of questions for you."

Simon looked as if that was a conversation he might hate or maybe tolerate or possibly even enjoy. He was much more hands-on in the running of the island than Jack was, and if talking to Padma was for the good of Deux Saints, he would do it. After a while, he might even have fun with it. He needed some fun, Jack always thought. And Simon thought Jack needed more seriousness in his life. In the next few days, they might each get what the other wished for.

The door leading to the kitchen opened. Jack glanced that way, expecting to see Maman Marisol, and sure enough he did, but right behind her, a head taller and less than half as wide, was Lisette. She was wearing one of her new outfits, colors so bright that they held their own against the competition of the tropical setting. With her smooth dark skin and her black hair more neatly contained than he'd thought possible, with the shirt clinging to her curves and the lines of her body softened by fabric dancing in the breeze, she looked exotic and lovely and, damn, incredibly sexy.

Her gaze skimmed the patio before stopping on him, and a sweet smile spread across her face. His breath caught, heat and pleasure and need exploding inside him. If he'd been on his feet, the impact would have been staggering. As it was, he had to set his coffee cup down so the faint tremors in his hand didn't cause it to spill.

Padma trailed Lisette, and all three women carried serving platters, with Maman wearing a stern look for Simon. Jack knew the meaning of that look: it was rare when guests wanted to help out around the house, and Simon didn't approve. It was the way he was raised—Jack, too—but helping out was the way Lisette and Padma had been raised. It was their nature, and one of the things he admired about them.

Maman's platter held Simon's favorite breakfast, a casserole made of salted cod, green bananas, ackee and callaloo. Lisette carried Jack's favorite: yams, tomatoes and cheese with sunny-side-up eggs tucked in among them. Both dishes contained Scotch bonnet peppers—the stuff tears were made of—and were accompanied by Padma's dishes: glazed plantains and *vitumbua*, coconut rice pancakes served with caramel sauce. The sight of them started his mouth watering.

Ali was approaching the table from the direction

of his office when Maman dusted her hands, satisfied with the placement of the dishes, then took two icy pitchers from the side table. "Papaya or orange juice?" Without looking behind her, she raised her voice. "Anyone who isn't seated by the time I pour the last glass doesn't get any."

Lisette and Padma hastily slid into the chairs opposite Jack. He laughed. "She's talking to Toinette," he explained, gesturing to Simon's assistant, hustling up from the beach. "Maman likes to keep a schedule. Toinette likes to dawdle."

"I don't dawdle." Toinette claimed the chair next to Jack. "My clock is set to island time."

"I've been on these islands twice as long as you, Antoinette, and yet I manage to be on time," Maman chastened. She rounded the table, filling glasses, nudging Ali in greeting with one elbow, before stopping suddenly next to Lisette. "Ooh, baby girl, them bruises... What did you do?"

Lisette stiffened, her face going pale for a moment. She wasn't superficial enough to care about honestly earned bruises, so Jack's mind skipped to the next possibility: Had her mother called her baby girl in that island-accented way? Surely she was missing her today on her first visit to the area Mom had come from.

After an instant, Lisette shook it off, lifted one arm to look at the dark marks on the back of it and grimaced. "I fell off a…" Meeting his gaze, she smiled faintly. "A boulder while rock climbing."

Maman would have planted one fist on her hip if her hands hadn't been full. "This your fault, Master Jack?"

His brows arched. She hadn't called him that in years. In fact, she only called him that when his parents were around or he'd gotten himself in trouble…again. Which made it rather fitting now, didn't it? He was in trouble, not only with David but with Lisette, too. "*No. I mean, I was there. It was my idea—the climbing. But I didn't* make *her fall. I tried to catch her.*"

Maman continued to glare at him until she bent to press her cheek to Lisette's. "He'll take you to see Annie after breakfast. She'll make you better."

"I was already planning to do that," he protested halfheartedly.

After fussing a few more moments, she went back into the house, leaving silence while everyone filled their plates. Jack hadn't thought to ask Lisette if she liked Caribbean cooking—or the Scotch bonnet—but she ate Indian food, and Mexican, and probably used wasabi with her sushi. Besides, she took small portions of everything except for the *vitumbua*, which filled half her plate. She'd rightly guessed that anything served with homemade caramel sauce was worthy of eating.

Simon was the first to break the silence. "Aunt Gloria called this morning. Wanted to know what you'd done to Candalaria. She said he's got—and I quote—'a burr under his saddle' and is looking for you."

His telling him in front of the others didn't surprise Jack. Toinette knew everything that happened on the island—business, personal, didn't matter—and as head of security, Ali knew practically everything, without Toinette's interest in gossip. Jack cut into his egg, freeing the yellow yolk to spread over the yams and tomatoes. "I'm guessing she told him to kiss her I-don't-give-a-damn."

"She did. Made him apologize for getting snippy with her. Once he'd groveled sufficiently, he politely asked her to let him know when she heard from you. She was on her way to visit a gentleman friend somewhere around Naples when she called, but she did suggest you make Candalaria suffer a bit before you take pity on him."

"I have no pity for him." And he preferred no contact with him. It was only good luck that Lisette hadn't been hurt in the fall, that she and Padma had escaped serious injury when the SUV plowed into them, and that they were now safely in hiding. But Aunt Gloria didn't know any of that. David wouldn't tell her, and Jack had no intention of worrying her until the danger was past. Whoever and wherever her friend was, she was safe.

"I took a call this morning from a man wanting to know if you were here," Toinette said, "but he wouldn't give his name. I told him do I look like my only job is to track Jack's whereabouts? No, I do not. He is a big boy with a big plane and a lot of money. He could be anywhere in the world. He could be in Denver. Just because the plane is gone, I told him, doesn't mean Jack is gone."

She speared a bite of food on her fork before going on. "Oh, there was one other call. Isn't it amazing how we go entire months without getting calls for Jack, and you hook up with these two ladies and suddenly everyone's calling?" She followed the words with a wink at the two ladies in question. "I like a woman who shakes up a man's life."

The last call was from Dominic, a message that he'd sent two men to spend the night at Lisette's house, where their sleep had been interrupted by two other men trying to break in. "After a little, um, persuasion from his guys, the men waited quietly for the police to pick them up." Toinette grinned at Ali. "I think we can all guess what kind of persuasion was involved."

Lisette swallowed the last bite of her last *vitumbua*, then sighed softly. "Poor David. Things aren't going the way he planned."

"Yeah, poor David." Padma followed her fake sympathy with a snort. "I wish someone's guys would use a little persuasion on him. I don't like it when people mess up my life."

"But it's a good mess up, right?" Toinette asked, raising her arms to encompass everything around her. "Look where you are, who you're with. You're safe. You can be as lazy as you want. You can study your water issues firsthand, maybe even meet with experts from other islands. There are worse ways to go into hiding."

"And you got to meet Toinette," Ali added drily. "That's usually the highlight of anyone's trip to paradise."

The highlight of Jack's trip was going to be spending time with Lisette—some of it, hopefully, in bed. Eh, make that a *lot*. Toward that end, he folded his napkin and laid it aside, then pushed his chair back. "Lisette, are you ready to meet our nurse practitioner?"

He was expecting a brush-off and might have gotten it if sliding her own chair back hadn't stirred some pain. "I believe I am. Padma—"

Padma's grin was quick and broad, and it was directed, just slightly, at Simon. "I'm going to get my feet wet, so to speak, and find out about the water situation here. I'm sure I'll find someone—" her gaze shifted between him and Toinette "—who can educate me."

Jack circled the table, waited for Lisette to join him,

then turned toward the nearest path. "We'll see you at lunch then. Have fun with the water stuff."

Simon looked at him as if he'd never heard the word before.

"Are you surprised she abandoned us?"

Lisette glanced over to see Padma and Simon walking away from the patio, then turned back to watch her step. "I am. I expected at least a day of goofing off, relaxing and doing nothing before she dived headfirst into work."

"So to speak."

She laughed. "Talk with her long enough, and you'll hear every play on words having to do with water that ever existed." Drawing as deep a breath as her ribs would allow, she took in the view from every angle. She wished she had a camera to record everything she saw, touched, smelled, heard, for those lonely times in the future when she missed her mom, her dad…and Jack. Knowing the island's no-photos rule, she would settle for sketches drawn from sweet memories.

None of it yet was unfamiliar. Simon might be able to control physical access to the island, but he couldn't stop satellites far overhead from posting pictures on the internet. She had printouts in her files that she'd studied until she knew them by heart. The trail they followed led to the village, where the nurse worked from a small pink cottage with a shingle out front, a red cross on a white background. The only places a person could see the ocean from the compound were on the upper floors; the roof of the main house held a luxurious living space that provided views to the far horizon. From a boat at sea, there was no hint of a mansion, work buildings, the village or a thriving population.

She knew everything…and nothing.

"Why did the saints build inland?" she asked. She knew that, too. She just wanted Jack to talk.

"Privacy. They discovered the island when they were blown off course in a storm. Sailors back then avoided this area. It had difficult currents, lots of unexplained sinkings—sort of a Bermuda Triangle reputation. According to the official family history, it took them a year to find it again, and when they did, they didn't tell anyone but their most trusted crew members. Once they'd scouted the entire island, they decided to build their headquarters here.

"They used prisoners and slaves—" he hesitated, discomfort and a bit of shame in his voice "—to build the houses, the cottages, the fishing boats; to plant the fields and the gardens and take care of the saints and their families; and they spent the rest of their lives here. They married and had kids, and their kids stayed, too. Some of the current residents have lived here less than fifteen years, but we have a lot who have spent their entire lives here."

If Lisette's girly skirt had pockets, she couldn't find them among the airy layers, so she clasped her hands behind her. Did he have any idea all those generations of people had stayed because they'd been forbidden to leave? That leaving had been an action punishable by death? Did he know that policy had extended into his own lifetime?

She doubted it. He was uncomfortable admitting that his and Simon's families had used slave labor to create their amazing island. How much worse would he feel if he'd known Simon's own father had held his people hostage?

How did *she* feel, knowing family had been prisoners or slaves? That before crossing paths with the Sinclairs and the Toussaints, they'd been free to do as they wished—to travel, settle down, pray, raise families, make decisions, live their lives? Then bad luck, being in the wrong place at the wrong time, had turned them into nothing more than a possession, to be used or disposed of upon a whim.

"So much to be proud of. Pirates, prisoners and slaves," Jack said ruefully, making Lisette realize that she'd been quiet since his admission.

"It doesn't reflect on you," she said, freeing one hand so she could lay it on his wrist. "I have this vague image of my family, back to the beginning of time, living quiet, simple, happy lives—the men fishing, like my father did, the women cooking and cleaning and birthing babies, like my mother. Getting together with family to celebrate on Saturdays, going to Mass to do the same on Sundays.

"Deux Saints isn't the only island with that history. My great-great-grandfathers could have been slaves or prisoners. My great-great-grandmothers could have been kidnapped from their homes and families to make new homes and new families with strangers. All of them could have been taken—" *had* been taken "—from the lives they knew to make someone else's life more comfortable or profitable."

He twisted his hand so his fingers wrapped around hers. "I'm sorry—"

Her fingers warmed where he held them. She studied them a moment—the differences in size and strength and color, and the similarities in function—and she wondered how such simple contact between them could seem like so much more. Like she could hold on to his hand forever. Like she would always be safe when her hand was in his. Like out of the billions of hands in the world, his two hands and her two fitted together exactly the way they were meant to.

Exhaling a loud breath to release some of the heat building inside her, she met his gaze levelly. "You're no more responsible for whatever life they lived than I am. We can't control the actions of people we never knew. We can't accept the blame for them, either. We can only be held accountable for ourselves. What we do right. What we do wrong. What we learn from our mistakes. We choose the kind of people we are."

Keeping her fingers twined with Jack's as they resumed walking, Lisette asked, "When was the transition made from prisoners and slaves to just employees? Workers whose home was here?" Her voice, she was relieved, didn't hint that she had a personal interest.

"I'm not sure. In the beginning, they were provided food and shelter. At some point, they began receiving that plus a salary. While the piracy continued, the rules were still pretty inflexible about letting people leave the island because secrecy was such a big deal. As the saints began transitioning to other industry, the compound became less structured. Some people left. New people came in. Though…"

His brow wrinkled. "A lot of things depended on who was in charge at the time. Simon's family almost always ran the island, and some of them were a bit tyrannical. My family took their business dealings elsewhere."

Though it shouldn't have been the first question to

come to Lisette, she asked it anyway. "Is that what you'll do eventually?"

Lit by his grin, Jack's eyes gave the azure sky a run for its money. The sky's blue was beautiful, but his was that and more: warm, appealing, good-natured, intriguing. "Can you see me conducting business? Simon's got three offices on the island—one in the house, one in his suite and one in the farm headquarters. He also has one in New York and another in Paris. I don't have a single office anywhere in the entire world. I can't sit at a desk with a computer unless it's got floor plans, alarm systems, security schedules, fake identities or something similar on it."

Lisette laughed. "Then you can imagine how I feel spending eight hours a day planning Candalaria's social events for the museum when I could be plotting our next job."

A little of his lightness dimmed. "There'll be a next job?"

She met his gaze, saw concern there, but answered without hesitation. "There's still a lot of stolen art out there that needs to go home where it belongs. You know, there are thirteen masterpieces still missing from the Gardner heist in Boston. Two Van Goghs from Amsterdam. Two Monets, a Gauguin and a Matisse from Rotterdam. And—" Abruptly her gaze narrowed. "I know you're too young for the Gardner heist, but you weren't behind any of the others, were you?"

After a lifetime of secrecy about her work, Lisette was momentarily dizzy with the fact that she could even ask the question of Jack, that he didn't take offense at such a question. It was an exhilarating feeling.

"No. I don't like museum jobs. I prefer to make it personal by going right where they live."

She felt the same way. "Museum thefts aside, they estimate more than thirty thousand pieces of treasure looted by the Nazis are still out there. Mom did a couple of those retrievals."

Just doing my bit.

The path rounded a huge guanacaste, the tree's spherical canopy shading everything growing nearby, and on the other side the village came into view, bringing Lisette to a full stop. The commissary, the church and the school, with the nurse conveniently next door, were centrally located around a patch of grass lovely enough for any golf course. The houses clustered around the plaza were similar in design, with the major differences being the size and the paint colors—pastels, every one. Every building featured broad porches, windows tall enough to double as doors, shutters in contrasting colors and a good-size spread of lawn for each family to do with as they wanted.

Her gaze skimmed across the village quickly, then once more slowly, taking in the massive yellow trumpet vine that crept to the church roof. The three small children playing with toy cars in the grass, accompanied by a dog who occasionally lifted his head to sniff the air. The reggae music coming from the open windows of the school. The old men sitting in rockers on one porch, sharing conversation and cold drinks. The girl on another porch, keeping an eye on the little ones while peeling yams into an enameled bowl.

Lisette turned to Jack. "This is…"

Jack grinned. "It looks like a movie set. *Stepford Wives Go Tropical. This Old House*, Caribbean style."

He tugged to get her walking again, taking one of the paths that branched toward the school.

"I told you, life here depended on whoever was in charge. Some of the Toussaints were good leaders. Simon's father, grandfather and great-grandfather weren't. Things had gotten run-down, so a few years ago, when his father died, Simon dozed it and started over. He spent weeks with every woman in the village, and a few of the men, getting their input on architecture and decorating and landscaping. Everyone wanted their house to be pretty, so he made them pretty. They're concrete with siding, so they'll stand up to strong winds. They have Wi-Fi service and solar panels and reliable indoor plumbing. There's no air-conditioning—mine doesn't have it, either—but plenty of paddle fans and cooling-efficient design. And because it was all done at once, it's visually…stunning."

"Simon," Lisette repeated in an amused tone. "The one with the perpetual scowl who, in my presence, has spoken only to you."

"Well, I'll admit, he tried putting Toinette in charge of the project, but…"

"Toinette isn't your typical girl who cares about paint or decorating or flower beds." Lisette tried to imagine the Dark Lord surrounded by fabric swatches, color samples, floor plans and excited chattering women, but she couldn't quite complete the image. It seemed this Toussaint really did care about the people who provided him comfort and profit.

They were only yards from Annie's cottage when a compact barrel of a woman stepped onto the path ahead of them. Lisette slowed her steps to allow her to pass, but the woman instead planted her feet, fisted her hands on her hips and stared unflinchingly at her. A shiver stirred by the prickling at her nape danced down Lisette's spine, and goose bumps raised on her bare arms, as if a massive cloud had blacked out the sun's warmth without warning.

"Aunt Jesula." Jack released Lisette's hand and stepped forward, bending to envelop the woman in a hug.

It was a lovely name for a woman who'd likely always been substance rather than show. She was an inch or two taller than five feet, and about the same in roundness. Her ebony skin gleamed in the sun, her mostly gray braids covered by a gold scarf. Her blouse was white, and her skirt was as bright in color as Lisette's. No doubt, she was one of the island's lifelong residents, an elder who commanded respect, judging by Jack's response and the imperious glare that hadn't yet wavered from Lisette's face.

After patting his back a half dozen times, Jesula ended the embrace and, still studying Lisette, said in a cool, lyrical voice, "So you come back. I t'ought would never happen."

"I always come back, Aunt—"

For the first time, something softer, kinder, crossed her face as she reached up to pinch his cheek. "Not you, Master Jack. 'Course you come back. Dis your home." After that brief moment of relief for Lisette, Jesula's black gaze shifted her way again. "I'm talking to *you*."

Chapter 10

Jesula's lack of friendliness didn't surprise Jack; neither did her odd comment. The Haitian woman had been born there and had lived under the reigns of three terrible Toussaints. She'd had a soft spot for kids but nobody else. She'd gotten an exemplary day's work from her staff and ruled with little more than sharp looks or gestures. Those on her crews, even her family, had always feared those looks and gestures, a fear fed by the fact that she practiced vodou—frightening to people more familiar with the dark-magic, sacrificial, ruling-by-fear mythology than the religion.

He and Simon had asked her once why she liked them. She'd given a shake of her head with her blunt answer. *You boys don't got good enough sense to be a-feared of me.*

Lisette looked *a-feared* of her. Her mouth was agape,

surprise and distress streaked across her face, and she crossed her arms over her middle as if to ward off cold. Danger.

Jack slid his arm around her waist. "Aunt Jesula, this is my friend Lisette."

When Jesula made no effort to speak, Lisette did. He wondered if she could channel Bella on command; surely she would feel more comfortable as Bella than with the quavering uncertainty she showed now. "It—it's a pleasure to—to meet you, Jesula."

Jesula didn't respond, didn't offer the traditional air kisses or a light pat of Lisette's arm. Her expression narrowed, lining her forehead and the corners of her mouth, but after a moment, her face relaxed back to its normal cantankerousness, and she turned abruptly, continuing across the path, muttering as she went. "Crazy old woman. T'ink she seein' ghosts. Ha!"

It took a moment for Jack to shake it off, another for Lisette to do so. "That goes down as my strangest encounter so far."

"Aunt Jesula has always been a character, long before she turned ninety, but that was odd even for her." Jack kept his arm around her, guiding her the last few feet to Annie's clinic. He had no doubt the Oregon-born-and-bred nurse would offer a much warmer welcome.

Annie did, and immediately kicked him out of the clinic. It wasn't as if he would peek into the exam room if given the opportunity, he groused as he sprawled on the grass. When he got Lisette naked, there would be no peeking, just full-on, wide-eyed appreciation. There wouldn't be anyone else around, and there would be nothing cursory about his exam. It would take hours. Maybe days. It could turn out to be one of those pleasurable needs in life, like eating and moving and breathing, that stayed with a person until his spirit slipped from his body.

Ten minutes had passed when the puppy roused himself and came over to investigate. Two girls and a boy trailed behind him, taking a seat a fair distance away. They were a mix of skin tones and eye and hair colors. No one on Deux Saints was just one race, except possibly Jesula. It made for good relations—and gave Jack a bit of surprise every time he went back out into the real world.

Rubbing the dog's belly, he said, "I'm Jack. Who are you?"

The blonde, maybe three or four, answered. "I'm Sassy, she's Tamita, he's Stanley, and he's Sneezy." She pointed at each one in turn, then pointed at him. "And you're Wheezy." All three kids collapsed in giggles, causing Sneezy to abandon Jack and frolic from child to child.

Jack kept a straight face, though inwardly rolling his eyes. None of these kids had even been born at the time of his run from the jungle, and yet the nickname he'd been blissfully unaware of lived on.

"Bless the little children who utter whatever pops into their heads," Lisette said, her shadow falling over him. She carried a jar of goo and wore a look of sweet relaxation. The time spent with Annie had certainly done Lisette good.

"Do I look like a Wheezy?" he asked, scrambling to his feet.

"Not really. Maybe a Whiny."

Before he could fake a hurt look, the same little girl

pointed at Lisette. "And dat one dere, her name be Trouble," she said in a decent imitation of Jesula's accent.

Lisette's smile quavered, faded, then re-formed through sheer will. "Trouble. Hmm. I like that."

She'd certainly created a lot of it in his life the past few days. Or David had. Or, hell, maybe Jack himself had. If he hadn't sought her out at the museum, followed her to Mrs. Maier's house and to Pecos Pete's, if he hadn't reacted when David mentioned the fancy red…

Bottom line: everything that had happened had brought them to where they were now. Fate, karma, destiny, good luck or bad, he didn't care. He was happy where they were now.

"So I can call you Trouble from now on?"

"Can I call you Wheezy?"

Another round of giggles hit the kids. There were far worse things in life than being the source of unfettered amusement. "Sassy, Tamita, Stanley, it was a pleasure to meet you. Sneezy—" On cue, the puppy sneezed, knocking himself off his feet, and the laughter started again. Joining in, Jack reached for Lisette's hand and was pleased to find her reaching for his. "You can call me Wheezy only if you call me a few other things first. By the way, want to see my house?"

His private, secluded, nobody-around-close-enough-to-hear house. His sanctuary with its big comfortable bed, his favorite pillow, those incredibly soft linens.

This time her look was long and steady. Just a little speculative. A whole lot intrigued. The tiniest bit unsure. But the smile that followed was everything a man could want from the woman he needed to seduce. "I would like that."

He chose a smaller trail this time that wound straight

to the beach, where they could pick up the path to his cottage while avoiding the main house and anyone with interruption on their minds. The only flowers along this trail grew wild, and the trees arched overhead to provide permanent shade. Only one house was near—Jesula's—so it was no surprise that this was one of the places he'd always felt watchful gazes. Today, though, the only person he was aware of was Lisette, and though her gaze was watchful, it was also sweet and affectionate and full of promise.

She asked him about the trees and shrubs they passed, how hot it got, how cold. He told her about the two hidden coves, one ahead where they kept a collection of boats for fishing and trips to the other islands, and a deep harbor on the far side, where bulk deliveries were made.

And suddenly, she stopped abruptly again, struck by the view that appeared as they topped a gentle rise: the ocean. Sunlight reflected in brilliant beams off the water, and the sand, somewhere between rose and tan in color, invited them to walk, laze, stretch out, to absorb the heat and the beauty and to explore...

Damn security cameras.

Dropping his hand where the path turned from packed dirt to sand, she stepped out of her sandals and scooped them up, walked to the water's edge and gazed out over the sea. When the wave rolled over her feet, she yelped and turned a good-naturedly accusing look on him. "It's cold."

He kicked off his own shoes and joined her. "This isn't cold. How *do* you survive in Colorado with island blood in your veins?"

"I hibernate." Tilting her face to the sky, she closed

her eyes and breathed. Pleasure and serenity softened her features, making him forget he'd ever seen fear or stress or pain or there, making his breath catch with the impact of a punch, with hunger and need so strong they made him weak.

A strand of hair blew across her cheek, and he tucked it back, his fingertips barely skimming her skin, yet still he felt the sizzle. She smiled slightly, turned toward him, and he slid his hand to the back of her neck, bent his head, took her mouth with his. He had no patience for time-taking but pulled her closer, until their bodies touched, until he felt the heat of her, the flutter of her skirt around his legs, the tightening of her muscles everywhere they touched. He slid his tongue inside her mouth, tasting, craving. The sun beat down on them, and the chilly water washed over their feet, receded, then returned. Seagulls croaked, and somewhere not too distant, someone cleared his throat.

Jack ended the kiss, rested his forehead against Lisette's and sighed. A man would think he could catch a break in paradise, but apparently not this morning.

"Damn," Lisette murmured, making him smile.

"Exactly."

Dark glasses hid Ali's eyes, and his head was turned so he saw them only peripherally. He wore jeans and a polo shirt neatly tucked in—no uniform for security officers on the island—but he needed neither uniform nor the weapon and the Taser on his belt to intimidate any but the worst of the bad guys.

"Isn't it enough there are cameras everywhere?" Jack asked in place of a greeting, leaving the surf to stop a few yards from Ali.

"I wondered if you'd forgotten that."

"I remembered. I just figured your men would be polite enough to not watch."

"My 'men' include three women. But yes, they would be polite in deference to Miss Lisette…and having already seen Master Jack's naked bum on more than one occasion."

Lisette choked before her laughter escaped. He dragged his hand through his hair. "Jeez, did no one get the memo that I'm trying to impress this woman? Do all the embarrassing details need to come out right now?"

She bumped shoulders with him. "I think it's cute. Though I do think the age and the circumstances under which you were showing your bum to all and sundry might be necessary for a full judgment."

"And the kid says you be Trouble. I'm surrounded by a whole bunch of Troubles, it seems. Did you need anything, Ali, or was your goal just to interrupt us?"

"It's always nice to kill multiple birds with one stone," Ali responded in his cool British accent. "Maman is planning a feast tonight for the entire island. The usual spot at six o'clock, and for that reason, Maman informs that lunch will be light—salads on the veranda." He started to turn but paused. "Oh, yes, a man matching Candalaria's description tried to hire one of Harry No-Hair's boats for a visit to Deux Saints. Harry told him no, but Candalaria will try again, and when the price gets high enough, someone somewhere will get stupid enough to agree."

There was always someone somewhere stupid enough.

Lisette looked from Jack to Ali. "Doesn't it seem the smartest move is for Padma and me to leave?"

"No," Jack and Ali answered together. When she

frowned, Jack went on. "He's not after you and Padma anymore. He just wanted to use you to get to me. We could fly you out of here right now, but he'll still be out there tomorrow trying to hire a boat."

"But *I* stole the painting."

"You'll never convince him of that."

Ali shifted, sliding his hands into his pockets. "Harry will let us know if or when Candalaria gets a taker. He's keeping in touch with the helicopter pilots there, too. We're fortifying our security plan. Once that's done, we'll figure out how to get rid of Candalaria once and for all."

His ominous tone made Lisette shudder, but she didn't protest. Jack waited until he left to bump shoulders with her. "It's not as bad as it sounds. Trespassing down here is taken very seriously, especially when it's done by a small but lethal army, which is the only way David travels. If they come here, if they stir up trouble, they'll be subdued and turned over to the authorities."

Having lost interest in the water—and, apparently, the kissing—Lisette turned toward the steps Ali had taken. Two hundred feet up, shaded by tall trees and fragrant vines, Jack's cottage sat out of sight. He would get her there—sooner, please God, rather than later— or he was going to explode.

After a few awkward moments of walking, she abruptly grinned at him. "Are you really trying to impress me?"

"I really am. Is it working?"

"Ask me after the feast tonight."

He grabbed his chest with both hands. "You're killing me, Trouble."

And he was liking it.

* * *

The feast took place in a cleared field, where a bonfire burned in the middle, surrounded by tables groan-
ing under their burdens, with quilts and blankets for
seats and a few folding chairs for those whose bones
didn't tolerate getting down and up again so easily. The
whole thing was impressive: the food, the sense of family, the joy. The live music, ranging from calypso to soca
to reggae. The dancing, the laughter, the pure satisfaction. It was an amazingly happy event.

Then came the singing. Not from the guests pack-
ing up as darkness settled. These voices traveled on the
still air, distant and dreamy. Voices long gone singing
songs long forgotten. Their words were indistinguish-
able, their melodies haunting, and they leached the bliss
right out of the evening. With nervous looks over their
shoulders, mamas and papas gathered their little ones;
grandmas and grandpas clung tightly to each other's
hands; and wispy moonlight and bonfire were replaced
by powerful flashlights that banished the shadows.

Padma leaned close to Lisette and whispered, "Do
you have goose bumps? My entire body is covered. If
I was outside alone and heard that, I'd die of fright.
Aren't you freaked out?"

Lisette couldn't deny the shivers gliding over her
skin, but they weren't fear. In any community, people
lived and died. In the three-century history of this particular community, a lot of people had died, without
much peace to accompany them on their final journey.
"They just seem sad."

"Sad? They're scaring the crap out of me, and I'm
surrounded by dozens of people." Standing, Padma
straightened her clothes, then offered a hand to Lisette.

"Let's get some of these big strong guys to take us back to the house and lock the doors behind us."

"Do you think locked doors will keep out spirits?" Lisette accepted her help, then regretted the question when she saw Padma's eyes widen. "They're not malicious. They don't mean anyone harm."

"How do you know?"

The answer came from behind Lisette in a voice that startled her far more than the singing. "Because dem lived with us for t'ree centuries and never done anyt'ing yet." Jesula lifted the cane she held to point northward. "Dems just joining da celebration. Everybody do love a good celebration, huh?"

It seemed wrong to talk about celebration in such funereal tones. Lisette's shivers multiplied, and she caught Padma trying to control one. Jesula didn't notice, though, as her gaze was fixed on Lisette. "Maybe dem spirits t'inking dem knows you, too."

"Auntie Jesula!" A young boy, about ten or twelve, skidded to a halt beside the old woman. "Mama says come, please, and Papa and Martin will walk you home."

Jesula continued to stare at Lisette. Then, as she'd done earlier, she abruptly turned and walked away, the boy sticking close to her side.

"More freakiness," Padma whispered, grabbing Lisette's arm. "That's the woman who recognized you? She's scary."

Jack and Simon returned in time to hear the last words. "Ah, you've met Jesula," Jack said with a grin. "Even Simon's father was afraid of her, and he was—"

Simon finished for him. "The meanest son of a bitch that ever lived."

There was little bitterness in his voice, just acknowledgment of something he'd long known. Not having a father could be tough, but sometimes *having* one could be tougher.

Jack slipped behind Lisette, resting his hands on her shoulders. That usual sense of safety spread through her, easing her nerves, calming her spirit. "Hey."

His voice was soft and ticklish in her ear, creating shivers of a whole different kind. Leaning into him, she nodded, took a breath and said, "Yes."

"Yes what?"

With Padma and Simon occupied with shaking out and folding the quilt, she turned in Jack's arms and reminded him of his question earlier that morning. "You're impressing me. Though I think it's terribly unfair…"

She paused, considering the words—the invitation—she was about to offer, wondering if Marley would put in an appearance to try to change her mind. But her mother remained silent, and his body felt so good against hers, and she was a grown woman who knew what she wanted and could deal with the consequences, and…

She wanted this. Needed it. Would never regret it, no matter how badly it ended.

Nuzzling her neck, he prompted her. "It's unfair that…?"

Letting go of everything but the moment, she twined her arms around his neck and smiled her best smile. "That everyone else on the island has seen your naked bum except me." She brushed her lips to his jaw, his mouth, then his ear. "You show me yours, Charming, and I'll show you mine."

She hadn't known arousal could manifest so quickly.

In less time than it took to breathe, his erection came to life, hard and hot, and he gave her a look more scorching than the bonfire. So used to his lighthearted manner, she was surprised and made weak by the fierceness in his voice. "God, Lisette, you're definitely killing me."

After kissing her quick and hard, he grabbed her hand, snatched a flashlight from a nearby guard and began pulling her toward his cottage. Giddy with her first carefree moment in days, she happily kept pace. She heard a few comments from behind, but the only one she clearly understood came from Toinette, her tone smug.

"My bet was before midnight. Pay up, guys. You, too, Padma. Ten bucks each."

Their friends had bet on when they would have sex, Lisette's discreet side pointed out. Her womanly side couldn't care less.

By the time they reached the path to the main house, they were more or less alone. Voices filtered through the trees, tired children fussing, fathers discussing the next day's work, mothers asking about homework and chores and recipes. It was startling, so much tradition and so much diversity in one people, one place. She could fit in here if she had a chance.

And she had that chance. It was simple, really: don't steal *Le Mystère*. Give up her life's goal, her mother's life's goal. Choose the man over the statue. Her father had been dead twenty-eight years. As far as she knew, she was the only Blue/Malone left, and she didn't want a priceless carving. She couldn't display it. She couldn't loan it out to museums. She could never sell it. Having it would just make her a target.

Don't steal it. Disappoint her mother. Disrespect

her father. Deliberately fail at the one thing she'd been raised to do.

Simple? It was too damn complicated a choice, and when they passed under a glowing light and she saw the hunger and appreciation and tenderness in Jack's face, she pushed the choice aside. There were more important things to think of now.

By the time they reached their destination, all the other voices had faded. The only lights flanked the door, with a lamp visible through the living room window. They climbed the steps, crossed the porch, and he quickly unlocked the door and shut off the alarm.

She hadn't gotten a tour of the cottage that morning. She'd admired its simple lines, its white siding and dozens of tall windows flanked by dark green shutters, but they hadn't stopped. She had imagined them relaxing on the broad porch, listening to the ocean, and wondered that Jack found such contentment in a house she could so easily fit in herself.

As he drew her to the curving stairs, she caught mostly impressions: space, comfort, again simplicity. Then they reached the top of the stairs, then his bedroom, and he pulled her into his arms and kissed her, and she forgot everything except him. Them. Lust and hunger and weakness.

Fever was too mild a word to describe the heat that consumed her, that made her blood boil and her brain go hazy, that heightened her senses, giving scents and flavors to things she had only felt in the past. It was crazy mad and scary intense, and it was more right than anything she'd ever known.

Jack was more right.

She didn't consciously move, other than to touch

him, more of him, and taste him, more, more, but in a daze she realized that her clothes were gone, fallen unnoticed, and the pins that held her braids had fallen, too, leaving her hair to cascade over her shoulders. The bed dipped beneath their weight, cool air sliding across her body before the substance of Jack's body blocked it and warmed her again, filled her, more and more, joining with her until she couldn't imagine how she'd survived this long without him.

Fever. Lust. Life.

The thudding of Jack's heart slowed to a steady drum, and his breathing settled from consciousness-threatening hypoxia to lazy, deep inhaling-every-scent-of-her-so-he'd-never-forget. Wheezy, he'd briefly thought when it had seemed he would black out, and he would have grinned if he hadn't been so captured by the torture/pleasure of an orgasm. Followed by another. And another.

Beside him, sweat formed a sheen on Lisette's skin. Her hair tumbled across the pillow, the damp curls spiraling tighter, and the look on her face was peace and calm and pure satisfaction.

It was the most beautiful he'd ever seen her.

Swiping strands of hair back from her forehead, she grinned at him. "I'm guessing you've done this before."

"Maybe a time or two."

"You learned well." She turned to face him, making no move to hide her nakedness. He hadn't held her to her promise yet—*show me yours, and I'll show you mine*—but he'd seen her front side, and that was sweet enough to make him forget the back for now. Besides, it was still early. They had hours—years—to go.

"Feel free to teach me everything you know. What you like." He touched his fingertips to the swell of her right breast. "What you don't." Skimmed them along the outside, avoiding contact with her nipple, to the curve of her waist. "Any kinky fantasies you might have."

Her laugh almost disguised her shiver as his hand moved to her hip. "Nothing about me is kinky. A little quirky, maybe—I do live a secret life as a thief—but never kinky."

"Damn," he said, feigning regret before admitting, "I'm not into kink, either. Enthusiasm counts for a whole lot more with me."

She echoed his fake regret. "Damn. Wish I'd pursued cheerleading when I was a kid."

With a laugh, he slid from the bed and crossed to the French doors, opening each set, letting in the breeze and the night sounds and the ocean's briny scent. The esperanza blooming at the base of the trees added its own sweet flavor, and all of it paled in comparison to the fragrance that enveloped him when he returned to bed: sex and sweat and perfume and wood smoke and Lisette. It created the sort of memory that would last forever, no matter where he was, no matter who he was with.

When he was relying on memories, where would she be? Would they still be lovers? Friends? Even casual acquaintances?

Part of the fun of a new relationship for Jack had always been would-they-or-wouldn't-they. Would they have sex? Would they last longer than six months? Would they fall in love? Would they part as friends? Would it last, or would it be just another stop on the journey?

This time he didn't find that wondering quite so

much fun. This time he was a lot more emotionally invested a lot faster than ever before. This time he wanted more than sex, more than six months, more than friendship, more than just another stop. This time he thought she might be the one, and though he'd thought that before, this time he really believed in the possibility.

Did she? Had it even crossed her mind?

Not accustomed to being the needy one, when he resettled in bed, he changed the subject. "What did you think of our ghosts?"

Her expression turned thoughtful. "You're sure they're ghosts."

"We're sure they're not trespassers. What does that leave? Aliens? Ghosts? Mass hallucinations?"

Her smile was a little blue as she agreed. "Ghosts." Then… "What does Jesula think?"

"She calls them the lost souls. She says they lose their way in death same as in life. Someday maybe they go home, or maybe they don't want to."

"Maybe they have no home to go. Maybe they lost so much that they can't bear to move on."

The possibility sobered him. Rolling over, he propped one arm under his head and gazed at the fan directly above them, its paddles shaped like long, slender palm fronds. "Thanks to the Toussaints and Sinclairs. They had no concern for anyone but themselves, and they passed their narcissistic sociopathic tendencies down through the generations." He scoffed. "No legacy at all is better than theirs."

Then, to lighten the mood, he cut his gaze to her. "That's what my legacy is—nothing. I'm not contributing to society. I'm spending my life not leaving my mark on the world, and when I'm gone, my footprint will be so tiny no one will even know I was here."

The linens rustled as Lisette pulled the sheet over her, then rested her head on his shoulder. "Don't kid yourself, Charming. People know you're here. They'll always know. Your family, your friends, the people here on the island. Your employers, your marks. Candalaria will never forget a thing about you. He'll be cursing you with his dying breath."

Jack considered it a moment before grinning. "That alone gives a man a reason to live, doesn't it?"

She laughed, a full-throated, blood-warming laugh that tightened his chest until something inside him broke...or was made whole again. He wasn't sure which. "A person has to find his reasons where he can. Tormenting Candalaria until the end of his days seems as good as any other."

"And what about you, Lisette? What gives your life purpose?"

Her expression dimmed as the last of the mirth seeped away, but only for an instant. Her brows arching, she gave a long-suffering sigh. "Wow, have amazing toe-curling sex with the guy, and he wants to know your deepest secrets."

Gently he stroked her arm, savoring the silken feel of her skin, skirting the bruises there. "I already know your deepest secret, Bella. Damn, they named you well. You're beautiful."

"They gave the name to my mother. I appropriated it."

"If they'd realized there were two of you, they would have named you Donna Più Bella. Doesn't that mean 'most beautiful woman'? My Italian's a little sketchy."

Her hair tickled his skin when she shook her head. "No one would look at my mother and me and choose me as the most beautiful. She was gorgeous."

"You're more gorgeous."

"You've never seen her."

"I don't need to."

Lazily she shifted until her body was stretched out over the length of his. She pushed herself into a seated position, her hips cradling his, and tossed her hair back into a sexy, enticing tumble over her shoulders, and she smiled a sexy, enticing smile that roused his erection with surprising speed. "Just for that, Lucky Jack…"

Bending forward, she brought her breasts into contact with his chest, the soft mounds swaying, and then her mouth touched his jaw, sliding back and forth. "I'm going to help us both live up to your pirate name."

A sound, half groan, half strangled sigh, escaped him as she took him inside her, sliding slow with taut control, until he filled her. Head back, eyes closed, she sighed, too, with contentment and satisfaction and anticipation, and the same sentiments echoed through him, tightening his muscles, shortening his breaths, feeding his own anticipation.

Somewhere in the distance of his rational mind, he realized she hadn't answered his question: *What gives your life purpose?*

And at the moment, damned if he cared.

Lisette was ravenous the next morning. It wasn't as if she hadn't eaten well at all three meals the day before, but this morning nothing within her reach was safe, especially the tender buttery flatbreads that went by the odd name of buss up shut.

It wasn't until she'd polished off her second plate of food and the third glass of papaya juice that the conversation turned to Candalaria. The mention of his name in bright sunlight cast a shadow over the warm, sated feeling that had settled over her sometime yesterday and completely enclosed her by the time she'd fallen asleep last night. Now it was as if a tiny prick had pierced the bubble, letting the good seep out.

It was Ali who brought up the subject. "Harry No-Hair says Candalaria hasn't found any takers yet. Rumor says he even offered to buy one guy's boat, but the guy turned him down."

"Does Harry really have no hair?" Lisette asked absently, though her brain was returning to reality too quickly.

"Actually, his hair is longer and curlier than yours," Jack replied. He'd had the option of taking the seat beside her this morning, but he chose to sit across from her again. The better to see him, a fairy tale-ish voice in her head had pointed out. "It's pure white, and it's been that way all his life."

Simon curtly said, "He'll branch out soon. If he doesn't find help in Santo Domingo, he'll go farther, someplace where the saints' names don't carry any weight."

Padma turned an innocent, open-eyed gaze on him. "Such a place exists? I had no idea."

His expression didn't change one bit, but Lisette was pretty sure she saw some tinge of humor hiding there. Were Padma and the Dark Lord flirting? Seriously? They'd known each other mere hours, and Padma had grown up with the same Toussaints-are-evil mantra that Lisette had.

"The farther you get from our headquarters, the less influence we have," Simon replied. "Maybe Ali should take some staff and persuade Candalaria it's a bad time for a visit."

Persuasion seemed to be their favorite way of dealing with troublemakers, but Lisette still didn't know exactly what that meant. Going toe to toe, flexing muscles, flashing weapons? Taking up position for a chat, Ali and Candalaria unarmed while their soldiers formed a circle around them? Keeping distance between them and exchanging threats by cell?

Killing Candalaria and anyone else who gets in their way?

Simon Senior's men had done just that to her father, and they'd left her mom to the same fate. But Jack and Simon weren't pirates. Even though she didn't feel nearly as at ease with Simon as with Jack, she was sure he wouldn't resort to murder to take care of a pesky problem. Relatively. Mostly.

Okay, she *wanted* to be sure.

"It can't hurt to talk to him," Ali agreed, his fingers flying over the screen of his cell. "We'll leave at nine. And, no, you can't go."

His last words were directed at Jack, whose mouth was open to speak. The muscles in his jaw tightened. "You know, he's here because of me. He's probably more likely to talk to me."

"Or shoot you on sight. He's not the first person who's felt that way," Toinette reminded him with an elbow to the ribs.

"You stay here," Simon agreed with Ali. "You can show our guests the family treasures."

The words had hardly registered in Lisette's mind

when Toinette laughed. "Ha! Lisette thought she saw the treasures last night."

A flush warmed Lisette's face even as she realized that *family treasures* translated to *art*. She knew Simon wasn't comfortable with having a thief other than Jack on his island, and she wouldn't have blamed him at all if he'd refused access to her. She had no clue whether the invitation would include *Le Mystère*, but even so every muscle and nerve in her body was dancing at the possibility.

Padma apparently felt the same way. She rose from her chair, her features set in full surprise, and said, "Really? We can see your collections? Now? Come on, sweetie, Charming, why are you wasting time still sitting?" Catching the hint of a frown marring Simon's face at her enthusiasm, she frowned back, managing fierceness to match any they'd seen from him. "You don't have to worry. I'm not the light-fingered one. The actual stealing is Lisette's job, and she's too busy being girly with Jack."

"He gets that look when Jack goes into the galleries, too," Ali pointed out. "It's hard for a collector to feel safe with a known thief on the premises, no matter that they were crib brothers."

"You meant to say 'renowned thief,' didn't you?" Jack stood and circled the table to pull Lisette from her chair. "Besides, he knows I wouldn't take anything from the family collections."

"Because he knows I'd take him past the divide again, and this time he wouldn't come back," Simon replied drily.

Everyone else rose, too, Ali heading for the helicopter on the side lawn where his officers had gathered.

All of them were heavily armed. Toinette picked up her coffee and strolled north toward her office, and Simon followed, giving a lingering look over his shoulder at Jack, Padma and Lisette.

She was flattered that he thought highly enough of her talents to worry. And saddened that he was right to worry.

"Do you want to start with impressed and work your way up to flabbergasted or get your socks knocked off right at the start?" Jack asked.

"The former, of course. It's always better to start with the least and finish with the best." Lisette loosely clasped her hands; she didn't want him to think that not having stolen anything since last week had given her the jitters.

"Hear that, Jack?" Padma said. "She expects you to keep getting better."

"I think I'm up to the challenge," he teased.

Behind his back, Lisette widened her eyes and fluttered one hand over her chest, making Padma swallow a giggle.

He led them past the kitchen and into the main corridor. Lisette hadn't seen much of the house so far. The floor tiles were deep rusty red, covered here and there with antique rugs, and the furniture visible in the rooms they passed was old and solid. The paintings and sculptures were lovely, created by talented artists but not breathtaking. That would change once they reached the entryway to the right of the front door.

It was a simple doorway, double wide, a pattern of leaves carved around the edges. It looked like the other doors opening off the hallway into mundane living spaces, except those appeared to never close and these stayed that way. And the keypad. These doors had an electronic lock.

Simon had already deactivated the alarms, so all Jack had to do was open the doors. Her breath caught in her chest when she got her first glimpse. Lights came on automatically, motion-activated, and climate-controlled air welcomed them. Padma squeezed Lisette's elbow, their looks both giddy when they stepped inside.

Lisette had been in museums where the smallest gallery was ten times the size of this room and held one-hundredth—one-thousandth—the value in art. She didn't know where to look first: at the Rothko directly in front of the door or the Turner competing for attention from the wall on the left. There was the sculpture by Modigliani in the center, the Chihuly blown-glass installation on the right and…

"Wow," Padma said, and Lisette echoed it. "You have, oh my God, your very own Caravaggio. And Kandinsky. And Church."

"I would have made straight As in art appreciation if I'd ever gone to school," Jack said smugly.

Padma stopped in front of a textile—eighteenth century, a palampore, made of chintz and hand-painted in vivid shades of red—and turned to him. "You didn't go to school? Ever?"

"I'm not barefoot and ignorant—" he glanced at his flip-flops and grinned "—but no. We traveled a lot, so I always had tutors."

Which meant the best education money could buy and little chance to slack off. How much more would Lisette have loved the traveling, the museums, the cultural opportunities, the one-on-one attention of a tutor over the daily drudge of public school?

While Padma studied the textile from every angle, Lisette wandered to the nearest object, a vase, hard-paste Oriental porcelain, overglazed in pastels. "Qing dynasty?" she asked, her voice soft as if sound waves might damage the piece, her fingers hovering inches above it.

"Yes. My great-great-grandfather lived in China a while." Jack paused. "You can touch it. You can both touch what you want."

Her gaze jerked to his. She'd seen so many priceless works of art in her life, but the only ones she'd ever touched were the ones she or Marley had stolen, and that had always been with gloves. Paints and canvas, clay and porcelain, threads and wood and precious metals lost strength over time. It was only common sense that treasures needed protection.

"Really?"

Jack moved closer behind her, taking her trembling hand in his, and laid her fingertips against the vase. He took a firm grip on the vase so she could slide her fingers from birds to flowers to background, the sheer importance of it penetrating from her fingers into her senses. Dear heavens, she was *touching* a centuries-old vase worth at least twenty million dollars. Goose bumps spread through her, her muscles contracting as if they could somehow imprint the feel on her memory, and her lungs seemed to have frozen midbreath.

"Incredible," Lisette said.

Jack's head was bent close to hers, his mouth brushing her skin, when he spoke. "This is one of the benefits of a private collection. One easy door to walk through. No pesky laser grids, vibration sensors, motion sensors or hard-eyed security guards who value their job more

than your life. No cameras everywhere capturing unflattering angles of you."

From the corner of her eye, she saw him lean back,
take a look at her backside and grin. "Not that I've yet
found an unflattering angle on you."

Carefully, she removed her hand from the vase and
swore her skin continued to tingle for a moment. Giving the sensation time to fade, she looked around the
room. Except for the cameras, all the other security
measures had been deactivated for their visit, and she
was hesitant to pay too much attention to the cameras.
She didn't want him to think she was wondering how
to defeat their system.

But he knew anyway and laughed. "Every time I
walk into a highly fortified place, I immediately start
figuring how I would bypass the security—even at my
mom and dad's houses. It's an occupational hazard."

"Does Simon know that?" she asked as he moved to
the next display, drawing her with him.

"I set up the security here. Tried to get past it a few
times but failed. Ah." Switching to a pirate-y voice, he
said, "Here there be jewels."

Three necklaces graced a primitive-looking table.
The first was rubies, multiple strands with a gorgeous
monster of a stone. The second contained sapphires of
varying sizes woven on thin gold wire to create an impressive collar.

The last was of yellow diamonds: thin chains of gold
connecting perfectly matched stones, the smallest at
the top, each succeeding pair larger, ending in a tear-
drop of about five carats. The necklace was perfectly
balanced, and when Jack fastened it around her neck,
it damn near sizzled against her skin.

In the nearby mirror, she envisioned the necklace with the proper dress: black, shoulderless, low-cut, fitted over her breasts but flowing like a silk column to the floor. Nothing to distract from the beauty of the gems themselves.

"It almost makes me regret that I'm a jeans and T-shirt girl. It's a good thing, too, given that I'm likely unemployed at the moment."

"You're out of a job, but you've still got your career. With a little change in attitude, you could be living on the next island to the west—it's for sale—and we could be neighbors. Maybe even partners."

Partners. The idea sent shivers down her spine at the same time her stomach turned a little queasy. Still having Jack in her life a few months or years down the road sounded wonderful. Stealing for no reason but to build up her own wealth? It would never happen.

Unfastening the necklace, she returned it to the table. Something else that was never going to happen? Him wanting anything to do with her once he'd found out the truth.

That certainty turned the shivers and the queasiness to something she'd never felt before: pain right in the center of her being. A rare sort of sorrow, as if things were rushing headlong down the wrong path and nothing she did could ever put them right again.

It was the feeling, she was fairly sure, of her heart breaking.

Chapter 11

They spent several hours in the first-floor gallery where they'd started and the basement wing directly beneath. Jack had seen all the pieces dozens of times before, but experiencing them with Lisette and Padma was different. Their enthusiasm was so genuine, their appreciation so damn near dazzling, that it made him look at familiar old friends in a new light.

Just as they'd suggested, he saved the best for last. When they returned to the elevator, he pressed the button for the second floor and waited. Tension filled the small car—curiosity about what could possibly outshine the items in the first two galleries; anticipation; even... he wasn't sure what. Something that always niggled inside him the moments before the doors opened to reveal the most extraordinary treasure on the island.

The elevator stopped, the doors slid open soundlessly, and he stepped off. Padma took Lisette's arm and pushed her ahead.

The third gallery wasn't really a gallery at all, just a single room, no bigger than his bedroom. The walls were tan, and the floor was planks of wood, salvaged from an ancient saint's ship and laid in their original condition. Cameras mounted in the ceiling covered every inch of the room, where the sole display stood in the center, resting on a weathered column of oak.

Padma's reaction outshone Lisette's: a shriek that ended in a gasp and uncharacteristic speechlessness. Lisette's response was much quieter—he heard her breath catch—but fueled with an intensity that radiated off her.

"*Le Mystère*," she whispered before taking a halting step forward, stopping abruptly as a shudder rocketed through her.

Probably fewer than a hundred people had seen the statue in his lifetime, and most had shown the same sort of awe and disbelief. A lot of people in the art world insisted the statue didn't exist. It had never been photographed, exhibited or shown to any but the people closest to the Toussaints and Sinclairs, so over the centuries it had become more legend than fact.

It struck him that Lisette—and Padma by extension—was the only person he'd ever shown it to. That said so much more than he wanted to acknowledge at the moment.

Lisette finally moved, circling the column, slowly easing closer with each rotation. "We saw *Martin Luther King in Sapphire* when it was on display at the Denver Museum of Nature & Science, and it was incredible, a bust carved from a single stone, but this…" Her voice clogged with emotion. "It's so…delicate. So perfect."

Le Mystère was. Unlike the more common carvings in diamonds—busts, faces—this carving was a full figure: a slender young woman, her hair pulled back and woven with flowers. Her arms and feet were bare, as was one strong thigh, and her gown floated over her torso, appearing gauzy and airy. She stood on rocks at the edge of a stream, with flowering trees in the clearing behind.

At four inches tall, she was damned impressive.

"It's hard to believe," Lisette said. "The size of the stone necessary. The willingness of the owner to commission such an attempt, and of the sculptor to risk such a stone. The talent. The precision. The vision. And all done without computers or high-tech drills or micro tools."

"Why don't you share it?" Padma asked. "Send it on a tour of the top five art museums in the world. Let a few magazines do a feature on it. Something like this should be shared."

"If more people knew it existed, more people would want the bragging rights for it. It's pretty much one of a kind, priceless, and there are people out there who want to add exactly that kind of piece to their private collections. It would become a target. It would make our families targets."

"True," Padma conceded. "And I can say from my limited experience that being a target isn't fun."

"Sixty percent of the Toussaint and Sinclair collections is traveling at any given time. This is the only piece we own that's never left the island and probably never will."

Lisette stopped directly in front of the column before glancing at him. "May I...?"

Jack joined her on one side, Padma on the other. "Just don't drop it," he teased. "I really don't want to die in the jungle with the ghosts."

She picked up the statue, cradling it in her hands, turning it side to side, front to back, her gaze soft and wary and filled with awe. She wrapped her fingers around its middle, as if amazed that something so rare that it truly was priceless fitted almost perfectly into her palm. Eyes fluttering shut, she rubbed her fingertip across the soft folds of the gown, touched the tiny, perfect feet, then the hair coiled atop the woman's head.

With a shaky breath, she set it on its base again, strode to the elevator and took up position in the back corner. He and Padma watched her, then their glances met. Clearly she wanted to go to Lisette, but just as clearly something held her. "Can I...? Just a touch?"

He nodded, and she held it the same way, fingers around the middle, without lifting it from the stand. Just as quickly, she let go and hustled to the elevator, too.

Interesting responses, Jack thought as he texted Simon to rearm the systems in two minutes. He was pretty sure there would be no lingering on the first floor.

They left the gallery and the house in a curious line: Lisette followed by Padma followed by Jack. They were angling toward the beach, as good a place as any to go when you were unsettled. Sitting in the sand might not solve a person's problems, but at least it made life more bearable for the moment.

Jack wondered what had caused Lisette's mood. *Le Mystère?* Was she wondering if it was touched by innocent blood like so much of the saints' lives? Did she think the family was cheating the rest of the world by hiding it away?

Or maybe it had nothing to do with the statue at all. Maybe it was remembering all the chaos in her life back home, or seeing the over-the-top exhibit, or trying on a necklace with a single stone that could support her and Padma and a half dozen more for the rest of their lives. Maybe it had fully hit her how unfair life was—losing her father, her mother, her job—while he had everything, for no reason other than he'd been born into the right family.

He sat on the sand, arms resting on his knees. Maybe he needed to start contributing to society, to start leaving a mark, some legacy that overshadowed the saints'. Maybe he needed to prove that there was more to him than a little charm and a lot of money.

After a moment, Padma joined him. They both wore shorts and sleeveless shirts, both in shades of tan, but that was where the similarity ended. His cargo shorts almost reached his knees, and his T-shirt was faded. Her shorts were snug and short, and her shirt was the same, barely covering her belly button. Simon hadn't been able to keep his eyes off her that morning.

"She gets a little…sentimental about pieces. I've seen her sit at the dining table for hours, entranced by some of the stuff she and Marley recovered. Well, not the baseball. She didn't want to even touch it. She said it was dirty and people had written on it." Padma took the band from her hair, shook out the braids, then pulled it into a ponytail, doubled to hold her hair off her neck. "And something like that carving… Man, it's epic. Awesome."

Lisette turned to face them, the odd expression gone from her face, replaced with a smile that touched on wan. "It was all epic," she said, kneeling on the sand with her back to the ocean. "I think Padma would have sneaked out that palampore if she could have."

"Hey, it was Indian. I'm Indian. There's a chance—" Padma held her fingers a negligible distance apart to describe just how little a chance "—that it could have belonged in my family."

Lisette laughed, her face softening, making Jack's fingers curl with the desire to touch her cheek, brush his thumb against her mouth, to just look at her for hours, as entranced by her as she'd been by the art.

Then her gaze flickered, awareness slipping over her—not of him or Padma but directed outward, literally. She glanced over her shoulder to the ocean, then slowly stood, shading her eyes with her hand. About the same time, he heard a distant buzz. The helicopter returning from Santo Domingo?

A helicopter, yes, but not Deux Saints'. Jack stood and stared at it.

"That's not yours, is it?" Lisette murmured.

"No." Their helicopter was bigger, its paint job royal blue and gold. This one's colors matched the sky, making it difficult to pick out. His muscles tensed, his nerves going on alert.

It wasn't common—all the local pilots knew Deux Saints valued its privacy and normally respected that—but they saw the occasional flyover, vacationers taking the shortest route to Aruba or tourists who paid handsomely for a look at the private compound.

This didn't feel common.

As Padma rose from the sand, they continued to watch the sky, Jack waiting for the pilot to turn one way or the other, but the helo didn't deviate from its

heading. It was on a direct course for the main house…
or for them.

Blindly Jack reached for Lisette's hand, her fingers tightening instinctively around his, then grabbed Padma's arm. "Come on, let's go. Head for the back trail. The trees will give us some cover."

Lucky they were all taller than average, all active. Their strides lengthened and matched, leaving great loose ripples in the sand, their goal the trailhead that led to the village. They were a dozen yards away when a shout sounded from the right, one of a pair of security guards stationed near the harbor.

"They're armed! *Run!*"

They needed no further encouragement. Padma kicked off her sandals, jerked free and shot across the sand. He and Lisette ditched their flip-flops, too, and raced after her, reaching the path seconds before the rifle shots reached his ears. Reports echoed back, shots fired by the guards, accompanied by shouts from the direction of the house. Engines revved in the harbor, powerful patrol boats that would draw the pilot away… or use their firepower to bring the helicopter down, whichever option the intruders forced.

Running full-out, they'd covered half the trail's distance, flinching at every shot, when Lisette drew up abruptly. Jack stopped, too. "Are you okay?"

She bent forward, her breathing ragged but strong. "We can't go to the village. It's too dangerous. People…kids…"

Damn. He didn't even think… "You're right." He gulped in a breath, then grinned. "Remember, I'm not good at playing the hero. Someone shoots, my instinct is to forget everything else and run like hell."

"Aw, you're doing a fine job of being my hero," she said with a smile, but neither the teasing nor the smile could pass for real.

Hearing their conversation, Padma came back. "So we just wait here?"

Jack glanced up. The canopy overhead was so thick that not even the brilliance of the midday sun could penetrate. Nature cocooned them, turning them invisible to anyone above. "If we can't see the men with the guns on the helicopter…"

"They can't see us." Lisette picked her way off the trail a few feet to lean against a massive palm before letting her unsteady legs draw her to the ground.

He joined her, and after a moment, Padma sat on her other side. He couldn't hear the helicopter anymore, but he didn't know if that was because it had fled or because the boats' roars were drowning it out. Hell, he didn't even know if the roars were from the boats or if it was his carefree-good-natured-not-used-to-getting-shot-at life facing reality awfully damn fast.

As soon as the adrenaline faded, the anger simmering at its edges would erupt. Damn David. Who the hell sent gunmen to an island filled with innocent people and instructed them to open fire? What kind of idiot thought he could breach the security of the Toussaint/Sinclair stronghold and not have to face the consequences? What whack job threatened the lives of two women just to make Jack more malleable?

And all over a painting that *David* had stolen, not Jack. Really, who was that mad?

A sociopathic billionaire.

Feeling the tremors ricocheting through Lisette's body, Jack slid his arm around her and pulled her close.

On the other side, his hand grazed Padma's where it was holding on to Lisette, and she widened her fingers, gripping both Lisette's arm and his hand.

"Simon will send someone to find us when it's safe."

"Not until they've kicked some ass, I hope," Padma said darkly.

Lisette smiled just a little, then rested her head against him, settling in to wait.

Jack hated giving up lessons he'd learned years ago, especially lessons that encouraged him to do what he wanted, but this one was definitely getting stricken from his rule book. Sitting on a beach wasn't *always* good for what ailed a person.

It wasn't long before multiple footsteps sounded on the path, approaching from each end. Simon and Toinette came into view first, both carrying deadly-looking rifles and followed by two guards. A half moment later, four more guards appeared from the south.

Jack offered Lisette a hand. She accepted it, pulling Padma up with her. Everyone was giving them intense head-to-toe looks, checking for injuries, she assumed, then relief swept over their faces. Smaller for Simon, perhaps, when he looked at Lisette. Why not? She'd brought this danger to his island.

Guilt heated her face, and she tried to hang back as Jack and Padma returned to the trail, but they refused to release her hand.

"All the markings on the helicopter were covered," Simon said, his voice steely, "but one of the men recognized the pilot. The guy flies tours between the islands—has brought people out here a time or two before to gawk. Ali was on his way back, but now he's going to find him. No one was injured, though it looks like your cottage took a few shots. A maintenance crew is checking it out." Simon's sigh was heavy. "This is not acceptable."

No, it wasn't. Lisette hated her stupid plan, and she meant to do something about it. She couldn't stay here while Candalaria continued tearing around like a wild animal. There were too many innocent people here, and sadly, she was least among them. For everyone else's sake, she had to leave the island, and for her own sake, she had to take *Le Mystère* with her. Much as she hated it, it would fulfill every promise the Blues had ever made.

Those vows had always been important but felt more so now that she'd actually seen and touched the statue. She'd held it the way Marley told her Levi had, in the moments before his death, when it had been ripped away and he'd been heaved into the sea like so much garbage. She'd felt his love for her mother and for her. His courageousness. She'd felt *him*. His essence. His life. His anger. His love. His soul.

Before this morning, retrieving it had been a family obligation. Now it was a family honor.

She would insist on leaving the island first thing in the morning, and at the last moment possible, she would retrieve the carving. She'd been working out the how and when since the moment she'd found herself face-to-face with it, and she had come up, not with an elegant Bella Donna plan but one so plain it was ugly—and had a decent chance of success.

A better chance of success at the theft, she thought, than of Jack merely agreeing to let her leave. Too bad she couldn't pilot a boat. She could slip into the harbor—always guarded, she knew, but guards had never stopped her before—but she knew nothing of engines or charts or things nautical.

Maybe she could bribe one of the fishermen or guards to sneak her away under cover of darkness. But the idea made her skin prickle. Her parents had bribed local fishermen for their escape, and look how that had turned out.

But there was one person she could negotiate an agreement with. One person Jack couldn't intimidate into a change of heart. One who didn't feel safe with a known thief other than his crib brother on the premises. Simon would help her for his own reasons.

The crackle of a radio pulled her from her thoughts. A couple of the guards had left, and everyone else was relaxing, shaking off the stress of the attack. Toinette headed toward the beach, returning in a moment with their shoes, then Simon led the way between trees and around bushes on a shortcut that came out at the edge of the lawn. Maman and Eduardo waited at the kitchen door, both crossing themselves after doing a head count.

"Inside, inside," Maman admonished, waving them across the grass and the patio and none too gently pushing each person through the door. "No meals outside while that maniac is on the loose. Toinette, show the girls to the dining room. And no excuses that you can't eat because someone just shot at you. You need energy and strength, all of you."

"I can eat just fine, Maman," Toinette retorted as she walked to the far end of the elaborately carved dining table and slid into a chair. "But I was the one shooting, not the one getting shot at."

Lisette sank into a seat, gave Toinette and her big

rifle an appreciative look, then turned her thoughts inward. Usually she planned with Padma, but this afternoon she kept looking at her partner and seeing instead her best friend in the world. She already knew Padma couldn't think of a safer place for Lisette to be than here, other than in a locked cell underneath the Denver County jail; Padma loved her, trusted her, but would put her faith in matters of security in those who had experience. And firepower.

This job she would do without Padma.

This job would be entirely on Lisette.

The meal was excruciating. Within a few minutes, everyone was giving her curious glances. Even Padma knew something was up. *Remember your training,* Marley had always stressed to her. *Put on your best nervous, stunned-but-happy-to-be-alive face.*

Lisette picked up her wineglass before glancing around the table. She forced her mouth into a smile that became real the moment it came in contact with Jack. "I'd like to thank all of you. I naively expected getting shot at would be easier the second time around, but clearly I was wrong. I can't tell you how incredibly happy I was to see your gorgeous faces this morning. Thank you."

Jack clinked his glass against hers, then Toinette's and finally Simon's. The toasts circled the table, with pleasant murmurs and laughter, then Padma's voice cut through all the others. "Wait a minute. Wait, wait, wait. What do you mean the second time around?"

Lisette was grateful her friend had caught that reference. "I didn't mean—"

"You said, 'I naively expected getting shot at blah blah the second time.' What *first* time?" Her eyes flashing, Padma spun to face Jack. "It was your fault, wasn't it? You got her shot at and told her not to tell me because you knew I'd beat the crap out of you."

Jack's brows arched as if surprised, but Lisette could see he was happy that things appeared normal again. "It wasn't exactly my fault. I wasn't the one with the gun. I don't even like guns. Never have."

"That's true," Simon agreed. "When my father decided we were old enough to learn to shoot, Jack always begged off. Said the noise hurt his ears and he got a crick in his neck and the rifle was too heavy to carry."

Everyone but Padma chuckled at the litany of complaints. "Damn right," Jack said. "Besides, Padma, I'm not afraid of you."

Toinette leaned closer to him. "Maybe you should be. According to the guards at the harbor, she outran both you and Lisette, and I'll bet she fights dirty."

"Damn right." Padma high-fived Toinette across the table before turning her attention back to Lisette, who sighed woefully, mostly for show.

"I told you I fell when Jack and I went rock climbing, and that was true. But I fell because one of Candalaria's men shot between my feet and startled me."

Padma stared, mouth open. It worked a few times, but only fragments of sounds came out.

Lisette gently pushed her friend's jaw shut. "I was going to tell you, but we got home and…well, everything happened. I was just waiting for a better time."

"Better time. Yeah, sure." But Padma leaned across and enveloped Lisette in a rib-cracking hug. "It's a good thing you're all right, because I'd have to kill anyone who hurt you." She pointed a finger at Jack. "Remember that, Charming."

Lisette luxuriated in the embrace, at the same time whispering a silent prayer that her best friend in the world would understand when she left the island with the statue but left *her* behind.

The guards were the first to exit the room, but they only went as far as the hall. Simon and Toinette left next. At the door, Simon turned back. "Ladies, I'd like you to stay close to the house until Ali returns. Go no farther than the patio, please. Jack?"

Jack followed Simon into the corridor. "Am I restricted to the patio, too?"

"Padma and Lisette will respect my request. They were raised right—no offense to Aunt Amalia. You, on the other hand..." Simon shrugged. "Do me a favor. Move your stuff into the house for a while."

"Hey, I like my cottage."

"The fewer places security has to concentrate on, the better. We'll have extra patrols here and at the village tonight, but if you want to stay at your place, go ahead. Just don't expect company."

Jack was stubborn sometimes, and he was reckless on occasion, but he wasn't stupid. If Lisette was in his bed, it didn't matter where that bed was. "I'll bring my stuff over before dinner."

His expression so dry it should have cracked his face, Simon drawled, "Nice of you to be so reasonable." He took a few steps away. "It just occurred to me... Go by Aunt Jesula's, will you? Persuade her to stay with someone in the village for a few nights."

Jack snorted. "Just occurred, my ass. You're still afraid of her, aren't you?"

"Every reasonable person is." With a nod to Toinette, Simon walked away, and she fell into step with him.

Lisette and Padma came to the door wearing sunny smiles. "You get to visit with Aunt Jesula." Lisette patted his arm, sending little sparks the length of it. Then she slid her arm around his waist, and the sparks set his entire body on fire. "Lucky you."

"Gee, I'd ask to go along if I hadn't just been confined to the house." Padma paused before adding, "And if she didn't scare the snot out of me."

Jack offered an easy lie. "I was going to check on her anyway. I'll tell her you send your regards."

Lisette walked as far as the patio with him, her body soft and pliant when he pulled her against him. How quickly could he talk to Aunt Jesula and get back to persuade Lisette to join him upstairs for a little fun?

Brushing a strand of hair from her face, he gazed at her, and she gazed back. Whatever mood had possessed her this morning, it was gone now. She was her normal self—sweet, beautiful, soft, a little mysterious. She didn't look like a woman who'd literally had to run for her life a mere two hours ago. She looked... *Damn*.

He opened his mouth but couldn't think of anything to say, so instead he kissed her, slow and hungry, letting the need build until his body hummed with it. She saved him—killed him—by ending the kiss. "You'd better check on Auntie," she whispered.

He dragged in a desperate breath. "I'll be back."

"I'll be waiting." With a sly, womanly smile, she walked back to the house, her hips swaying provocatively, her every movement languid and tempting and incredibly arousing. He ached—literally—when he started toward Jesula's.

With two guards trailing him, he set out for Jesula's house. It was similar to the others in the village, though where everything else was pastel and soothing, her house beamed in yellow, purple, orange and pink. The top step creaked beneath his weight, and chimes dangling at the corner tinkled, but other than that, there was silence.

Passing between two rockers, Jack stopped at the open screen door and knocked. It was dark inside, shade plentiful from the overgrown trees. To one side, a candle burned on a table-turned-altar, giving the air a faint smoky scent.

"Aunt Jesula?" He knocked again.

"Dat big bird gone?"

He jerked around to find her standing at the top of the steps, the tails of her head scarf fluttering but otherwise so still she might have been a statue. How did she manage such stealth?

Glancing past her, he saw the two guards stop a safe distance away, far enough that Jesula couldn't accuse them of eavesdropping, near enough that if there was trouble, they could deal with it. He wasn't ashamed to admit that their presence gave him comfort.

"Yes, it's gone. Are you okay?"

She sat in the nearest rocker. "No big bird in da sky gonna hurt me."

"Probably not, but to be safe, Simon would like you to stay in the village tonight. Will you do that?"

She tilted her head to one side. "If Simon want, why he send you?"

"You know why."

After a moment, she gave a great laugh that shook her entire body. "He learned to be a-feared of me over da years, but not you, eh?"

He laughed, too. "I know what a sweetheart you really are."

Her mirth subsided, but enough remained to give him a smile. "Maybe for you I do it." Then, before he could respond, she asked, "Dem come because of her, didn' dey?"

"Her? You mean Lisette?"

"Lissette." Jesula made the *s*'s hiss, then shook her head slowly. "Dat girl always had a way of attractin' attention. Dem men. Da spirits. Dey watchin' her, you know."

He sat in the second rocker, leaning toward the old woman. "Aunt Jesula, maybe Lisette reminds you of someone else, but this is her first visit to the island. She has no ties to Deux Saints."

Stubbornly she shook her head again. "I know her. Da spirit 'round here—" she swirled her hand in a circle above her head "—him know her. Him know she come for da shiny girl, just like dem said she would. Him want her to have it, to take it far, far from here."

A shadow fell over the clearing, fleeting but cold, as if the lone bit of sunshine that cleared the maze of branches had turned to ice. It raised gooseflesh on his arms and along his neck, and it stirred in him an irrational need to take flight.

The island was haunted, he'd told Lisette, but it wasn't just the spirits. There were secrets and sorrows and surprises, and they were everywhere: part of every building, every tree, the rocks, the beach, the people.

"The shiny girl?" he repeated. "What shiny girl, Aunt Jesula?"

One strong push put her chair in motion, the rockers creaking with every backward stroke. "What live in da tower. I seen her in da village a long time ago, when dere wasn't no Lissette. She lived wit' da Blues, all pretty and sparkly. Lord, she sparkle. Like fine glass. Dey said she was carved from stone, but I ain't never seen no stone sparkly like glass."

Jack's system shut down. His heart quit beating, his lungs stopped processing air, his ears just buzzed instead of picking out sounds. All that worked was his eyes, and what they saw wasn't the scene before him but earlier: the second-floor gallery, sun streaming through the windows, Lisette holding *Le Mystère* so carefully in her hands. Her stunned look, her quavery voice, her fingers tenderly touching the statue's gown, the hair, the perfectly rendered feet. Then her retreat, both physical and emotional. Her flight to the beach.

Shiny girl. Oh, yes, the description fit perfectly. The purity of the stone's color, along with the hundreds of facets, made it look sometimes as if the sun lived inside it.

She come for da shiny girl, just like dem said she would.

Lisette? Come to steal *Le Mystère*? Jack's first response was to scoff at the idea, and his second and third, too. But each time the thought repeated in his mind, the words got a little stronger, his certainty a little weaker.

She was a thief, and a damn good one. It took a lot of practice to get that good, and as far as her claim that she only returned stolen property to return to its rightful owners, he had no proof of that. Who took the word of a thief as gospel?

Like any art lover, she'd been dazzled by the pieces on display in the first and second galleries this morning, but her response to *Le Mystère* had been so much more, almost a religious experience rather than mere appreciation.

She'd known that the only way to get close to the statue was through an invitation from Simon, who'd never been suckered in his entire life, or Jack, who apparently had the word tattooed all over him. She'd intrigued him from his first glimpse in the ballroom, and he'd officially hit besotted on the balcony outside David's suite, when he'd caught her in the middle of the job.

No one had ever caught Bella Donna.

He'd even rescued her.

No one had ever rescued her. She'd never needed it. Until she met him.

A few essentially harmless incidents over the next few days were all it had taken for him to sweep her onto the plane and off to the island. She'd cleared the first hurdle to taking *Le Mystère* as easily as the helicopter had set down in the side yard.

Oh, God, he felt sick. Pressing his hands to his face, he rubbed the throb in his forehead, forced the tension from his jaw and swallowed the bitterness that filled his mouth.

"She's come to steal the statue." The words were little more than a whisper. He repeated them, stronger this time, and knew it was true. Knew it in his bones and his blood and his heart.

Jesula shrugged. "Steal. Reclaim. Da same t'ing, dep, endin' whether you owns it now or you owned it afore."

"But *Le Mystère* has been in the family forever. She can't reclaim what was never hers."

Sympathy softened Jesula's features. "You know da problem wit' people, Jack? We too trustin'. People say what dey want us to believe, and until someone else comes along with proof to da contrary, we believe it. Da shiny girl ain't always belonged to the Toussaints. One of dem bought it, and another one give it away. Simon's great-great-great give it to Lissette's great-great-great for savin' his life time and again. Den when dat gen'leman died, his son, him wanted it back. Killed her great-great-great but never found out where da shiny girl was hid."

There it was again, that sense in his bones and his blood and his heart that what she said was true. *Le Mystère* wasn't the legitimate-legally-acquired-honest-and-aboveboard treasure of a lifetime. It was just one more thing the family had spilled blood for.

Lisette's family blood.

He leaned back in the rocker, unsure whether the creak accompanying his movement came from the chair, the floor or somewhere deep inside him. His stomach heaved, but he clenched his jaw. Sweat dotted his forehead, and he shoved his hand across it, trying to breathe in nothing but pure air.

Short, shallow breaths fed his need for oxygen and calmed his stomach for the moment. He still felt sick, still felt tightness and anger and hurt in every pore, but he wasn't going to break yet.

"You said you saw the girl in the village. If Simon's great-great didn't find it when they killed the man it had been given to, when did they get it back?"

Jesula stared off into the distance, slowly rocking. After exhaling a long breath, she fixed her solemn gaze on his. "When dey kill Levi Blue. Her cursed 'em. Said she wouldn't rest until da shiny girl was back where she belong. Marley Blue… Lord, she love dat man. Woulda died wit' him if not for dat baby."

Jack had heard the name before, while cleaning the broken china in Lisette and Padma's dining room: *Marley bought all these dishes.* And just a while ago on the beach: *I've seen her sit for hours, entranced by some of the stuff she and Marley recovered.*

Marley Malone. Marley Blue. The original Bella Donna. Lisette's mother.

Dear God above, what was he going to do?

Chapter 12

After lunch, with guards on watch, Lisette and Padma dragged chaises onto the emerald green grass and stretched out in the sun. No sooner had they settled than the stone building that housed the island's administrative offices caught Lisette's attention. She took a deep, apprehensive breath, swung her feet to the ground, then said in a hopefully casual tone, "Hey, Padma, I need to talk to Simon. Do you mind?"

Instantly Padma's gaze sharpened on her. "About what?"

"Candalaria."

"I'll go with you."

"No, please. It won't take long. Just stay there."

Padma stared at her a long time. There was mostly curiosity in her expression, but also a little bit of suspicion. Doubt. The fact that she'd earned them hurt.

But Padma covered the emotions by putting on dark glasses and tilting her face up to the sun. "Okay. Sure. I'll be around."

Lisette told the nearest guard what she wanted. He spoke into the mic attached to the shoulder of his shirt, then gestured to the trail leading north through the gardens. It wasn't a bad commute to work—all of two minutes if one dallied, which she very much wanted to do.

But then they were there, and an earnest young man showed her to the boss's office. An earnest young woman offered her coffee, water or tea before closing the door behind her as she left.

"Interns," Simon said from behind the desk. "We have six kids in college this year. They come home when they can and work, and if they want a job when they graduate, they get it. It's fall break for those two."

She eased a few feet closer. "Does the island pay for their education?"

"Yes."

"Live in paradise, learn a trade, find a career. Is the next question they face, 'Should I stay or should I go?'"

"For some of them. Some careers demand more than we can offer. No police department, military, hospital, law firm and so on." Simon pushed a pile of papers to the side, then settled back. "Have a seat."

Lisette didn't want to. Didn't want to talk to him at all. But she stepped around the oversize armchair and sat. He didn't offer small talk, and she didn't want it. She just wanted to say what she needed and get out, hopefully with his promise of help.

Simon shifted, obviously impatient for her to get to the reason she'd interrupted his day. Wishing she'd taken time to rehearse her proposal, she took a breath, opened her mouth…and entirely the wrong words came out.

"My family was among the original settlers of Île des Deux Saints. One of your ancestors rewarded one of my ancestors for his allegiance with the gift of a statue. Unfortunately, another of your ancestors killed mine in a failed attempt to take it back. Twenty-eight years ago your father regained possession of it. Unfortunately for my mother and for me, my father was killed in the process."

Simon stared at her, his eyes gone flat, his jaw dropped open. She was equally stunned. Only the worst fool gave her target advance notice of her plans. She'd be lucky if she didn't wind up locked in a closet with armed guards until the first opportunity to banish her from the island. What the hell was she thinking?

Lisette believed he was an honorable man. True, she didn't know him well, but Jack did, and he loved and respected him. But this outrageous declaration…

It was live or die. Either Simon acknowledged her claim on the statue, or its security became impenetrable. There'd be no second chance to fulfill Marley's lifelong goal, to protect Levi's legacy. She would have failed at the most important task she'd ever been given and disappointed her parents completely.

Lisette tried to take another deep breath, but her lungs were too tight. "That statue was *Le Mystère*." Her voice quivered, then grew strong as she straightened her spine, lifted her chin and steadied her gaze. "I'm Levi Blue's daughter, and I've come to take it back."

Silence settled, sharp and edgy. Simon continued to stare at her, his expression dark with disbelief. Whether it was for her story, she didn't know. No one wanted to hear that his father was a murderer, no matter how strained their relationship had been, and certainly no one would ever expect an apparently sane individual to walk into his office and demand a statue that truly was priceless.

"What the hell are you doing?"

The emotion-slashed voice came from behind Lisette, startling her. She swiveled around to see Jack, his face flushed bronze, his eyes stormy, his jaw clenched so tight it must hurt. Pain throbbed in her chest, so real she pressed one hand to her heart, as she realized that he knew. He knew who she was. Why she was here. That she had used him.

Dear God, this was going to kill her.

On the trek from Jesula's cabin to Simon's office, Jack had prayed to the gods, the angels and saints and spirits, for this day to end. He would have said all the same prayers and given half his fortune for it not to have begun at all, but then he walked down the hall to Simon's office and heard Lisette's sweet, sexy, lying voice, and he'd added his whole fortune to the deal. *Just please, someone, make it stop.*

He stalked into the room, seeing Simon first. He looked the way he had when his mother died in an earthquake in some remote Peruvian valley. Jack wanted Lisette to feel the same pain as he turned in a menacing circle around her.

"God, you're a good liar. I believed damn near everything you said to me. Hell, I believed everything you didn't say. But that's what you do, isn't it? Be whoever your target wants you to be, lie and deceive and pretend. What's your game this time? What's the point of telling him you came to steal 'da shiny girl'?"

Looking surprised and hurt—*damned* liar—she got to her feet. She took a step toward him and flinched when he backed away. Before she could say anything, though, Simon did, distantly, numbly.

"Da shiny girl. I remember hearing stories... Da shiny girl ran away from home and was placed in a tower where her parents couldn't see her. Or she ducked out of school and was taken by a monster who locked her away, or she disobeyed and the spirits flew off with her and broke her parents' hearts. She always broke her parents' hearts." His smile was thin and bitter. "I thought it was some kind of cautionary tale. I didn't know... I never connected it to *Le Mys*..."

He let the word trail off. His gaze shifted from Jack to Lisette, then back again. "Is what she said true? That my father...killed her father?"

Sorrow competed with the pain inside Jack. He'd never liked Simon Senior, had always distrusted and feared him, but he'd never imagined having to answer a question like that. "I—Jesula says... Yes. Not himself, of course. He had someone do it."

Simon's shock wavered into something sad and painful to see, then into a grimace. "Of course. He never liked doing dirty work himself." He pushed away from the chair and walked to the window. "I feel like I should be angry. Insisting you're wrong, Jesula's wrong, Lisette's lying. He was my father, after all. But...he *was* my father. It feels..."

Right. Jack laid his hand on Simon's shoulder. There wasn't much he could say. Simon wouldn't find comfort in hearing that had been Jack's reaction, too, that he'd known immediately Senior was guilty. Senior had just been that way: power colored by wealth, corrupted by superiority and wearing the ugly tinge of just plain meanness.

"Is there any proof?"

Jack shrugged.

"Toinette!"

Simon's shout made Lisette cringe. She'd never heard him raise his voice, Jack realized, and had never heard that much emotion in it. The petty place inside him was glad it startled her and hoped it stirred some serious fear. Simon could be fierce, and she damn well deserved to see it for herself.

Toinette hustled into the room, gaze skimming, curiosity piquing, before settling on Simon.

"When did *Le Mystère* show up in our collection?"

Toinette tapped the screen of her tablet. "Just because I digitized all those old records does not make me the Deux Saints art historian, now does it?" Without pausing for breath, she went on. "It was first listed 239 years ago when Raphael Toussaint acquired it. It shows up in the inventories for forty-five years, and then it doesn't. According to my notes, two pages of the original records from the time it dropped off had been torn from the ledger. It reappeared in the inventories twenty-eight years ago."

Jack and Simon exchanged looks, then Simon said, "If you're trying to regain a valuable that your father had given away…"

"First you destroy the evidence he'd given it away. You claim it was stolen. Turn the victim into the villain. But Jesula says the statue was hidden so well, no one outside the family could find it. What about the name

Blue, Toinette? What do your records say about that?"
Jack's gaze locked with Lisette's as micro-expressions
flitted across her face, so natural, so real, she probably
wasn't even aware of them. Sadness. Heartbreak. Guilt.

Toinette's fingers tapped again. "There's a long list
of Blues on the island census. The first was on the original crew, and the last was Levi, son of Elijah and Sarah,
husband of Marley Malone Blue. Hey—" She smiled at
Lisette. "Is that—"

"Go on," Jack said curtly.

After another look around the room, Toinette returned her attention to the tablet. "Both Levi and Marley Blue died on the water twenty-eight years ago. They
went out at night, presumably to fish, and their boat
sank. Their bodies—" she gave Lisette a cautious look
"—were never found. Just bits of belongings."

The statue disappearing from the inventory, the
pages that would have told why ripped out, the diamond reappearing at the same time Levi Blue died…it
was proof enough for him, probably enough for Simon.

It was impossible to tell how much Toinette had
gleaned from the discussion so far, but he figured it
was enough when she spoke quietly. "We have a fair
number of residents who were alive when—when Levi
and Marley Blue died. Do you want me to ask them to
share their accounts?"

Gingerly Simon sat down again, moving as if he had
new aches in old places. Jack had new aches in new
places. Like his trust. His ego. His judgment.

"Just a few," Simon replied. "Father Beto, Maman,
Eduardo, Esther."

Toinette was walking away before he finished speaking. That left Lisette the focus of Simon's attention.

"Lisette, Emilio will take you back to the house. He's waiting in the lobby."

"Why don't you put her in the cell back there?" Jack jerked his head to the rear of the building even as something in him recoiled at the words. The cell was at least two hundred years old, iron and stone, dirty and cold and creepy. Putting her there, leaving her there like a common criminal, would be wrong.

She is a criminal, his wounded spirit retorted. Though there was nothing common about her.

"She can wait at the house."

Jack glared at Simon. "She weaseled her way in here for the sole purpose of stealing *Le Mystère.* She took advantage of you and me and everyone else. The islanders have been doing their damnedest to care for her, treat her like an honored guest and keep her safe, and the only thanks she intended was to sneak off with the statue. And that doesn't change anything for you? You're going to let her wander around like she belongs here?"

Simon scowled back, and his voice matched. "She's still our guest. Please go, Lisette."

She took a few steps toward the door, then stopped. For a long moment, she just gazed at Jack, so collected and poised. A person would never guess that the last minutes had been so emotional. It was as if she'd turned a switch and someone else had taken over. Bella Donna. Even Jack, who'd thought he knew her damned well, couldn't see anything but what she wanted him to see.

Then she walked out. She didn't reach out, didn't speak, didn't give any hint of what she was thinking, feeling, maybe even regretting.

It must be nice to control one's life like that. He

didn't have a switch. He couldn't turn off anything. His life right now was ugly and messy and wasn't likely to change for a long time.

Damn Bella Donna.

Head up, Lisette left the building, Emilio on her heels. Even the sun couldn't chase away her chill. She'd done it—made the stupidest move in her entire life—and she didn't know where the words had come from. Who had taken possession of her caution and good sense?

Lisette truly felt the fool today. She'd destroyed any chances of recovering the statue, and along with them any hope, however small, for her and Jack. How could she live in a world where he existed, outside her reach forever, and know it was all her fault? That she had single-handedly ruined both dreams?

There was no sign of Padma on the patio. With a wan smile for her guard, Lisette went inside, slipping past the kitchen without catching Maman's attention. She refused to even glance at the doors leading into the galleries, instead taking the stairs two at a time. In her room, she closed the door, walked to the middle, turned in a slow circle and sank to the floor with a sob.

She felt Marley's presence, but her mother stayed silent. All she could do was what she'd always done when Lisette needed comforting: hum softly and stroke her hair. Lisette could actually feel the gentle brush over her curls that sent goose bumps in a wild dance, until the shift of fabric against her legs made her realize the French doors were open to the breezes.

The realization loosed her tears in a flood.

She didn't know how much time passed before she

felt the real touch, hands on her hair, arms wrapping around her, the sudden cooling of a damp towel and wet skin against hers.

"Sweetie, it's okay," Padma murmured, hugging her tightly. "Whatever's wrong, we'll work it out. We'll take care of it."

Clinging to her, Lisette cried harder until, soggy and starving for air, she hiccuped, breathed deeply and pulled back. Padma's damp black hair hung down her back, and a beach towel knotted at her waist covered the matching bottom of her yellow bikini. She smelled of salt and sunshine and love and home, and Lisette wanted to hold on until everything *was* okay.

Which would probably be never.

After drying her face, she told her what she'd done. How shocked Simon had been. How angry Jack had been. How she'd ruined everything. A range of expressions crossing Padma's face, she listened until Lisette fell silent, then she sighed. "Jeez, Lizzie girl, when you blow it, you do it spectacularly, don't you?"

There was nothing funny about the whole situation, but a laugh choked out anyway. She could always count on Padma to not sugarcoat things.

Patting her hand, Padma went on. "Maybe this is for the best. Have you given any thought to what it would be like to own the statue? Where you would put it, what you would do with it, how you would pay to insure it… I've thought about these things, and even before I saw it, I knew the sugar bowl in the dining room wasn't gonna cut it. Maybe it's better to just know that it's safe and being cared for and to not have responsibility for keeping it that way."

Lisette sighed. "I know in my head you're right. I

can't afford to own a priceless carving. Sure, I could loan it to a museum, and they'd have to protect it, but... I thought it was so sad that Mrs. Maier had to send *Shepherdess* to a museum, that she can't just walk into the bedroom whenever she wanted and look at it and remember her husband giving it to her. What would be the point of having *Le Mystère* if I couldn't see it whenever I wanted, if I couldn't touch it or hold it?"

Padma went into the bathroom to trade her wet towel for dry ones, then returned to sit next to Lisette. As she pressed the water from her hair, she slowly said, "I know your mom meant well, but... It wasn't fair to put this on you. You didn't choose to become a thief, she did. I did. But you didn't. And you didn't choose to fixate your entire life on recovering the statue—she did." She lifted her gaze upward. "Aunt Marley, I love you dearly. Please don't forget that. I just think Lisette should have had a choice."

It had never occurred to Lisette that she *should* have had a choice. Stealing to recover someone else's treasure was one thing; her responsibility ended when she returned the item to them. Stealing the statue—her father's treasure, Simon's, the island's, anyone's but hers—when she didn't even want it...

Maybe that was what this journey was all about. Realizing her truth. All she had to do was be happy and safe and live her life to the fullest.

An unexpected smile tugged at the corner of Lisette's mouth. "I actually do like the retrieval business. We help people when no one else does. That makes me feel good."

There was a rustle of air—physical, metaphysical, Lisette had no clue—but Padma shrieked and jumped to her feet. Her gaze darted side to side, searching for something that couldn't be seen but was real even so. She touched her hand lightly to her face, then stared at her fingertips as if something might have appeared there. "Lisette," she whispered, reaching blindly for her. "I felt her. I heard her. She called me Padma-cakes. She touched me. She said she loves me. She..."

With the same awe she'd shown the diamond statue, Padma whispered, "Wow."

At least there was one part of Lisette's life that still earned a heartfelt *wow*. She hoped it would be enough. But judging by the devil's hold on her heart, she didn't think it was likely.

The last of the employees Simon had summoned left, leaving Jack alone in the office with a raging headache caused by disgust, shame, Lisette's lies—and truth. As Simon walked to the main exit with Father Beto, Jack paced out of the room, made a sharp left at the corridor and headed for the rear door.

Simon called his name, but Jack kept walking. He needed physical exertion before all the emotions building inside exploded and left nothing but pitiful little sorrows behind.

His steps increasing to a run, he kicked off his flip-flops and crossed the grass onto the nearest trail. Ignoring the pricks and pinches on his feet, he took a path that grew smaller, weaving through trees. It was an anchoring tendril on the spiderweb of the island's network, crossed again and again by other tendrils but staying its northern course. The elevation climbed steadily, bisecting heavily wooded areas and a few old ruins from ancient outposts.

His lungs were struggling for air, and sweat drenched him when he finally reached the divide that slashed from east coast to west. Foliage on the north side grew so thick that, even though only thirty feet separated the crowns of the gorge, the only thing visible on the other side was the first screen of trees, bushes and rocks.

Gasping, he sank onto a boulder at the cliff's edge. The employees Simon had questioned had told the same story. Eduardo's mother had heard rumors about the Blue family's shiny girl from her own grandmother. Maman's great-great-aunt had written of the close bond between an early Blue and a Toussaint in her diary. That same Blue had died mysteriously, his family put out of their home, everything they'd owned broken and destroyed. The fear fueled by it was still felt: Esther's family continued to hide their valuables to this day.

The big question had been put to Father Beto: What happened the night Levi and Marley died?

They were trying to escape, the priest said. They'd wanted to be free more than anything, and when Marley realized she was pregnant, the decision had been made.

Escape? he and Simon had echoed. *Escape what? Escape to where?*

Freedom. Like everyone else in the village—Father Beto had been the exception—the Blues had lived on the island, worked, worshipped, celebrated…and were prisoner there. Simon Senior, in the tradition of the Toussaints before him, ruled with an iron fist. Their salaries went into accounts he controlled; they were overcharged for clothing, food, medical care, spiritual care. Setting up a new life required money, and Senior made damn sure they didn't have any.

Jack drew up his knees and rested his forehead on

them. He and Simon weren't descended from just pirates but from kidnappers, slavers, tyrants and killers.

This day couldn't possibly get any worse.

And then it did.

He heard the footsteps long before they reached him, but he didn't react, sure only Simon would follow him here. He stopped behind Jack, tossed something to the ground—flip-flops—then quietly spoke. In Lisette's voice. "I'm sorry."

Jack scrambled around so quickly that one foot slipped from the rock and he scraped his knee. "What the hell—!"

"I'm sorry. I mean, I'm sorry I startled you. I should have said something sooner. I'm sorry—" An exquisitely sorrowful look came across her face. "I'm sorry for everything."

Yeah, losing her only chance to steal the statue could certainly make her regretful. It was good to know that it, at least, meant something real to her.

He stared at her. She stood as tall as ever, as beautiful, the sun gilding her left side warm, rich gold. But there was a roundedness to her shoulders, and her eyes were puffy and red-rimmed. "Did you decide you couldn't do it?" he asked, sitting again, staring across the gorge. "Is that why you confessed to Simon?"

"Couldn't— You mean, steal the statue?" The surprise in her voice seemed genuine, but so had everything else about her. "Of course I could do it."

"Right. So it's just coincidence that you saw the galleries, the security, and suddenly felt compelled to appeal to Simon's honor instead."

She took a few steps to come even with him, making him wonder how he'd mistaken her light, delicate steps for Simon's.

"I can break the system." Gracefully, she seated herself on a smaller rock to his right. She glanced toward the cliff's edge, and discomfort flitted across her face, but she ignored it. "I don't know why I confessed. Maybe dem spirits possessed me."

"You meant for me to catch you at David's, didn't you?"

"Yes."

"To be intrigued by you."

"I hoped so."

"To manipulate me into bringing you here."

She gave a regretful sigh that traveled across the gorge and echoed back a dozen times. "Yes."

Bleakness settled over him. "Why?" The word was a croak, barely half-formed, and he couldn't be any more specific. *"Why...?"*

Slowly she turned toward, the sun shining fully on her. Her skin glowed, her eyes glistened, and her hair formed a halo around her face. "My whole life, everything I've ever done, was for this—stealing back the statue, getting justice for what Simon Senior did, honoring my father's memory. It wasn't something I ever really thought about. It just *was*."

Jack didn't want to hear that. He'd rather be used because of a passion so great she couldn't help herself. He didn't want to know that she'd broken his heart because her mother had pushed her, shaped her, trained her like a robot to do the job.

"You could have approached Simon the way any normal person would have, with a letter, an email, a lawyer."

She smiled faintly. "For nearly three hundred years, my family was held prisoner here by one Toussaint after another. One Toussaint murdered one Blue for the statue, then another did the same. Neither my mother nor I had any reason to think Simon would be different."

A four-inch statue. Cursed, Jesula had said, and Jack believed it. He would never look at it again with wonder and awe. It would just be an ugly reminder of the lengths people would go to to get what they want, and damn whoever got hurt along the way.

In the past, all that hurt had been on the Blues' side. It was only fair that this time circumstances should be reversed.

"So now you've lost the statue. You'll never get it."

Her gaze was distant; so was her voice. "I can live with that."

Anger surged through him, pushing him to his feet again. "You can *live* with it? You manipulated me, you used me, you made me believe you *cared* for me! You threw away the best chance I've ever had to love someone, and you can *live* with it?" He dragged his hand through his hair, then glared at her. "Well, damn it, *I* can't. I thought we had something. I thought we *were* something. I thought I was falling in love with you and you with me. I was planning a future with you, and you just threw it all away. You concocted your stupid plan, you betrayed me, and now you say, 'Eh, I'll be fine.'"

Misery etched every line in her face, and her eyes, bright with emotion a few moments ago, were dark and mournful. "That's not what I meant. I do care for you, Jack. I think I'm falling in love—"

Noise erupted to the south, harsh staccato reports, a sudden long burst, a moment's pause, then another.

Birds catapulted from trees into the air, squawking, swirling northward in panicked flocks. Confusion drew Lisette's brows together, along with fear, then as another round of gunfire echoed, she jumped to her feet and shot away from the cliff.

"Damn it!" Jack ran after her, catching up within a hundred yards. This was surely another attack by David, who only *thought* he wanted Jack. If he got his hands on Lisette, if she convinced him that she stole *Shepherdess*—and God knew, she was damn good at convincing people—David would leave Jack and the islanders alone.

But if he got his hands on Lisette… A shiver ran down Jack's spine, damn her, and propelled him forward enough to grab her hand and drag her to a stop. "You can't go back there."

She twisted violently, but he was stronger, even if his strength did come from fear. "Let go, Jack! I have to— Padma's there, and Simon and Toinette and—and—"

Gripping her other arm, he dragged her up close to him, close enough to die a little as he stared into her eyes. "They'll be safe. The guards, Ali, the defenses— They're safe."

She met his stare unflinchingly before her shoulders slumped and she swayed on her feet. For an instant, he thought she would sag into his arms; then she caught her balance and breathed, blowing out panic, taking in control. "All right. I won't run into the middle of it. But we have to go back."

Of course they did. Jack couldn't hide in the trees while everyone else dealt with the trouble he'd brought here.

Releasing her left arm, he started along the path,

using his grip on the other to keep her at his side. He strained to hear any noises other than the gunshots and, as they grew closer to the compound, the *whump-whump* of helicopter blades.

When they reached the administrative building, the scene was chaotic. Two helicopters circled overhead, first one swooping in, then the other, close enough for their passengers to fire a barrage of shots, then swooping back up out of reach of the island's defenses. From their vantage point, he spotted fourteen, maybe sixteen, islanders, taking cover where they could, taking shots when they could. Simon was among them, and so was Toinette, smiling as she stepped away from the house to fire on one helicopter, pumping her fist triumphantly when the engine sputtered and smoke began to rise.

Pressed tightly to the side of the building, Jack grumbled, "I should lock you in that cell."

Pressed tightly to his side, Lisette gave him a narrow-eyed stare. "I'd make you sorry."

Pain twinged deep inside, weakening his knees and his anger. Turning his gaze back to the attack, he sadly murmured, "You've already done that, Lizzie."

Chapter 13

It seemed the assault lasted forever, but by Lisette's calculations, it was less than fifteen minutes. There was one minor injury on the ground, a gardener hit by shrapnel when the first shots were fired, but the helicopters had suffered damage. She hoped they both crashed into the ocean.

She and Jack hustled toward the patio where people were gathering, her gaze skimming for Padma. Her stomach knotted when she didn't locate her, but Jack had said she was safe. Surely they'd taken her somewhere; surely they were just waiting for an official allclear to bring her out.

After giving terse orders to the security force, Simon started toward them, his focus on Lisette. He walked right up to her and locked gazes with her. "You should go."

The question she'd asked earlier in the office: *Should I stay or should I go?* Ignoring the pain in her chest, she nodded. This was what she'd wanted, right? "I'll contact Candalaria when I'm back in Denver. I'll send him a message he can't ignore."

"What kind of message?"

"Wait, wait, wait a minute." Jack scowled at them. "You can't send her away. You can't set her up as bait for a crazy man!"

Recognizing Jack's concern as the same he would show anyone in this situation saddened Lisette, but she smiled anyway. "I won't be the bait. I'll be providing it. When can I leave?"

"He wants *Shepherdess*," he reminded her. "You can't give it to him."

"No, but I can give him something better."

"What?"

She hooked a strand of hair behind her ear. "Number one on his list is Aunt Gloria's rubies, but there are a lot of other beauties there. Some pieces he's made quiet offers on and been rejected. Others, he complains, have been in the same families so long, their owners won't even entertain offers."

Simon's gaze didn't waver. "You think you can liberate one of these beauties, and he'll be satisfied enough with the trade to let this feud with Jack go. What if he reneges?"

Lisette shrugged. "Then it'll be up to him just how much he loses— His art. His museum. His reputation. His castle. His freedom." *His life.* She had never caused a person pain before—before Jack—but she would stop Candalaria, no matter what it took.

She hesitated before going on. "I have one favor.

Keep Padma here. Introduce her to some conservation experts around here. Keep her busy and safe."

"I'm not in the habit of holding people against their will," Simon said drily, then the lines across his forehead deepened. "It's neither the best time nor the best place, but I apologize for all the Toussaints before me who did have such habits. Yes, we'll keep her safe."

Emotion radiated from Jack in waves. "You can't do this, Simon. She's in way over her head. She doesn't know how to play David's games."

Simon gave him a grim, sympathetic look. "You wanted her gone, Jack. Soon she'll be gone. Lisette, if you'll wait in your room, I'll let you know when Ali's ready."

She nodded and Simon headed away to deal with one of the dozen crises going on. Beside her, Jack muttered, "This is stupid."

She began walking toward the rear entry of the main house. "I created a problem, Jack. Now I'm resolving it."

"Bella Donna never put herself into this kind of danger."

At the door, she stopped and faced him. "No. But she helped me get here, and she'll help me out of it."

"You can't take on David alone."

"One lesson I learned from my mother, Jack—I can do what has to be done." She wouldn't accept Padma's help, and no one else was offering. She hesitated, thinking of all the things she could, should, say, but in the end, all she had to offer was regret. "I truly am sorry, Jack. I can't fix this—" she gestured between them "—but I can make everything else right. I will. I promise."

Without waiting for his response, she hustled inside and to the stairs. She was halfway up them when Padma caught up, grinning ear to ear. "Oh, sweetie, I have a surprise for you. You won't believe—*I* can hardly believe it. It's the most amazing bit of luck we've ever had. Hurry, hurry. I don't think I can hold it one second longer."

Padma pushed Lisette into her room, closed the door and dashed to the bedside table, scribbling on the notepad there before presenting the paper to her proudly. On it was eight characters: letters, numbers, symbols. Padma didn't wait for her to figure it out. "It's the code to the galleries! That's where they sent Maman and me during the attack, and I saw her type it in. It disarms everything—*everything,* Lisette!" Her voice dropped to an excited whisper. "You can get the statue. You can just walk right in and take it."

Lisette stared at the sequence, then wadded the paper and pulled her suitcase from the closet. As she laid it open on the bed, she said, "I'm leaving, Padma. As soon as Simon arranges it, I'm going back to Denver, and I'm going to stop Candalaria."

Padma stared at her, jaw dropped, then suspicion narrowed her gaze. "What did Jack say when you found him? Is he throwing you off his precious island?"

"No. It was my idea. I was planning it before I talked to Simon. I put these people in danger—I put *you* in danger—and it's up to me to fix it."

It was clear from the confusion and curiosity that Padma was struggling with Lisette's decision, but her response was typical. "I'll get packed. I wonder how I'll fit all those clothes into my bags. You *are* taking the clothes, aren't you? I mean, they were a gift—"

"Padma." Lisette dropped her own clothing into the

suitcase, then stopped Padma on her way to the door. "You're staying here."

"Oh, no. Huh-uh. No way. Aunt Marley would kill me. Mommy and Daddy would kill me if I let you go off to battle the evil dragon by yourself."

"Please. They'll kill *me* if anything else happens to you. Just for a few days. Besides, Simon's setting up meetings for you with local water experts. You'll never have another chance like this. You can't pass it up to go home and wait while I…do what I do." Hopefully, the long flight home would help her figure that out.

Padma shifted her weight as if an imaginary bond was pulling her both toward her room to pack and to Lisette's side, where she'd always been. No, not imaginary. Very real, and Lisette was deeply grateful for it.

A sharp rap at the door interrupted Padma's indecision. She went to open it while Lisette continued to pack. Her heart wasn't pounding, her nerves not fluttering, so it wasn't Jack. The knowledge saddened her.

Simon's gaze flickered to the suitcase, and the closet still full of Jack-purchased clothes, but his expression remained passive. "The jet is being readied in Santo Domingo. As soon as Ali and the chopper pilot get something to eat, they'll take you there. You'll be back in Denver by midnight. You'll stay at a hotel tonight, and then…"

He took a few more steps to reach the bedside. "Lisette, I really do regret…everything. Some wrongs can't be righted, but some can." Reaching into his pocket, he pulled out something small and brilliant that collected all the light in the room, then reflected it back. "Keep it. Sell it. Use it as bait. Whatever you want. It's yours."

He opened his hand, and there was *Le Mystère*, del-

icate, beautiful beyond words, the object of love and
hate, passion and life and death. When Lisette did nothing but stare at it, Simon placed it in her hand, wrapped
her fingers around it, nodded once and left.

Long after the door closed behind him, Padma's gasp
shimmered on the air. "Oh, sweetie. He *gave* it to you!
What are you going to do with it?"

Lisette stroked the folds of the gown, the trembling
leaves in the tree, the ripples in the flowing water.
She thought about all the Blues through history who'd
touched this statue, about her father who had died for it
and her mother who had found purpose in it, and slowly
a smile spread across her face.

She knew *exactly* what she was going to do with it.

Dusk had settled by the time the Deux Saints helicopter took to the sky, circling the island's south point
before turning north. It disappeared from sight almost
immediately, its engine noise fading a moment later.

Jack was in his favorite childhood hiding place,
twelve feet above the ground in the branches of the island's oldest tree. Its canopy was thick with leaves, but
underneath fat limbs joining to the broad trunk provided excellent spots to read, snooze and maybe down
a bottle of rum or whiskey.

"I figured I'd find you here." It was Simon, damn it.
Couldn't he go piddle in someone else's life?

"I'm not that predictable." Irritably Jack uncapped
the bottle and took another long swig.

"Please. All your other favorite places are over by
the divide, and you won't go there after dark."

Jack had brought a second bottle with him, in case
one wasn't enough. Maybe he could drop it on Simon's

head and make him go away. "When's the last time you went up there at night?"

"We're not talking about me." After a moment, Simon leaned against the trunk. "Lisette's gone."

Jack pretended those words didn't break his heart. Was this what his entire life had been leading up to? Falling in love with a stranger, a liar and a thief who didn't give a damn who she hurt as long as she won? "Of course she's gone. She got what she wanted. The game's over for her." He wasn't surprised—hadn't even been surprised that Simon gave her the statue. Simon was one of the good guys, but thanks to his father and family history, he felt compelled to be even better than good. Add the fact that it was *his* father who'd had Lisette's father killed…

"About that…"

Because he was exhausted, he dropped the bottles down to Simon, then gripped the branch and swung off into the air. He'd seen Lisette do it that night on David's balcony—no slow and easy baby steps, but literally flinging herself off the structure. That was when he'd started falling.

When he let go, he landed with a wobble beside Simon. "What 'about that'?"

Simon handed him the open bottle but kept the full one as he turned toward the house. "I want to show you something."

Jack badgered Simon to just tell him, even though badgering him never worked. He would talk when he was ready. It was one of the things that made Jack want to strangle him.

They entered the house through the main entrance. Two guards stood at the open doors leading into the galleries, where the lights were on and the elevator waited with open doors. "Oh, God, what else did she take?"

Simon walked into the elevator, waited for Jack and pressed the second-floor button.

How stupid could he possibly have been to bring a thief here? Even he got itchy fingers in the gallery, and half the stuff belonged to his family. To put Lisette in the midst of such temptation...

Wait. If anything had been stolen, first, Simon would be ticked off, and second, they wouldn't be going to the tower. It was empty now.

Except when the door opened, it wasn't. The oak column stood in the middle of the room, and sitting atop it was *Le Mystère*, a piece of paper anchored to it.

Simon stepped out of the elevator, but Jack couldn't move. He stared at the statue, sure it must be a fake, a trick. Maybe Padma had fashioned some sort of projected image; when he blinked hard, it would waver. But it didn't.

"Don't you want to read the note?"

Numbly, Jack walked to the pedestal and fixed his gaze on the pale stationery with Deux Saints' logo at the top. The writing was graceful, full of loops, exactly the way he would have expected Lisette to write.

Dear Simon, I loved owning the statue for those few minutes, but truth is, I live in a two-bedroom house in a middle-class neighborhood and my sugar bowl is broken so I have no place to keep it. But those few minutes made my mother and father happy, which was the point of the whole thing. Thank you.

As for bait, I've got some pieces in mind. Since

they already belong to Candalaria, I don't think he'll be able to resist them.

Tell Jack (without sounding too smug, please) that I beat his system. Don't tell him how, though, not right away. Let him stew on it a bit.

Her name looped across the bottom.

"Is sugar bowl code for something?"

Jack skimmed the note again. "Whenever she stole a red diamond, they hid it in the sugar bowl until they sold it. David's men destroyed it." Though his voice was calm, his brain was racing. She'd brought the statue back. She'd had it in her hands free and clear, with a helicopter waiting to get her off the island and a jet to take her wherever she wanted, and instead she'd returned it. Why? What kind of thief did that?

Then she'd headed home for a job that just might get her killed, into a situation that she bore little of the blame for. No one had known David would go off the rails here. But she had to do the right thing. That was the way she'd been raised, to care about injustice and to right wrongs. *We're bad guys because it's the only way we can help the good guys.* Because she cared about good guys and bad guys and helping.

What kind of thief returned the target she'd planned so long to recover, then put herself in danger to protect others?

One with honor.

He loved a thief with honor.

A woman with honor.

He headed toward the elevator. "I've got to go."

"Aren't you going to ask how she got in?"

"Later. I need someone to take me to Santo Domingo."

"The helicopter won't be back for a few hours. They've been flying a lot today. I'd rather not send them out again tonight for anything less than an emergency." Simon stepped inside and pressed the button.

"You've got plenty of boats. I need the fastest one and the best captain you've got."

Simon stared at him. "A boat? You're voluntarily going out in a boat? On the water?"

The thought made Jack's stomach heave, but he ignored it. He'd be feeling it for real soon enough. "Just find someone to meet me at the harbor and get me a plane. I've got a thief to catch."

In the crisp morning air, the Castle rose out of the forest, strong and massive and impenetrable. Lisette knew getting in wasn't impossible; she and Padma had devised several plans allowing just that. Getting out was generally the problem, especially with souvenirs.

In the light of day, plan M didn't seem as workable as it had in the middle of the night. Granted, she'd been exhausted then, worried and heartsick. Hell, she still was.

She sat on the shoulder of the road, studying the scene through binoculars. Thanks to the high-thirties cold, there was no outdoor activity at the Castle in front or on the west side, and the employee parking lot was mostly empty. Not much staff on hand when the boss was gone.

Too bad it was easier to go unnoticed in a crowd.

With a sigh, she set the binoculars aside and touched the museum ID badge. It had been deactivated, but that didn't make it useless. It would get her through the gate with a tale of a delivery for Mr. Chen. Once inside the house…well, she would wing it from there. Good thing she worked well under pressure.

Pulling onto the road, she drove to the front gate. Cold air blasted in when she rolled down the window to greet the guard. "Good morning. I'm Lisette Malone from the museum. I've got the package."

The uniformed man studied her badge, then turned a blank look on her. "What package?"

"The thank-you gift that the sheikh sent Mr. Candalaria. He was a guest here for last week's party. Didn't Mr. Chen tell you I was on my way? He said he would call so you'd know I was coming. God, I hope I don't have to take it back to the museum and try again. It's a bit of a drive, and—"

"I'll check. Wait here." He walked away, cell phone to his ear.

So he says he'll deliver the package to the house. Then what?

"I'm so sorry, I'd love to leave it with you, but it requires some setup, and I have strict orders to do it myself. My boss would be livid if he found out I disobeyed."

All right, you can go to the house. Stay on the drive. Don't take any turns. Park at the entrance. You get into the house, with more security guards plus staff. What do you do?

Lisette bit back a sigh as the guard headed back to her. "You always liked a detailed plan, didn't you?"

I always liked getting out alive.

The guard said he would take the package. Lisette gave her excuse. He opened the gate and repeated Marley's warning, and Lisette drove through. With her cell on speakerphone, she called Dominic, who'd picked her up at the airport last night at Simon's request. "I'm on the property. Give me ten minutes, then make the call."

"Why don't you just turn around and drive back out?"

"Admit failure before I even reach the target?"

"It would be the wise thing to do."

"I'll be okay. I have plans." And a stun gun. A handy little lock. A GPS, her favorite running shoes and exit routes mapped through the woods. An extra cell phone and a whole lot of lies ready to roll off her tongue.

And motivation. Jack.

"Nine minutes. Okay?"

"Yes, okay."

Ending the call, she caught a glimpse of the Castle through the trees. It was impressive from a distance. Up close, it *loomed*. Shivers danced down her spine when the drive came out of the woods and cut its way across acres of manicured lawn. The grass was yellowed, the fountains turned off, the scene still and quiet and cold. She parked directly in front of the double doors, which opened before she got out of the car. Another guard stood there, watching as she lifted the box from the backseat.

There really was a sculpture inside that required setup. She had found it at a crafts show, rusted pieces of iron that dangled on the treelike form of the base. It was impressive in its fine balance, but it certainly wasn't anything Candalaria would give a second look at.

She greeted the guard cheerily before asking, "Where should I put it?"

He led her into the nearest room, a library too dark and austere for comfortable reading. An oak table sat in the middle, and she set the box on it. Her movements were slow and methodical: taking out a pocketknife, slicing through the tape, bending back the flaps. She kept an eye on the time, making sure she didn't reach the midpoint before the guard's cell rang.

He looked at it, frowned, yelled a name out the door, then answered, his tone curious. Dominic knew of the security chief for the Castle, and the guard apparently knew of him. He would offer him a job, Dominic had said. The Iannuccis were well known for their generous salaries and perks. Everyone in the business wanted to work for them.

A woman as formidable as the guard joined him, spoke for a minute, then came into the library as he disappeared down the hall. Her suit was conservative and expensive, her spine straight as a ruler. "I'm Ms. Jennings, the estate manager. I'll keep you company while Mr. Parker is busy."

Lisette took a deep breath to calm her nerves, maneuvered a piece into place on the sculpture, then took a step back. "I apologize, Ms. Jennings, but could I use the ladies' room? I had a large coffee on the way up here, and…" She feigned an apologetic smile to go with her shrug.

The woman curtly gestured. "This way."

As Lisette followed her along the main corridor, then into a smaller one, she drew the stun gun from her pocket. It was hot pink and was small enough to conceal in her hand. It delivered a 50,000-volt shock without any permanent damage, and the lock she cradled in her left hand would keep Ms. Jennings in place for a time.

The estate manager opened the door to a powder room and stepped back. Lisette met her, steadied her hand and pressed the stun gun to Ms. Jennings's neck. She scrambled to catch the woman as she collapsed, lowering her to the floor, then inserted one half of the lock in the door. It was a simple design: a notched piece that fit into the cutout for the knob latch and a round barrel that slid into the notch, locking the door.

Exhaling deeply, she dashed back to the main hallway and into the ballroom at its end. Taking the same route as before, she ducked through the servants' door, jogged up the stairs and to the end of the passage. She had no clue how long Ms. Jennings would remain incapacitated or how long Dominic could drag out his conversation with the guard, so the clock was ticking. The only problem was she couldn't see it.

Good under pressure, she reminded herself.

Candalaria's suite was quiet when she entered. Once again she wished she had time to study his treasures. Once again she didn't. She grabbed her backup phone, braced it against the lamp on the desk, settled herself in the luxurious chair and began recording.

"Good morning, Mr. Candalaria. It's Lisette Malone. We met at the museum last week. Oh, yes, and you've had people shoot at me, break into my house and try to run me off the road. I understand. It's a bit frustrating when you've gone to the effort and expense of stealing a painting you want desperately to own, then someone waltzes in and steals it right out from under your nose.

"But you're wrong about who stole it. It wasn't Jack. It was me, and I returned it to its rightful owner. By the way, I wanted to leave this for you." She made a show of removing a rectangle of cardstock from her pocket and laying it on the desk. "It's an invitation to the Fenwick

Center's unveiling of the newest addition to their collection. I thought you might want to see it. Or maybe not.

"The real reason I'm here, though—I'm sure you recognize that 'here' is your suite at the Castle—is that I want to offer you a deal. I'll take only a small part of your collection, and you'll leave Jack Sinclair alone. You'll also stay away from Île des Deux Saints. If you keep your word, eventually I'll return the pieces to you. If you don't…"

She was shrugging carelessly when the hairs on the back of her neck stood on end. Her gaze shifted from the camera, gliding around the room. There hadn't been a noise, a movement, nothing so obvious, but *something* had changed. She wasn't alone any longer. She would bet her life—

And then she saw him. Jack. Leaning against the corner of the waterfall wall, looking incredibly handsome and sexy and watching her with a look of… She couldn't say what it was, but she knew what it wasn't. It wasn't hatred or betrayal or anger or never wanting anything to do with her ever again. It was sort of sweet, tender, amused, smug, sort of everything she loved about him.

It was a struggle to refocus, to drag her gaze back to the camera, to pick up her derailed train of thought. Her hands trembled just the slightest, and she pressed them together in her lap to still them. Her voice threatened to quaver, too, but a good deep breath steadied it.

"If you don't accept my offer, and if you don't live up to your end of it, I'll be back, again and again, until I've taken every single thing you hold dear. I'll destroy you, David." She easily imagined him flinching at the idea of an inferior presuming to use his first name. "So

come back home. Take a look around. See what's missing. I'll be in touch."

Leaning forward, she stopped the recording, pock-
eted the phone and slowly stood. "Wh-what are you
doing here?"

He pushed away from the wall and started toward
her. With each step, a little more breath left her body
until she felt as insubstantial as a sigh. There was something threatening about the way he moved, but in a good
way: arousing, not scaring; with purpose and determination, like a big sexy graceful cat, making her hot and
weak and filling her with need.

He came around the desk, and she stumbled a step
back, then another, but the credenza stopped her retreat. Just as well, when what she really wanted was to
throw herself into his arms. "You talked your way past
the guards? You're good."

He was right in front of her now, so close she felt the
power radiating from his body, so close her own body
tingled with at least 50,000 volts of attraction. "H-how
did you get in?"

He nodded toward the French doors, and she saw a
grappling hook and line similar to the one she'd used
last time. Next to the balustrade sat a large duffel. When
she looked back, he'd ducked his head so that her cheek
brushed his, then his mouth feathered along her jaw.
"I've already chosen a dozen of my favorites. Anything
in particular you want?"

"N-n-no."

He nuzzled her lips, the merest of kisses, then inhaled deeply as if filling his lungs with her scent. "Then
we'd better get out of here. You can send that video to
David once we're safe."

Her own cell phone in her pants pocket buzzed, shocky against her hip. "Dominic's distracted the guard as long as he can. Are we making a run for it?"

"Better. You flew *Shepherdess* out. I'm flying *us* out."

He stepped back, grasped her hand and pulled her to the balcony. Clinging to him, she tried to make sense of his response even as she prepared herself for another experience with giddy, height-induced terror. Vaguely she became aware of a newly familiar sound, the rhythmic popping of helicopter blades, and her gaze jerked to the sky.

"Oh my God," she whispered as a helicopter descended above them, some sort of rig dangling mere feet over their heads and coming nearer. "No, no, no, Jack, I can't— You don't mean— Oh God, I'm really going to die."

Grabbing hold of the gear, he harnessed himself, slung the long duffel strap over his head and pulled her close. "Hold on tight, Trouble. We're going for a ride."

Shuddering desperately, Lisette wrapped her arms and legs around him, pressed her face to his chest and squeezed her eyes shut. When her feet left the ground, her heart doubled its already manic pace and her muscles flexed as if her life depended on them.

Jack showed no such fear. His pumped-up *Woo-hoo!* echoed inside her, and she knew without looking he was wearing the biggest grin ever. "Wave goodbye to the guards," he shouted, then chuckled. "Never mind. You don't want to let go, do you?"

"Never." She wasn't sure if she yelled back or if she even said the words aloud. Maybe they were just a whimper in her soul.

The flight lasted minutes—lifetimes—then the pilot hovered before descending again. When their feet touched the ground on the empty highway, miles from the Castle, when there was enough slack in the line for Jack to unhook, he pried free of her long enough to do so and handed first her, then the duffel into the helicopter.

Lisette huddled in the seat, her shaking out of control now that she was inside instead of out. She'd never had a panic attack before, but at the moment, she planned to never get any higher off the ground than she could jump all on her own. Of course, in the next moment, the pilot took to the sky again.

Jack leaned close to her. "You're safe now." The look he gave her this time was very definitely sweet and tender and amused and smug.

After forcing air into her lungs, she weakly smiled. "That was one hell of a rescue, Charming."

"Aw, Bella Donna never needs rescuing."

"Maybe not. But I do." Her unsteady fingers touched his jaw, his skin cool and smooth and so familiar, as if she'd been created to do just that with only him. His eyes turned smoky and intense, and he grabbed her hand, pressing a kiss to her palm.

"Besides," he went on, "what kind of thief leaves his partner to go into a dangerous situation alone?"

"Partners? So we're going into business? Sinclair and Malone, Heists International?"

"Or Malone and Sinclair. Until we become Sinclair and Sinclair." He said it blithely, as easily as he might have commented on the clouds around them, but his expression belied the tone. He looked at her as if he was entirely serious. As if he'd forgiven her everything and still cared about her and wanted her and might even, someday, lo—

"I meant what I said yesterday, Lisette. I *am* falling in love with you."

Tears filled her eyes. She'd been blessed to have been very well loved by several people in her life, but Jack… Jack was the greatest blessing of all. "I'm falling in love with you, too."

"Of course you are. Everyone always said I was destined for trouble." His grin was charming and breathtaking and made her want to kiss it away.

"It appears they were right."

* * * * *

*If you love Marilyn Pappano,
be sure to pick up her other stories:*

*BAYOU HERO
UNDERCOVER IN COPPER LAKE
COPPER LAKE ENCOUNTER
COPPER LAKE CONFIDENTIAL*

*Available now from
Harlequin Romantic Suspense!*

✦ HARLEQUIN®

ROMANTIC suspense

Available January 3, 2017

#1927 UNDERCOVER IN CONARD COUNTY
Conard County: The Next Generation
by Rachel Lee
Kel Westin is assigned an undercover role to draw out illegal trophy hunters in Conard County, but his feelings for the beautiful yet wary game warden, Desi Jenks, are anything but a front. When signs point to an inside job, can Desi and Kel learn to trust each other before they wind up dead?

#1928 DEADLY FALL
by Elle James
Billionaire Andrew Stratford, desperate to keep his small daughter safe, hires tough-as-nails—and sexy-as-hell—Stealth Operations Specialist Dixie Reeves as a nanny to protect his daughter, but sparks begin to fly when they are forced to set aside the walls they've hidden behind for years in order to save little Leigha from a mysterious threat.

#1929 SPECIAL FORCES SEDUCTION
by C.J. Miller
Alex "Hyde" Flores had hung up her spy gear for good, at least until her currently off-again lover Finn Carter shows up with one last mission in mind. But taking down the drug lord who killed their friend isn't Finn's only objective. He's determined to win Alex back, whatever it takes.

#1930 DR. DO-OR-DIE
Doctors in Danger • by Lara Lacombe
Dr. Avery Thatcher was sent to investigate a mysterious illness at a research base in Antarctica. Instead, she finds a deadly new bioweapon—and help in the form of her ex-boyfriend, Dr. Grant Jones, the senior doctor on staff. Will they be able to stop the spread of a deadly disease *and* face the never-quite-forgotten feelings bubbling back to the surface?

YOU CAN FIND MORE INFORMATION ON UPCOMING HARLEQUIN® TITLES, FREE EXCERPTS AND MORE AT WWW.HARLEQUIN.COM.

but that wouldn't remove the experience or stinging words. Only fresh experience would, and she apparently hadn't allowed herself any.

Opening his eyes, hanging on to his temper, he gave her another soft kiss. "I want to do it again. But like I said, let's take it slow."

"Because of me?"

Double damn. Was he messing this up? "Because I want it to be perfect and right for both of us. Okay?"

She nodded, then let her head fall against his shoulder. Relieved, he snuggled her in, astonished that this self-assured woman had exposed so much vulnerability to him. Vulnerability he had never imagined could be part of a woman who presented such a confident face to the world.

He felt a little shiver run through her, then she softened completely. Staring at nothing, he held her and wondered what he was walking into. What he might be dragging her into. Because something was rotten, and it was easier to think about that than to think about the ache in his groin and how much he wanted Desi.

Don't miss
UNDERCOVER IN CONARD COUNTY
by Rachel Lee, available January 2017
wherever Harlequin® Romantic Suspense books
and ebooks are sold.

www.Harlequin.com

Her eyelids fluttered. "I didn't know," she murmured, her voice breathy.

"Didn't know what?"

"That a kiss could be so nice."

At once he found his self-control. It snapped into place like the jaws of a crocodile. She didn't know a kiss could be so nice? Her words speared him until his chest ached for her. My God, what had this woman been through? Had her rapist been her first and only?

Forget his attraction to her, he had a strong urge to rend something, smash something, hunt down the SOB…

"Did I do it right?"

He closed his eyes, battling fury, battling pain for her. "You did it right," he said. "Very right." That she should have to wonder about the smallest touching of lips? That guy must have assaulted her in ways that weren't physical. She might say he wasn't able to walk for a week,

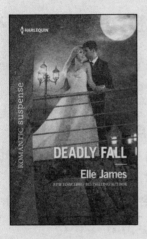
HRSELBPA1216